The Widow's Séance Society

Rebecca F. Pittman

DEDICATION

This book is dedicated to John Drzemala.

"You know why."

CONTENTS

1 BEYOND THE VEIL

The darkness enveloping the room swallowed the six people seated around the parlor table. Rain patted the windows like skeletal fingers tapping for admittance. Sandalwood incense clung to the heavy draperies and Victorian furniture, its cloying perfume choking out the pervasive smell of mildew and tired fabric. Suddenly, a candle flame leapt to life, illuminating a black-draped table and the pallid faces surrounding it.

Abegail Landry shifted in her chair, her diamond earrings sending fractals of light from the candlelight into her carefully coiffed blonde hair, piled in smooth profusion atop her head. She ran a tongue over her lips and studied the faces of the other five people seated at the round parlor table. A gentleman to her left, somewhere in his mid-seventies, sat with his shoulders back and jaw set. The only telltale sign of his nervousness was a muscle jumping near his mouth. A matronly-looking woman on her right was worrying a hangnail and breathing deeply, her blouse rising and falling with each breath. Her eyes darted about the room. Two young teenage girls sat to her right, giggling softly and whispering to each other.

Across from Abegail sat a woman with a hawklike face, her cheekbones threatening to cut through her pale skin. She wore no makeup, giving her a corpse-like appearance. Her dark hair was piled atop her head in a messy bun, wisps of gray springing from it. She had been seated for several minutes with her head down and her eyes closed.

The small party around the table shifted restlessly. The faint sound of a chattering parrot could be heard coming from somewhere in the back of the house.

A rasping sound came from the medium Abegail had been watching. The teenagers stopped their twittering. Slowly, she raised her head, inhaling deeply. Her eyes opened to reveal the most startling green irises Abegail Landry had ever seen.

"Place your hands upon the table," the medium intoned. "Palms down, fingers spread until your little finger is touching that of the person to your right and to your left. This forms a protective circle. Do not break the circle as events unfold."

The older woman to Abegail's right inhaled sharply at the words "as events unfold." It underscored that something was about to happen. Abegail could feel the woman's ice-cold finger pressed to her own, and she fought the urge to move her hand away.

"Silence," the medium called out. "We will begin by summoning my spirit guide, Jaziel. You must be silent."

The group waited and watched as the medium lifted her chin to the ceiling, eyes squeezed shut, and called out, "Jaziel! It is I, Madame Lorraine. Will you come through the dark ether and pierce the veil of the dead? Do you have someone with a message for one of these earthbound souls seated here tonight?"

Suddenly, the candle in the center of the table sputtered out. The room sat in complete darkness. Several people gasped. The woman to Abegail's right grabbed her wrist in a deathlike grip, her hand the temperature of a meat locker. Abegail shook her hand loose and tried to calm her own breathing.

"Do not break the circle!" Madame Lorraine called out angrily. The dowdy woman once again spread her fingers and pressed her pinkie to

Abegail's. Seconds passed.

"Jaziel!" Madame Lorraine's voice called from within the inky darkness. "Light the candle."

An orange and gold glow appeared in the center of the table, at first faint, and then brighter as a large candle seated atop a black onyx slab came into view. The candle's glow highlighted the frightened faces around the table, giving them an eerie jack-o-lantern appearance. The two teenagers stared at it with heightened excitement.

"Now, we will begin," Madame Lorraine said solemnly. "Is there a spirit with Jaziel that has a message for someone here?"

The group waited, holding their breath. The matronly woman looked up, as if expecting ectoplasm to swirl into the room. It was impossible to see more than a few inches past the confines of the table. The shadows of the room seemed to advance towards the group. The rain had picked up, striking the glass with fury. Wind moaned through the open fireplace, wafting through the room like a haunted soul.

Abegail felt a spectral breath against the back of her bare neck and shivered. Just then, a faint green mist eddied into the room from the left of the table. It was gauze-like and glowed as it swirled on an unseen current, rising and falling as it grew in mass. The group's bulging eyes watched as it floated behind Madame Lorraine and rose toward the ceiling, finally dissipating into the dark shadows. The woman to Abigail's right whimpered.

"I see a man," Madame Lorraine called out suddenly. The group jumped. "A man of wealth. Great wealth. Not a kind man. He is glowering at me. He is showing me a watch. This seems to be of great importance to him."

Abigail Landry blanched. Her breath caught in her throat, but she remained still. Her heart was pounding against her ribcage.

"There is sudden pain. I see dark water." Madame Lorraine paused, her face contorting in grimaces. "Blackness!" she screamed. Everyone flinched. "Confusion! This is not right. He is thrashing!"

The matronly woman screamed, pulling her hands from the table and clutching her chest. She was hyperventilating, and Abegail was afraid she was going to faint.

"Do not break the circle!" the medium yelled. But it was too late. The woman slammed her chair back and struggled to stand, one hand on the chair's back.

The lights suddenly came on in the room. The circle of people blinked in the blinding glare of electric bulbs. Madame Lorraine was glaring at the woman, who was taking great gulps of air. She finally took several tentative steps toward the archway leading to the hallway and stumbled through it. Her flat-heeled shoes clicked hurriedly along the marble floor. The sound of another woman's voice could be heard, solicitous and kind. Then the sound of a door opening and closing.

Abegail turned her attention to the medium whose face was flushed with color.

One of the teenagers, sensing the séance was over, leaned forward eagerly and asked if she could ask the Tarot cards a question. The girl nodded toward a deck of well-worn cards lying near Madame Lorraine's elbow. The medium stared at her coldly until the girl leaned away, frightened. Awkward seconds passed. Finally, Madame Lorraine spoke, her voice strained.

"I will give a short reading for the group," she said benevolently. "You have paid to be here, and it is only fair that the evening is not cut short by one person's interference. The spirits, unfortunately, have gone."

She turned her gaze to the two girls and let it linger there. They fidgeted under the penetrating stare of the medium's green eyes. A light seemed to emanate from within them. That same stare turned to the gentleman and paused. Finally, it came to rest on Abegail. Here, the medium stopped. Her lips pressed into a thin white line, and her look took on an intensity that made Abegail feel naked and exposed. After several moments, the medium pulled her gaze and leaned forward from her high-backed chair. The soft sound of a bird's fluttering wings filled the room as the medium shuffled the worn cards. Satisfied, she laid seven cards face down on the table and looked at the young teenage girl.

"You must think of a question. Focus only on that question and then choose a card," she said.

The teenager who had asked for a reading jabbed a finger atop the third card from her right. Madame Lorraine turned it over slowly, revealing the Seven of Swords.

"Deceit, secrets, and sneakiness. You are being betrayed by a friend who is not your friend. She will steal from you. Not an object. Something worse. The damage will be great. Stop her now, or the consequences will be dire."

The two teenagers looked at each other in astonishment. One whispered into the other's ear, and she nodded.

"How do we stop it?" the girl asked quickly.

"That is all the card has for you," Madame Lorraine said. "It will become obvious, but maybe too late."

"Do you wish a reading, also?" she asked the young girl seated next to her. She nervously pushed her glasses up onto the bridge of her nose and shook her head no.

Madame Lorraine turned to the only gentleman at the table. His face was a mask. He showed no emotion as his hands lay steady upon the table, palms down.

"Choose, once you have a question in mind," the medium said, after repeating the shuffling of the cards.

The gentleman hesitated and finally pointed at the card closest to him.

Madame Lorraine slid a tapered finger under the card and flipped it over. It depicted The Lovers. It was an image of two people in a tender embrace, roses entwined about them.

For the first time that evening, the man's composure slipped. His chin trembled. With great effort, he pulled himself together and waited.

"Two lovers," Madame Lorraine said softly, watching his face. "But there are thorns in the roses surrounding them. It is not as it seems. Red. Not from the flowers. Red, the color of blood."

The man's face twitched. His hands moved from the table and gripped each other in his lap. Abigail could hear his heavy breathing. A muscle jumped near his jawline.

Madame Lorraine watched him for a moment, taking in all of his discomfort. Her lips pressed into a nondescript grin. It faded as quickly as it appeared. She scooped the cards together and shuffled them purposefully. Slowly, the medium laid out seven cards.

Abegail felt her heart rate increase as the steady glare from those iridescent green eyes met hers.

"Choose."

Abegail studied the cards, praying the one she chose would benefit her. She pointed to the second card from her left. Madame Lorraine turned it over deftly and smiled.

"The Tower," she said, her tone dripping with menace. "It is the card of destruction."

Abegail stared in horror at the image on the card of a castle tower in flames and a woman plummeting to her death from its precipice.

"Your world is crumbling," the medium said, a slight note of pleasure in her tone. "The golden goose will fly. Diamonds to glass. Champagne to water."

The color drained from Abegail's face, leaving only a soft coral blush highlighting her cheeks. She shifted self-consciously, aware of the other faces watching her intently. She ran her tongue over her teeth and sniffed.

"I see," she said, her voice faltering. "Towers can be rebuilt, surely?" She searched the medium's face pleadingly, hoping for some hint that the influence of the card could be altered.

Madame Lorraine slowly pulled the cards together and set them to one side. She looked at Abegail, considering her response.

"If one knows how," she said. "You will each remember the words I have spoken to you. They are important."

A tall, slender woman appeared in the doorway. The guests recognized her as the one who had greeted them at the door of the mansion earlier that night. She was quiet and moved without sound. She was younger than the medium, perhaps in her forties, and wore her brown hair long. She had welcomed them all earlier at the door and had them each sign into a ledger resting on a side table before escorting them to a small waiting area. All cell phones were placed into a basket on the table. A gong sounded, and she led them into the dark parlor, lit only by a large pillar candle in the middle of a round table. The medium seated herself at the table soon after. Now that the séance was over, the woman stood inside the archway and spoke.

"Our evening is concluded," she said, almost purring. "The spirits have departed, and Madame Lorraine must rest. We hope you have benefited from your session here." She held her arm out to wave them toward the hallway.

The elderly gentleman rose at once, eager to leave. The two teenage girls slid their chairs back slowly, clearly wanting to ask more questions. They picked up their backpacks hanging from their chairs and reluctantly walked out of the room. Abegail, her hands shaking, reached to the floor and retrieved an expensive gold-chained purse. She rose gracefully from her chair and walked past the tall woman, who smiled at her warmly.

Abegail turned in the hallway and waited for the woman to take the lead to the front door, where the others were gathering their cell phones from the basket. They were surprised to find the front door locked. Abegail could hear a bird twittering somewhere from inside a small, dark room they passed. The woman produced a key from a side pocket in her dress and unlocked the heavy oak door. A blast of rain-sodden air flew at them. Despite the storm wailing outside, the fresh air was a relief after the cloying smell of incense that clung to their clothing.

The teenagers laughed and darted out into the rain, holding onto each other's elbows. The elderly gentleman hunched over and pulled his collar higher onto his neck. He nodded goodbye and walked hurriedly down the sidewalk and out through the wrought iron gate.

Abegail Landry paused on the front porch gallery beneath the protection of the overhang from the balcony above. A flash of lightning cut behind the magnolia tree at the end of the walkway. She turned to look at the woman still standing in the open doorway, who gave her a soft smile.

"Nasty night," she said quietly, and shut the door.

2 THE FIRST ACCIDENT

Roger Landry took another swig of beer, ran a dry hand over his mouth, and glanced over the boat side at his fishing line. The iridescent monofilament line disappeared into the brackish water, green from the abundance of algae blooms. He knew the water would change to the color of tea near the shoreline, where tannins from the roots of trees leached into the foam. An occasional breeze carried a strong odor of rotting plants. Other boaters were out on Lake Pontchartrain, their whispered conversations echoing across the water

"Toss me a beer," Dale Bertolet ordered, pulling in his line. "Did you see that gator over there?"

"All part of the experience," Roger said, opening the cooler Abegail had packed for them and extracting a can of beer from the packed ice.

"Larry Owens lost a foot to one," Dale said, tilting his head back to allow the cold brew to flow into his throat.

"Says Larry," Roger laughed. "Odds are he shot it off while cleaning his gun. Gator story sounds better." The two men laughed.

"Hey!" Dale whispered eagerly. "You got a bite!"

Roger jerked his head to see his line straighten at an angle, pulling the tip of his fishing pole down. He grabbed the handle of the

8

expensive rod, reeled the line in a few inches, and waited. The line remained taut and then suddenly darted off to the left, the line whirring.

"It's a big one!" Roger said excitedly. "I bet it's that largemouth!"

"Could be a sheepshead or flounder," Dale said knowingly, leaning over the boat's side to peer into the impenetrable water. "The bass are usually over by the pilings at the bridge."

Roger leaned back, pulling the rod with him and reeling at the same time. The whir of the line sounded as the fish pulled the pole back over again.

"Damn!" Roger exclaimed. "I hope it isn't a bull shark!"

"Shit, if it is, cut the line as soon as you know," Dale said. The lake was home to both freshwater and saltwater species because of its connection to the Gulf of Mexico. "Just pretend it's the Brookhart deal you just lost and cut it loose." He smiled at his own joke.

"You can be a real ass," Roger said, glowering. "You lost your shirt on that deal, too."

"Yeah, but I wasn't the one who worked for two years to land him," Dale said. Suddenly, the line snapped, and Roger fell back into the boat. "Guess you didn't land that either," Dale laughed.

Roger threw his rod angrily to the floor of the boat. Dale stopped laughing. Roger's temper was not something you wanted to light a fire under.

"Did you find your watch?" Dale asked, changing the subject, as Roger looked at the damage to his line.

"No!" Roger said, hotly. "I've looked everywhere."

"How about your locker at the gym?" Dale asked, flinching. The topic was only making his friend of twenty years angrier. He knew the watch was worth a cool forty thousand dollars. It wasn't like Roger, with his OCD meticulousness, to misplace things, especially something that valuable.

Roger didn't answer him, which was an answer in itself. The subject was closed. Instead, he opened the cooler, pulled out the tray of ice and beers, and set it on the floor. He lifted out two sandwiches wrapped in wax paper, some gourmet crackers, a small tub of caviar, and a lidded bowl of mixed fruit, including a bunch of purple grapes.

"Let's eat something and then motor over to the bridge," Roger suggested, still pouting. "The sun is too hot here. They'll be biting better in the shade."

He handed a sandwich and a bag of crackers to Dale, who took them and placed them on his lap. He leaned over and grabbed another beer.

"I will say this for your old lady," Dale said, "she never forgets the lunch. Hell, Linda wouldn't risk messing up her manicure to make me an egg."

"Yeah, she never forgets a lot of things," Roger said while smearing caviar on a cracker. He offered the small can of sturgeon roe to Dale, who waved it off.

"I thought you two were working things out," Dale said.

"She's high maintenance," Roger said. "Her spending is off the charts, and all she does is complain. I can't take another talk about it. I spoke to my lawyer about a divorce last week. Frankly, it would be a relief."

Dale frowned but thought better of giving his friend advice. Instead, he bit into the baguette bun with creamy brie cheese and salty prosciutto with gusto, wiping the fig jam spread from his fingers onto his stained camo pants. Roger followed suit. The food assuaged his anger at his lost catch. He shook his head, thinking of how close he had come to landing a big one.

"Pass me the grapes," Roger said. He broke off a branch of the blackish-purple fruit, pulled two berry-shaped ones from the branch with his teeth, and chewed them. He made a face. "I'm not so sure these are ripe yet," he said. Undeterred, he pulled off three more and popped them into his mouth. He offered the remaining bunch to Dale, but Dale said he'd pass.

"If it ain't ripe, you can spend the rest of the day in the john," he joked.

Roger finished his sandwich and the rest of the grapes, leaving a single pruned one still clinging to the vine. He wiped his hands on his pants and reached behind him to start the outboard motor of the small fishing boat. It sputtered to life. Dale hefted the anchor up onto the boat. Roger took the rudder and swung the boat around in a large arc. They finally pulled in near the bridge pilings. Dale threw the anchor over the edge and finished off his lunch. Picking up his rod, he focused on attaching his new jig to the line. The small, red, fishlike hook glimmered as it hit the water.

"You know, with your portfolio, you could get a better boat, man," Dale said. "J.J. has an Allsea Profisher he's selling for $25k." There was no answer. "What lure are you using?" Dale asked over his shoulder as he watched his bait sink into the water. He jerked the line around, hoping to catch the attention of a passing trout. Roger didn't answer him. Dale jerked on the line again and finally turned his head toward his friend. He sat upright.

"Rog?" he asked, leaning toward the man who was bent over, clutching his stomach. His face was covered with sweat. "What's wrong?"

Roger suddenly leaned over the boat and vomited. Dale saw an angry red rash around his lips. Roger vomited again and again, each time leaning farther over the boat as the retching caused him to go into spasms. Dale sat helplessly watching him as his friend finally broke into dry heaves.

"What can I do?" Dale asked helplessly, looking around him in embarrassment as a few nearby anglers on the bank glanced over curiously.

Suddenly, Roger let out a scream of pain, his body bolting up from the aluminum boat seat. As he did so, the boat tilted to the side, and he lost his balance. Dale lunged to catch him, but he wasn't fast enough. Roger fell overboard into the fetid water.

"Shit!" Dale yelled and lunged to the side to grab him. "Give me your hand," he yelled, but Roger remained motionless in the water, his head barely above the surface. He had a wild, tortured look on his face, which was bloated and red. The rash around his mouth had become scarlet. "Give me your hand!" Dale yelled again, leaning over as far as he dared. Roger was sinking, just out of reach.

A movement from the nearby shore on the left caught Dale's attention. He looked in horror as an alligator slipped soundlessly into the water from where it had been basking in the sun on the shoreline.

"Help!" Dale screamed. "Somebody help him!" He could see the disturbance in the water's surface as the serpentine-like movement of the alligator made a beeline toward where Roger had just disappeared from view. The fishermen on shore ran to the water's edge, yelling in excitement. Only one pulled his cell phone from his back pocket and punched in 911.

Agonizing minutes passed as Dale scanned the water and banks for any sign of his friend. Finally, sirens erupted from the Causeway Bridge as two police cars, a truck hauling a trailer with a rescue boat, and an ambulance raced to a pull-off trail leading down to the water. Dale was hunched over in the boat, his shoulders shaking. The calls from the police officers on the bank to get his attention finally filtered into his consciousness.

"Where did he go in?" one officer screamed.

Dale stared at him for a moment, obviously in shock. He finally pointed over the side with a shaking hand. He knew Roger was gone. The alligator had probably lodged him under a log at the bottom of the lake by now, marinating in the debris. Or, he was caught in one of the cement blocks that littered the lake floor. The alligator had not resurfaced. A wave of nausea hit him, and he leaned over the side of the boat, away from prying eyes. He took several gulps of air, but all it did was coat his mouth and throat with the taste of lake water.

A boat's motor revved to life from the shore. Three men from the rescue team out of New Orleans were making their way to the location where Roger had gone under. One threw a multi-pronged grappling hook into the water at the site Dale indicated. They began dragging the bottom of the lake. One of the anglers on the shore was telling an officer that a "gator" had gone into the water after Roger went under.

"None of us were willing to go in after him," the elderly man said apologetically. "You understand, right?"

The officer didn't answer him. He was talking over a two-way radio to headquarters.

"They're saying an alligator went in after him," the officer said in low tones, sunlight glinting off his aviator glasses. "They're dragging it, but the current is pretty bad, and if a gator… Yeah, okay. Will do."

He released the radio button and muttered something to his partner, who nodded. "I think his friend is in shock," he said. "We're going to have to go bring in the boat ourselves." He looked out at the three men struggling with the grappling hook as they moved it along the lake bottom.

"Gleason!" he yelled. "Pick up the guy in the boat and one of you bring it in, okay?" He watched as they pulled up the hook and angled the boat over to where Dale sat, staring ahead of himself blankly, his body trembling.

The member of the rescue team carefully stepped from his boat into Dale's, steadying himself as the small boat tilted under his weight. He noted the parchment wrappers smeared with jam, empty beer cans, and plastic lunch bags littering the floor. He reached behind Dale and began reeling in the boat anchor. The rope was slimy with algae. After several tries, he hefted the small anchor inside.

"Hang in there," he said to the man shivering in the bridge's shade. "We'll get you looked at on shore, okay. Just hang in there." Dale remained hunched over and unresponsive. The rescue member turned and walked awkwardly to the other side of the boat to start the motor. His shoe crushed a grapevine with a single berry still clinging to it.

＊＊＊＊＊＊＊＊＊＊＊＊＊＊＊＊

Abigail Landry peered through a beveled glass side window on the left of the front door and saw two uniformed officers standing there. She took a deep breath to steady herself and opened the door, feigning surprise to see them there.

"Yes?" she said, nervously.

"Mrs. Landry?" the female officer asked.

"Yes," Abigail said softly.

"Ma'am, I'm afraid there's been an accident. May we come in?"

Abegail paused and then stood back to allow them to enter. She shut the door behind them, and they followed her a few steps into an enormous foyer with tufted benches, an entry table, and some abstract statuary. She did not offer them a seat.

The female officer took the hint and began.

"My name is Officer Hinckley," she said. "And this is Officer Deltoro. Your husband was in a boating accident at Lake Pontchartrain this morning. I'm afraid he fell into the water, and…well, I'm truly sorry to tell you this, but despite rescue attempts, he wasn't recovered." She paused and waited for the wife's reaction.

Abigail stared at them, her facial expression one that the officers could not place. She merely nodded, put a hand to her throat, and waited.

"They will continue to look for him," Hinckley continued," but I do want to be candid with you. With the lake's moving current situation, the Gulf, etc., the outcome may be something you need to prepare yourself for. Do you have someone who can come and be with you?" Officer Hinkley asked kindly. She wondered if the woman was in a state of shock.

A few seconds passed, and Abigail finally met her gaze.

"Yes, I'll be fine," she said quietly and began leading them to the door. Officer Hinckley looked to her partner with raised eyebrows. As Abigail opened the door and stepped back, Officer Hinckley stopped and addressed her.

"Mrs. Landry," she said, her tone more official. "Did you notice anything unusual about your husband this morning before he left? Was he showing any signs of illness? His friend, who was with him in the boat, said your husband suddenly became violently ill. Is he on medication, or has he recently gone off any medication?"

Abigail tensed. It was clear she was eager for them to leave.

"I didn't see Roger leave this morning. I packed them a lunch, like I usually do when they're going to be out there all day, and I left for my yoga class. He was fine last night."

"What time would you say he left to go fishing this morning?" Hinckly asked.

"They go early, but as I say, I wasn't here when he left. My class is the early one, at 7:30. You can check. It's New Wave Yoga."

Hinckley took a breath, looked at her partner, who gave her a blank look. They had run into non-cooperative people before.

"One last question," Hinckley said. A fly buzzed in through the open door, and Abegail sighed, her face tightening. "The lunch you packed for the guys. Usual stuff? Nothing that your husband might be allergic to? I'm only asking because his friend said he became ill quite suddenly. We just need to check the boxes, you understand?"

"I packed his favorite things—the sandwiches, fruit, caviar, beer, etc. All things he's eaten a million times. If the caviar was off or something like that, I can't be held responsible for it. It was new and had not been opened."

Officer Hinckley took a moment to respond. Finally, she handed Abegail a card with her department and phone number on it. "You'll be notified with updated information," she said. "Please don't hesitate to call if you need anything."

Abegail merely nodded, took the card, and waited for them to leave. The two officers stepped out the door. It was immediately shut behind them with a soft click.

They remained silent until they were out of earshot as they walked down the long walkway to the driveway.

"She didn't even ask how the accident happened," Officer Hinckley said in a low voice. "Wouldn't you want to know what happened? Like, how did he end up in the water? Was it a boat crash after he became sick? At least we were spared telling her that an alligator attack is suspected."

"It's hard enough having to be the ones to notify," Officer Deltoro said as he rounded the hood of his patrol car and opened the driver's side door. "Let somebody else fill in the details."

Officer Hinkley nodded, but felt they hadn't taken enough time with the woman.

"She took it better than I would have," she said, sliding into the passenger seat. "It's interesting that she immediately jumped to the caviar as a possible reason for her husband's sudden illness. And that she was quick to offer up the name of the yoga studio, like she had it all set up in case she needed an alibi."

"An alibi for a gator attack?" Deltoro asked, amused. "It was an accident.

"He was sick and *then* fell in," Hinckley said. "My Spidey sense says there's something fishy here, and it isn't the trout." She picked up her cellphone and clicked on the officer's name responsible for questioning the friend who witnessed the accident.

"Donavan?" she said, as a male voice answered. "You guys brought the remaining food in, right?" She paused as he answered. "From the boat! Yes! Is it at the lab?" Another pause. "Was there any caviar left? Or any of the other food?" Pause. "Yes, test it all and the wrappers. Oh, and another question…was there more than one brand of beer?" Pause. "Ok, well, if there was only one brand, it probably wasn't the beer. There would be no knowing which of the men would be picking up which bottle." Pause. "I know he fell overboard, but he was sick before that! What about his friend? Any signs of his being nauseous or sick?" Longer pause. "Ok. Did he already go home?" Pause. "Yes, text me that address, please. And tell the lab to take a good look at the food, including the items it was wrapped in, etc. Thank you."

Deltoro sighed, and she ignored him. She hung up and glanced out the window at the massive mansion. Abegail Landry was watching them from the bay window near the door. Their eyes met for a brief moment before the woman moved from view. It gave Officer Hinkley a queer feeling.

"You think some women prefer to be a widow?" she asked quietly, still staring at the vacant window.

"My wife would," Deltoro said, grinning. He turned the car around and headed down the long, winding drive bordered by manicured hedges. Hibiscus flowers bloomed in neat profusion.

Abegail waited until she saw the cruiser clear her wrought iron gates and ease out into the street. She walked into the foyer and retrieved her purse from the hallway table. Opening it, she removed the small pale purple notecard and reread the instructions inside. The envelope of money had already been taken care of. She smiled. Part of the money she was paying out had come from selling his precious $40,000 watch. All that was left to do was to dispose of the remaining grapes.

3 MADAME LORRAINE

Madame Lorraine walked into the dark library and crossed to the velvet, forest-green draperies. She pulled them aside and tied them back, hooking them with long gold tassels. Sunlight poured into the room, glinting off an ornate mirror over the fireplace whose edges were chipped. Dust particles danced in the light as they escaped the folds of the curtains. The warm rays fell upon the worn brown leather armchairs and ancient books with brittle spines. It was a masculine room with heavy wood details and the lingering smell of lemon furniture polish.

"Wake up, Socrates," she said, tapping lightly on the towering bird cage standing near the window. The large yellow-naped Amazon parrot opened his golden eyes and peered at her. He ruffled his feathers, his neck doubling in size. "Good morning," Madame Lorraine cooed at the bird.

"Good morning," Socrates repeated, his voice shrill but carrying the same inflection as the woman filling his food cup.

"I'll be back in a few minutes and let you out," Madame Lorraine said. "It's a fine day."

"Fine day," Socrates repeated and bent his head to the feed bowl.

Madame Lorraine walked along the long hallway toward the kitchen. The reflection of her long green dress showed dully in the white-and-black checked marble floor as it disappeared down into its depths. She entered the kitchen and crossed to the small door near the pantry. The moment she opened it, the smell of damp earth and herbs assaulted her nostrils from the greenhouse.

"Ruby!" called the tall woman with brown hair, tied snugly into a ponytail. She was standing near a row of potted herbs. "The caldarium bounced back. The treatment I gave it worked."

"I told you not to call me that," Madame Lorraine said, stepping down the four wooden stairs and crossing to the plant, cupping one of the red-and-green leaves in her hand. "You might forget when we have guests."

"I'm sorry," the woman said, her voice clipped.

"Rachel, we have to be careful, or the entire thing could fall apart," Madame Lorraine said, her voice tired. "We've been lucky so far. One little slip, like using my real name, could be just enough to have someone start digging."

"You're right," Rachel said, glancing guiltily at her sister. She continued checking the name tags affixed to the herbs' pots and entering their information into a stained leather ledger. "So, it all went as planned?" she asked, her pen poised above a lined page of plant names.

"Yes…well, that is, there was an unfortunate accident," Madame Lorraine said, a wan smile creasing her face.

Her green eyes took on a strange light that Rachel knew too well. She had seen it all her life, from when they were children. She remembered seeing it the night the little Bridgers boy went missing. All they found was his bicycle, the wind spinning the rear tire in the fall night air. The bike was found two days after her sister's husband disappeared.

"It seems Abegail Landry's husband went overboard and may have succumbed to an alligator attack," the medium continued.

Rachel's eyes flew open in surprise. "An alligator?" she gasped.

"He's dead?"

Madame Lorraine eyed her with disdain. Rachel's compassion was not exactly an asset in their occupation. "Yes... an alligator. Yes, he's dead. The spirits predicted it."

Rachel stared at her sister in shock. The familiar queasy feeling returned.

The room's humidity was cloying as the sun beat down through the greenhouse's overhead glass panels. Rachel felt a sudden feeling of being closed in, despite the size of the greenhouse.

"You told her there was danger and dark water," Rachel said nervously. "And he died in…"

"Yes, Rachel," Madame Lorraine spat. "The spirits warned her. Isn't that what we're here for? Why do you think these people come to us?"

Rachel stared at her sister, who was five years her senior. The same fear she had of her as a child had never abated. Her head was spinning over the information that another person had died. Madame Lorraine had moved on, studying the potted plants, crawling vines, flowers, and berries. A small door to the rear led to a room where Rachel brewed her "potions" in an old metal pot atop a propane camp stove. Shelves of brown apothecary bottles with corked lids lined the crude walls. The door was kept locked.

Madame Lorraine surveyed the room, her eyes lighting on a sweeping grape vine on the trellis at the back. Its purple-black clusters shone with the moisture from the mister overhead.

"It's a good crop of grapes this year," she said.

"Yes," Rachel said, her voice quavering. "They should ripen soon, but Moonseed grapes are poisonous. Don't eat them," she said.

Madame Lorraine smiled secretly to herself as she turned her back on her sister and walked away. She climbed the short stairs to the kitchen door, opened it, and walked out of the humid room, relishing the sudden coolness of the kitchen. Closing the door to the greenhouse behind her, she smoothed her silver-streaked hair where it was escaping its bun and glanced up at the clock above the sink. *My delivery will be here soon*, she thought. She leaned across the old farmer's sink and peered into the side yard. Rows of flowering bushes and ancient moss-laden oaks sheltered the area from prying eyes. A small pond reflected the scorching morning sun in dull hues of greens and blues. Water Hemlock bloomed along its edges; the small white umbrella-shaped flowers floated atop its toothed leaflets. Elderberry, privet, baneberry, and Star of Bethlehem shrubs were covered in a profusion of berries and small flowers.

Madame Lorraine washed her hands beneath the sink faucet and paused. She ran her mind over the séance from eight nights ago. The Landry case had been more than satisfactory. She hadn't counted on Abegail's husband succumbing to an alligator attack. It was perfect. No body, no autopsy. The elderly gentleman from the seance would be harder to persuade. He had signed the guest ledger as Colonel Malcom Harris. He had yet to respond to the note Rachel had placed inside his coat pocket as he exited the séance. He was focusing instead on the storm outside and hadn't noticed.

A sound came from outside the kitchen window. She leaned across the sink and was just in time to see the disappearing back of a young man in a blue denim shirt as he rounded the corner of the house. She smiled and crossed to the door leading outside to the landing and a short flight of stairs to the flagstone walkway bordering the side yard. The incessant buzz of cicadas abruptly stopped. Descending the steps quickly, she paused at the bottom and looked toward the corner of the house. He was gone. She looked quickly at the greenhouse set back from the yard. She stepped over to an azalea bush next to the small statue of a woman cradling a basket of stone flowers and bent to look behind it. A large brown paper bag was hidden there, its top neatly folded and taped shut.

Madame Lorraine smiled, picked up the bag, and hurried back up the stairs and into the kitchen. The paper sack was limp with the Louisiana humidity.

A knock sounded at the front door, and she paused. She hurriedly tucked the paper bag behind some cleaning products under the kitchen sink and walked out into the hallway. The knock came again, soft, and timid. As she paused by the open library door, Socrates squawked,

21

"Knock, knock. Knock, knock."

Madame Lorraine opened the heavy door and peered at the two teenagers standing there. They were the girls from the séance. She stood to one side, silently permitting them to enter. The two girls hesitated and then stepped inside the shadowed foyer.

Madame Lorraine clasped her hands in front of her, studying them with her green eyes. After several awkward moments, one of the girls took a deep breath and spoke.

"We, uh, well, we wanted to know if maybe…" She stopped and looked at her friend for reassurance. The other girl nodded, her eyeglasses sliding down the perspiration beading on her nose.

"We," the girl began again, "just wanted to ask if maybe you could make it stop." She waited, wondering if the medium would toss them out. "There was a note inside my backpack that said if we needed further assistance that you might be able to help with that."

Instead, Madame Lorraine's sharp features softened, and her face formed into a semblance of a smile.

"You're the girls from the séance the other night," Madame Lorraine said, cocking her head to one side. "I take it the betrayal I warned you of has begun?"

"Yes!" the girl said anxiously. "You were right, but it began a month ago. But it's all lies. I never did the things she is saying I did, and now it's all over social media. People are calling me names and bullying me. It's awful. Can you make it stop? Please?"

Her eyes looked pleadingly at the medium.

The other girl spoke up.

"Haley didn't do anything with Robin's boyfriend, but this Miley is putting it out there that Haley is sleeping with him. She's been saying trash about me, too."

Madam Lorraine took several slow breaths but remained quiet. The light in her green eyes intensified. The two girls looked at each other, panic on their faces. She wasn't going to help them.

"We can pay," Haley said, her voice trembling. "I don't have much, but…" She reached into her small purse with a gothic rose image on it and pulled out a hundred-dollar bill.

Madame Lorraine took the money and studied it.

"I'm sure Rachel can help you with something," she said finally, and motioned the girls to follow her down the hallway toward the kitchen.

Twenty minutes later, the two girls followed Madame Lorraine back to the front door, looking happier than when they arrived. Haley was clutching a small burlap bag, tied with a black ribbon.

"Thank you!" they said, gratefully, and walked out into the bright sunlight.

****

Officers Hinckley and Deltoro found Dale Bertolet an emotional mess. His wife had led them from the front door of his home into a stylish living room, all done in a taupe palette. Officer Hinckley marveled at the amount of décor in monotone shades of gray. Her attention drifted over to the man who was hunched over on the couch, his shoulders shaking. In front of him on the glass coffee table sat a half-full glass of whiskey.

"Mr. Bertolet," Deltoro said, his voice respectful. "I'm really sorry to have to bother you right now with this, but just a couple of quick questions, okay?" Dale didn't look up. "Uh, this morning, did your friend seem alright when you first started out? Did he look ill?"

Dale raised his head to look at the officer through swollen eyelids. His face was bloated.

"He was fine," Dale choked. "He was ticked about losing some big fish he had on the line, but other than that, no. We had finished lunch and had moved to the bridge. I was getting my lure in the water, and when I looked over at him, he was in bad shape. It came on so fast."

"Did you both eat the same things?" Officer Hinckley asked. Dale's wife had quietly taken a seat near the window, looking helpless.

"I don't know…I…no. I didn't want any caviar."

Hinckley shot a meaningful look at her partner.

"Is that the only thing that you remember not eating?" she asked.

"I think so," Dale said, his body trembling. "No, wait, I didn't want

23

any of the grapes. He said they weren't ripe, but he kept eating them."

Hinckley made notes in her small pad.

"How long after you finished eating did he become ill?" she asked.

Dale suddenly snapped.

"I already told the other guy all this at the station," he exploded.

Hinckley backed off.

"One last question," she said gently. "It was reported that you, too, leaned over the boat, like you were going to vomit as well. Did you feel sick?"

"Yeah!" he yelled, his face twitching. "I just saw my best friend drown, and a gator going in after him. I had a few bad moments! For the record, I didn't vomit, but I thought I was going to. Not from food poisoning… Look, it was a normal day of fishing. We go twice a month. He was in a bad mood about the fish getting away, a deal he just lost at work…and he said he had talked to a divorce lawyer. As for the food, I don't know."

****

Colonel Malcolm Harris's eyes scanned the document before him. After skimming over the second paragraph, he realized he hadn't retained a thing he had just read. Sighing, he laid the papers on his desk and stared off into space. He opened the drawer to his desk and pulled out a small purple notecard. He had found it inside his coat pocket the morning after he returned from the séance. He had fully intended not to attend such silliness, but the person who told him about the medium suggested Madame Lorraine could help him with his problem. He had no idea what form that help would take.

He pulled the folded note from the envelope and scanned the cryptic message he had memorized by now. It was all so odd. The words made his stomach clinch. There was no denying the message's intent.

He replaced the note in his drawer and placed a bank ledger over it. Rising from his leather desk chair, he paced about his office, pausing before the display cabinet of his medals awarded to him during thirty-four years of service to his country. Photos of him shaking hands with military dignitaries lined the fireplace mantel and bookshelves. Mementos from foreign countries he had frequented were placed about the room, each carrying memories of his glory days. He had returned home from his final call of duty to find rumors that his wife was having an affair with his lawyer. The same lawyer who had drafted their wills, prenups, and legal papers requiring a keen eye for the jargon and pitfalls.

Just then, the sound of the front door opening and closing caught his attention. He cleared his throat and put on the mask he had learned to wear around her. The scent of her expensive perfume announced her arrival into his study.

"There you are," she said, her smile tight and unnatural. "You were supposed to meet the Halversons and me for lunch. Did you forget again?" Marjorie Harris stood inside his office, her hand on her hip.

Her accusatory tone triggered the resentment he carried daily. She had been teasing him about his failing memory for months now. Treating him like a doddering old man. It made the twenty-year difference in their ages all the more apparent. It angered him that the sight of her still stirred his emotions. She stood there now in a form-fitting suit with a champagne-colored silk top, her full breasts straining the smooth fabric. Her auburn hair cupped her face in soft waves. The same hair that once spilled out across her pillow next to him at night. The same hair that now spilled across another's pillow at night. Her blue eyes watched him.

"I have the lecture tomorrow night, and I got caught up in preparing for it," he said, his voice void of emotion. "I lost track of time. I'm sorry."

She eyed him for a moment, noticing the jumping jaw muscle.

"Yes, of course," she said. "It's of no consequence. We had a pleasant lunch without you." She pecked his cheek and walked to the study door. "You did remember that tomorrow is Tuesday? My day to attend the gala opening at Ridgerton's? I'm sorry to miss your lecture, but all that military talk is beyond my retention."

She forced a smile and walked out of the room. Harris listened as she climbed the curving staircase and closed the bedroom door behind her. He traced her footfalls overhead with his eyes. Her muffled voice filtered down through the fireplace from the matching one overhead near their bed. She was on the phone.

Fifteen minutes later, the bedroom door opened, and she descended the staircase. She entered his study again, buttoning a pearl clasp through her silk sleeve. She had ditched the suit and was wearing tan slacks and a top.

"Emergency!" she said lightly. "Stephanie is in dire need of my opinion on which outfit to wear to the Hamptons this weekend. I swear, you'd think this party was an invitation to the White House."

She frowned at the stubborn pearl button and finally forced it through the opening. Sighing, she looked over at her husband of twelve years and smiled at him innocently.

Malcolm Harris looked at her, his heart feeling like a dead weight.

"Stephanie?" he asked quietly. "I thought she was in Denver."

Marjorie's face blanched, but she recovered quickly.

"She was!" she said, her voice faltering. "Just got back. All in a flurry now. You know how she is." Her phone pinged, and she looked down at it. "Speak of the devil," she said, a little too brightly, "She's bugging me to hurry up. Gotta dash!"

She backed toward the study door, tossing a silk scarf over her shoulder and cramming her phone into her shoulder bag. Malcolm's eyes were on her phone.

"See you tonight," she said, blowing him an air kiss.

With that, she was gone. And in that moment, Malcolm Harris made up his mind.

4 LIKE A WHEEL WITHIN A WHEEL

Rachel chose a book from the stack of four she had placed on the dining room table and flipped through the pages on plant propagation. Madame Lorraine was seated next to her, her fingers busily tapping the keyboard of an open laptop. She paused and looked over to her sister, happily ensconced in pictures of indigenous plants.

"I remember you asking for a book on plants for Christmas when you were just eight years old," the medium said. "Eight! What kid wants a book on plants?"

"It doesn't matter," she said. "I never got one, did I?"

There was a note of sadness in her voice.

"We didn't get a lot of things," Madame Lorraine said shortly. "We're doing okay now, right?"

"According to the bookings," Rachel said, "we made $3,700 this month. Maybe we need to charge more for the readings. The seances are the only thing keeping us afloat, and not everyone can afford $1,500 a pop. We have four in attendance for Thursday night." She ran a finger down the list of plants, periodically jotting down notes in her ledger at her elbow.

The medium didn't answer her. She was leaning closer to the computer screen, her lips moving soundlessly as she read what she found there. Finally, a grin creased her face.

"Look!" she said, and turned the screen so her sister could see it. "It's working."

Rachel bent toward the screen and stared at the face of a pretty young teenage girl with flowing blonde hair and blue eyes, framed in spider-like eyelashes. Her make-up was overdone, and a small gold ring pierced her right nostril. Below her face was her name, Miley Wilkins. She was on a social media platform, and a stream of conversation was running so quickly that it was hard to keep up with it.

"Then how come it's you in the pic with Mark?" one sentence ran.

"Yeah! You're the tool, Miley, not Haley! You totally lied about the whole thing!"

The stream of accusations rolled on. Miley kept objecting, but she was cut short. The tirade increased against her as several people in the chat posted the same photo over and over of a handsome, tanned teenage blonde boy with Miley seated on his lap. They were poolside, drinks in hand, and kissing.

"You call yourself Robin's friend?" one line screamed. "You're hooking up with her boyfriend and blaming Haley! I hope Robin rips your fake eyelashes off!"

"Not just Robin's friend, but you're supposed to be Haley's, too! You're disgusting!"

Rachel leaned back from the screen and watched the look of satisfaction on her sister's face.

"Where did you find the picture of the boy with her on his lap?" Rachel asked.

"Took some digging," her sister said. "I saw Mark's name come up a lot in Haley's socials, so I looked him up and went through his. It was buried, but I found it...along with pics of him and several other girls. He gets around. I just dropped the photo of him with Miley on his lap into a post on her page, and Voila."

She closed the laptop and sighed contentedly.

"What did you tell Haley the potion would do?" Madame Lorraine asked her sister.

"I just told them to sprinkle the contents in the girl's car," Rachel said, "and then the tables would turn on her. It was just some crushed wormwood. After you told me about what was happening to them at the hands of that girl, the rest was easy. Did you plant the picture on all the social media apps or just the big one?"

"Go big or go home," the medium said. "These teenagers get mean online. I had no idea. That should take care of Miss Miley Wilkins. Haley's $100 was well spent, I would say, and we can chalk up another satisfied customer."

"Speaking of that," Rachel said, laying the book aside. "It's not like you to help someone for such a small amount. "Are you getting soft?"

Her sister leaned back in her chair and studied the cut-glass fruit bowl in the center of the table. She reached for it and extracted an apple from the array of fruit there. Taking a bite, she licked the juice from her lips and turned her attention to her sister, grinning.

"You know me better," she said. "I had checked the girls out the minute we received their information before the séance. Do you know who Haley's aunt is?" She cocked her head, an affectation she adopted when studying someone's reaction.

"No," Rachel said simply. She would allow her sister the satisfaction of the great reveal.

"Tiffany Belmont LeBlanc," she said slowly, drawing out each syllable.

Rachel's face showed the surprise the medium had hoped for.

"You didn't really think I'd accept those silly girls into our séance without an agenda?" Madame Lorraine asked, taking another bite of the apple. "All it took was internet searches, seeing the problem they were having with the lovely Miley Wilkins, announcing at the séance that they were being betrayed and that it would get worse. I knew they'd come back. $100 potion, planting a scandalous photo where it would do the most damage, and problem solved! They tell their mother how this amazing medium and her side-kick—that's you—predicted that the whole mess would go away. It's up to them if they tell her they bought a potion."

"What makes you so sure they will tell their aunt or that Tiffany LeBlanc will even need a psychic?" Rachel asked, secretly impressed with the scheme her sister had not shared with her. It was not the first time.

"Let's just say, I can see the future," Madame Lorraine said, and sank her teeth into the firm, red apple skin. "Don't I always figure out how to make things happen?"

"Like a wheel within a wheel?" Rachel asked.

The medium shot her a quick look, but couldn't read her sister's stony expression.

Rachel gathered her books and rose from the table, Madame Lorraine watching her as she exited the room.

****

Majorie Harris slipped out of her sequined evening gown and tossed it over a small, tufted chair in her bathroom, atop a black velour robe. She rolled her head, releasing the tension in her neck. The small gold clock on the bathroom counter read 11:00. Malcolm would be out having celebratory drinks after his lecture tonight, she thought smugly. She had hurried to beat him home. She'd pretend to be already asleep in case he was in an amorous mood. Alcohol exacerbated his already high libido. She hadn't expected that in a 77-year-old man.

She studied her reflection in the mirror as she released her long auburn hair from a diamond pin holding it in place. Majorie walked to the bathtub in her bra and panties and bent over to push down on the drain cap. She turned on the gold faucets to full blast, adjusting the hot water pouring from the waterfall spout to her satisfaction, and studied the array of bath products in a large basket sitting on the tub's marble ledge. She plucked a red bath bomb nestled atop an array of others like it in various fragrances. She peeled away its cellophane wrapper and lifted it to her nose. It smelled of rose petals and something she couldn't place. Almonds? Shrugging, she tossed it into the bath water where it immediately began to fizz.

Marjorie reached for her cellphone and clicked on her playlist of music. The sounds of soft jazz filled the room. She turned it down so that she could hear Malcolm in case he returned home early, and slipped out of her bra and panties, laying them on the counter. She glanced at them guiltily and then again at her reflection in the mirror. Her lips twitched with a sudden stirring of emotion until the steam from the hot water began cloaking the mirror and obliterating her image. Sliding off her silk hose, she pinned up her long hair into a clamp, lit two candles, and turned to the bathtub.

The scent of roses filled the air, rising in the steam as the bath water climbed past the Jacuzzi jets. Majorie lifted her right leg and stepped over the rim of the large garden tub, stepping down into the suds. She lifted the other leg and stepped in. Holding onto the tub's edges, she sank into the scented foam. The bath bomb was almost fully gone, its fizzing motion sending the small remaining ball into slow spirals.

Majorie leaned her head back against the padded bath pillow and sighed. She sloshed the sudsy water over her breasts, a tingling sensation going through her. The soothing tones of Miles Davis played from her phone as she felt herself relaxing. *It will all work out,* she told herself. *He doesn't know.*

Malcolm Harris laughed heartily as he sat in the bar of the hotel where he had just delivered his speech to a standing ovation. He was overwhelmed at the reception his lecture on military policy in the Middle East had garnered. These were his peers. No greater acknowledgment could be given him.

"Helluva speech!" his friend Major Cliff Banfield yelled out, raising his glass of bourbon into the air. The fact that it was his fourth was represented in his slurred delivery.

The other three men raised their glasses, clinking them loudly above the empty hors-d'oeuvres trays. Malcolm sipped the smooth liquid and glanced at the clock above the bar. It was 11:30.

Marjorie's hands began to tremble as she struggled to push herself up in the deep bath water. The room began to spin as the song *Stella by Starlight* played from her phone. The rose-scented steam formed a cocoon around her, swirling in nauseating rotations. She screamed and looked down at her arms, blistering in angry red blotches. Her body was on fire, itching and burning at the same time. She tried to breathe, but her airway was closing off. Gasping for air, she struggled again to pull herself out of the water, but her vision was fading, and her arms had lost their strength. Their muscles trembled beneath her weight, and she collapsed. She fell back into the water, sending it sloshing over the sides. All the while, her body felt as if it were being baked alive.

"Help me!" she gasped. It was the last breath allowed her. A choking sound like a death rattle escaped her lips. Blackness overtook her, and she slid into the water, her head falling back against the bath pillow.

Malcolm's liberal pouring of drinks at the hotel bar accomplished his objective. Cliff Banfield slung a limp arm over Malcolm's shoulder and said, "I think we are impaired, old friend."

The other men laughed but agreed that a taxi was in order.

"The hotel put me up for the night," Malcolm said. "It's a double suite if you want to stay," he said to Cliff, whom he had known during ten years of military service. "You don't have a wife or dog to report to, so why not?"

Cliff grinned at him idiotically through the haze of alcohol.

"Why not indeed?" he laughed. "Doubt I could tell the taxi driver my address, anyway. You okay leaving Marjorie on her own for the night?"

Malcolm reddened. An awkward silence followed. The other men hurriedly rose from their chairs.

The three men who had tapered off during the evening and ended with club soda told Malcolm and Cliff goodnight, slapped Malcolm on the back, and left to call a cab. Cliff rose unsteadily from his seat and held onto the table for a moment until the room stopped spinning. Malcolm mimicked him, feigning intoxication. He had pretended to keep up with Cliff's bourbon consumption during the two hours the men had been at the bar. He fished his room key from his pocket and walked over to the bartender, showing him the room number and requesting that he put the bill for the evening's tab on his final hotel tally. Then the two old friends walked arm in arm out into the lobby and into the waiting elevator.

5 THE HUNT BEGINS

Detective Archer Hilliard and Lieutenant Adelaide Calvo pulled into the driveway of 5524 St. Charles Avenue and jockeyed for a space behind three police cars and a coroner's van. They got out of their unmarked car and walked up the pathway to the mansion's front door, taking time to marvel at the Italianate three-story home. The Garden District of New Orleans was well known for its historic estates, a mixture of Italianate, Greek Revival, and Queen Anne stunners. The homes had once boasted lavish gardens covering acres of property, hence the district's name. Now, they had been pared back to modest back and side yards, making way for newer homes to join their ranks.

Detective Hilliard paused before climbing the three stone steps to the covered porch, letting out a slow whistle.

"How much you guess?" he asked his sidekick.

Lieutenant Calvo, familiar with his abbreviated sentences, took in a deep breath and ran an eye over the Italianate façade. The ubiquitous wrought iron gallery above them mirrored the architecture for which New Orleans was famous, its lacing giving the house a feminine touch. Louvered shutters flanked the towering windows of the first floor, while the second-floor windows flaunted the rounded tops that smacked of Italianate décor. Two large urns flanked the stone steps, ferns pouring from them in symmetrical precision.

"I'm guessing six bedrooms, 5 bathrooms, about 4,119 square feet, built in the 1880s...I'd say around $1,895,000.

Hilliard jerked his head in her direction, a look of surprise on his face. She looked up at him with a smug expression. The detective stood 6'6" tall to her 5'3" frame, so she was always looking up at him.

"How the hell do you know all that?" he asked. "Are you messing with me?"

"No," she said, smiling. "My Aunt is a realtor for this area. She took me inside when it was up for sale twelve years ago. I'm good, but I'm not that good. Oh, it also has an in-ground pool that runs partly beneath a breezeway to the carriage house." She grinned at him and took the lead up the steps to the lower gallery.

A young police officer stood guarding the door. Hilliard flashed his badge, and the officer opened the door for him. He stepped into a massive foyer rising two stories, a gigantic chandelier dangling above his head. To his right, hardwood stairs with cream-and-gold carpeted runners rose to a balcony.

Voices were coming from a double-door parlor to his left. Calvo had already headed in that direction, less impressed with the opulence that spread out before them. Hilliard followed her in and stepped down into the sunken room onto a carpet so thick that the soles of his shoes disappeared. Two officers, a male and a female, were seated in Queen Anne chairs across from a sobbing woman wearing a maid's uniform, seated on a champagne-colored couch. The officers glanced over as Hilliard and Calvo entered the room. The male officer, Sergeant Burnard, recognized Hilliard and nodded at him. He rose and walked over to the towering detective.

"The body's upstairs," Burnard whispered, glancing over his shoulder at the maid who continued to wail, a sodden handkerchief pressed to her face. "The maid found her this morning, about an hour ago, in the bathtub. It's pretty ugly. Not sure yet what happened, but the victim looks like she was boiled in acid or something. We've been

35

trying to get something from the maid, but she's hysterical."

"The Missus!" the maid suddenly cried out. "How can this be to such a good woman? My Missus!" she yelled again.

Calvo looked at the middle-aged woman with mocha skin and recognized her accent.

"You take the upstairs," she said to Hilliard in a low voice. "Let me have a go at the maid."

Hilliard nodded and exited the room with Sergeant Burnard leading the way, grateful to leave the distraught woman to the Lieutenant. Calvo introduced herself to the female officer, Sergeant Mason, and asked if she could speak to the maid. Mason waved her on, her face showing perturbation at having her investigation handed off. Calvo took the chair Burnard had vacated and faced the woman, bent over and sobbing. She noticed the small tape recorder placed on the gleaming coffee table between them. Its green light blinked.

"What's her name?" Calvo whispered to the Sergeant, who looked surprised at the question. She merely shrugged. Calvo hid her irritation and turned to the woman.

"Eskize mwen," Calvo said, leaning toward the maid. Mason looked at her in confusion.

The maid immediately stopped crying and looked at Calvo with surprised, swollen eyes.

"Ja?" the woman said, sniffling.

Calvo smiled at her warmly. "I know this is hard for you," she said softly. "What is your name, please?"

"Camille," she answered, wiping her face.

"Camille," Calvo repeated, smiling. "How long have you worked for the Missus, Camille?"

"Three years, Lapolis," she said, using the Haitian word for police.

"You can call me Adelaide," Calvo said warmly. "I want to help you get through this.

The maid studied the female officer before her. Her accent was definitely Creole. She didn't look like a police officer except for her uniform. She had mocha skin with small black moles dotting her cheeks. Dark braids peaked out from beneath her cap. Her blue eyes were kind.

Camillie nodded and waited, her breathing coming easier.

"Tell me what happened this morning," Calvo said. "Start with getting here. Which door do you come in?"

Camille bit her lips and studied the carpet. Tears continued to spill down her face.

"I live here," she said. "I wake up at 6:30, take my shower, dress in uniform," she said. "I start the coffee at 7:30, feed Richy, and then go up to see what the Missus and Mister want for breakfast. If the mail is on the floor by the front door, I take it up with the Mister's newspaper from the front steps."

"Very good," Calvo said encouragingly. "Who is Richy? Is there a child here?"

"No. Richy is Missus' Persian kitty." She paused and then continued, "No mail yet, but I get the newspaper and go up the stairs."

Here, Camille stopped, and her face began to spasm. Sergeant Mason sighed, preparing for another onslaught of tears.

Calvo pulled her chair closer and placed her hand on the woman's knee. "You're doing great, Camille," she said soothingly. "It's okay. I'm right here. You don't have to go upstairs again at all, okay?"

Camille sniffed loudly and dabbed at her eyes.

"Ok," she said, taking a deep, shuddering breath. "I knock on Missus' bedroom door. No answer. They tell me it's okay to knock and ask about breakfast, so I open the door. No one in the bed. The bed not slept in. Curtains are still open. Missus didn't say she was going away, and her purse is on bed, so I wonder where she is. I see door to bathroom is closed, so I go to the door and knock. I call out, 'Missus?' No answer. I open the door. I first smell roses. I did not see Missus at first. I see her clothes on the chair, and I go to pick them up, and then I see…I see…"

Camille broke into hysterics again, wailing, her hands flying about her body. "She is there, in the bathtub. I see her hair. I go to her, and she is…" At this point, the maid completely broke down.

Calvo looked at the other officer and shook her head, indicating that they should not press the maid further at this time. She patted

Camille on the knee.

"Mwen dezole," Calvo said kindly.

Sergeant Mason pressed her shoulders back and glared at the Lieutenant.

"What are you saying to her?" she asked hotly.

"I first said 'Pardon me' before I asked her name, and just now I told her I was sorry. It's Haitian. She and I are Creole."

Mason lifted an eyebrow and reached to turn off the recorder.

"Good for you," she said and closed her notebook.

Calvo ignored her. She was used to it. Louisiana was a mixture of cultures. You were known by your address, Jambalaya, and which ingredients made up your Holy Trinity. She stepped up to the foyer just as the front door flew open. A man with silver hair and blue eyes burst into the hallway, a small overnight bag in one hand. He dropped the bag to the floor and glared at her.

"What is all this?" he demanded. "Why all the police? Why a coroner's wagon?"

Calvo regained her composure after the initial surprise of the man hurtling into the house.

"You are?" she asked.

"I'm Malcolm Harris!" he spat. "Where's my wife? What's happened?"

Calvo eyed him for a moment. She made a mental note of his statement as well as the time on her watch. It was 8:30 am.

"Mr. Harris, I'm afraid your wife has passed," she said softly.

Malcolm Harris staggered sideways and gripped the hall table. He looked stunned, his face twitching. Calvo waited. The silence was interrupted only by the maid's sobbing. Malcolm looked in her direction.

"What did the maid say about it all?" he asked.

Calvo squinted at the man. She chose her words carefully.

"We are still getting information from her," she said. "She is quite upset."

"I can hear that!" Malcolm barked.

Calvo eyed the overnight bag sitting on the floor near his feet.

"Have you been away?" she asked.

He paused, and his eyes moved to the floor. Then, in a flurry of words that took her by surprise, he said, "Yes. I was the guest speaker at a military conference last night at the Roosevelt. My accommodations were supplied as these things tend to run late. I had drinks in the bar with four of my colleagues and stayed the night. My friend stayed with me in the suite as we had both had a little too much to drink. I arrived just now to find this."

A noise came from the balcony, and Calvo looked up to see Hilliard standing there, watching them from the railing. Malcolm glanced up as the large detective made his way down the stairs. When Hilliard reached the landing, he extended a hand to the man.

"Detective Hilliard," he said. "I take it you are Mr. Harris?"

"Colonel Harris," the man said, standing even straighter than he had been. "Is anyone going to tell me what's happened here?"

"Well, I'm afraid your wife is deceased," Hilliard said, watching the man. "I overheard where you were last night, but what were your wife's plans? Was she home all night? When did you last see her or talk to her?"

"She had a gala event," he said, shaken by the barrage of questions. "I don't know what time she got home. You'll have to ask the maid. She stays here with us... has her own room in the rear." He took a moment to concentrate, his eyes fixed on the floor. Finally, he said, "I, uh, talked to my wife yesterday morning. She reminded me of her gala and wished me luck with my speech."

"What time was that?" Hilliard asked.

"Around nine, I should say. She was heading out to run errands. Marjorie shops a lot. She's also helping a girlfriend with some Hampton emergency."

Hilliard looked confused but continued on. "Can you supply us with this friend's name and a phone number, please?"

"It's Stephanie...Clemens. I'll have to find the number." His eyes drifted to the sunken living room where Camille was still sobbing, although slightly less hysterically. "I need to talk to her," he said and took a step in that direction. Hilliard blocked him.

39

"Actually, what I really need is your statement while your memory is fresh," he said. Malcolm's face reddened. "And that phone number."

"I don't have it on me," Malcolm said sarcastically. "She's my wife's friend. Marjorie has a little address book in her purse." His face became suddenly animated. "Is her purse gone? Is that what this is? A burglary and Marjorie got in the way?"

"It doesn't appear to be a robbery," Hilliard said with a slight chill to his voice.

An investigator and photographer came down the stairway from the second floor. Hilliard took the officer aside and conversed with him in low tones. The man nodded and stepped over to the Colonel.

"Mr. Harris," he said, and the Colonel grimaced. "My name is Sergeant Fallows. I would appreciate it if you would come with me, and we can get a statement from you."

"A statement about what?" he asked, his face hardened. "I've been gone. I don't even know what's going on here. What can I tell you?"

"It's procedure," the officer said. "We won't keep you long." He walked to the front door and opened it, looking at Malcolm with a face that brooked no refusal.

Malcolm shot a look at Calvo, pressed his lips together firmly, and stomped to the open doorway. He and the officer stepped outside. A small group of curious neighbors was gathered on the sidewalk a mere thirty feet away. Malcolm's complexion flamed in embarrassment as he walked to the police car.

Hilliard turned and yelled up the stairs to one of the officers.

"Martinez!" he yelled. "Is there a woman's purse up there?"

"Yeah. On the bed."

Hilliard climbed the staircase and entered the room. Someone had opened a few windows to air out the smell of roses. A few of the men were complaining about their eyes. He walked to the bed where an expensive Chanel bag was standing. He opened it and removed a small blue address book.

"Are you supposed to remove that from the crime scene, Boss?" Martinez asked quietly, fearing the retort.

"I'm not taking it," Hilliard said, flipping it open and running a

40

finger down names beginning with 'C' in the small, lined pages until he got to Stephanie Clemens. He pulled out his notebook and jotted down the name and phone number. He made a point of replacing the small book in the purse as he glared at the officer. Martinez shrugged.

"Make sure they bag the purse," Hilliard said and left the room. He rejoined Calvo at the base of the stairs. They walked down the hallway past several large rooms until they came to a massive kitchen. Everything was decorated in pale hues of honey gold and black. The black onyx countertops gleamed in the sunlight pouring in from floor-to-ceiling windows. Ochre pottery with fresh greenery was placed sparsely about the room. Copper pots and pans dangled from an overhead pot rack. The sweet smell of jasmine wafted through the air from a polished gold aromatherapy infuser near the sink.

Hilliard crossed to a glass-fronted cabinet and helped himself to a tumbler. He filled it with water from the sink and drained it. Calvo could see the strain around his eyes.

"How bad is it?" she asked him, not sure she wanted to know the details of what the detective found in the bathroom.

"Worst I've seen for a bathtub death," he said. He wiped his mouth with the back of his hand. "She's been in the water a while. Her body is blistered like someone set her on fire, all but her face, which was above the surface. The coroner is still up there with her, but he said it looks like a chemical burn. The tub water is red, but he said it was a dye, possibly from a perfumed bubble bath. The whole room smells like roses, but there aren't any in there, so it's probably from whatever bath stuff she added. No signs of head trauma. No strangulation marks, but there are petechiae in her eyes and other places on her face. It's odd."

"Yeah," Calvo said, leaning with her back against the island counter. "Petechiae can be from anything where you suffocate, not just strangulation. If her head was above the water, does that rule out drowning? Someone pushing her head under?"

"I don't think her head went under. Her hair is piled up in one of those clips, and it's dry and still curled. What did you get from the maid?"

"She started work this morning at 7:30, went upstairs, found the bedroom empty and the bed still made, found the bathroom door shut, knocked, and went in and found her. She commented on the rose smell as well. She's been working here for three years. That's about all I got. She's pretty wrung out."

"Well, seeing what I saw in that tub would wring anybody out. That's a memory she won't get out of her head for a long time," he said, shaking his head.

"Now the husband…," Calvo said slowly. "That guy is all wrong."

"How so?"

"When I told him his wife was dead, he never asked how she died or where she died. No wanting to rush to her when I told him she had passed. No curiosity about it at all. The second sentence out of his mouth was 'What did the maid tell us?' Seemed concerned about that. When I asked if he had been away, he rattled off a string of things that were over the top. The name of the hotel, how many friends were with him, and even one guy sharing the hotel room. I only asked if he had been away. I could have meant this morning. He automatically went into the details of where he was last night. I get the feeling the 'Missus' died last night. Am I right?"

Hilliard nodded. "Coroner thinks she's been in the water for at least 9-11 hours. Her cell phone was on the bathroom counter, but the battery was dead. We'll have it checked out. Meanwhile, we need a search warrant so we can grab his electronics and see what we can find."

Calvo sighed and pushed off from the counter. "We need more than a jerk showing little emotion over his wife," she said. "We need probable cause. Maybe the autopsy and tox reports will tell us something." Her eyes fell on a pet feeding station to her right by the butler's pantry. It was a fancy stand with china bowls holding both a water bowl and a dish piled high with wet food, a hard crust forming on its surface. She stared at it for a moment.

"Richy," she said beneath her breath.

"What?" Hilliard asked, following her stare to the pet dish.

"Camillie said she started coffee and put food in Richy the cat's dish. The food hasn't been touched. Where's the cat?"

"I fail to see the importance of it," Hilliard said. "Maybe it doesn't know it's chow time."

"Cats can hear a bowl being filled with food a mile away! He, or she, would have pounced on it. Besides, that was hours ago."

"Inside information, is it?" Hilliard grinned.

"I know cats," she said impatiently.

"Yeah, I know. You're New Orleans' cat lady."

"One cat does not make a cat lady. You need at least five."

Calvo walked to the back kitchen door, opened it to the back yard, and called for the cat.

"Kitty, kitty, kitty," she yelled. "Come here, Richy."

Moments passed.

"Were all the rooms checked?" Calvo asked.

"First thing responders do," Hilliard said. "No one, and no kitty, is in the house."

The two left the kitchen, and Calvo walked the long hallway to the front door. When they reached the grand foyer staircase, and Calvo continued walking, Hilliard asked her, "You don't want to go up and see for yourself?"

"No, I'll wait for the report and photos. Too many people up there right now."

Calvo glanced in at Camille as they headed for the front door. She had stopped crying, but her body was shaking. The Lieutenant stepped down into the room beneath the steady glare of the female officer who had been told to stay with the maid. Calvo leaned over the trembling woman and spoke softly into her ear. The maid seemed surprised by the question and then answered her in Haitian. Calvo nodded and squeezed her shoulder. She ignored the officer and stepped back up to the foyer.

"Fòs la pou ou," Calvo called to Camille. The maid nodded and managed a wan smile as the Lieutenant joined Hilliard.

"Translation?" Hilliard asked, pushing something down into his pants pocket. He seemed out of breath.

"I just told her to be strong," Calvo said, glancing at the detective's pocket.

The two exited the building to a crush of reporters who hurtled across the lawn toward them. The detectives hurried to the car and flung open their doors. Hilliard barely missed crushing a reporter's arm who was trying to force a microphone into the car as the detective crammed himself into the driver's seat.

"Get out of the way," he growled at the man, who hastily withdrew his arm while shouting at him.

"Come on! Just a few words. Who died? Was it murder?" the man yelled as Hilliard started the motor and whipped it into reverse. He swore as he maneuvered past the other patrol cars, coroner's wagon, and a dozen reporters.

"I didn't know it was professional for the media to flip off officials," Calvo grinned as she watched the angry reporter walk away. They finally backed onto St. Charles Avenue and turned right.

"I'm starving," Hilliard said as he peeled around the corner of Napoleon, headed for the Bear Cat Café. Calvo pulled her cell phone from her pocket and punched in a name.

"Deeters," a male voice answered, succinctly.

"Deeters," Calvo said, "Get over to the Roosevelt Hotel and ask for their CCTV footage of last night. Ask the desk clerk if anyone saw Malcolm Harris coming or going? What time did he check in? What time did he check out? You know the routine. And, get to Fallows. He's interviewing Malcolm Harris. Tell him to ask the Colonel about the cat."

Hilliard sighed deeply.

"The cat?" Deeters asked, a note of sarcasm in his voice.

"Yes! Ask him where the cat is."

6 SECRETS BETWEEN SISTERS

At 7:00, the guests began to arrive. Four people waited on the front gallery outside, nervously wondering what the night would bring. They studied each other surreptitiously as they pretended to check their cellphone or adjust their hair. The evening was still, except for crickets and katydids playing their nocturnal melody. The constant humidity wilted the small group's clothing and left a glistening mist on their forearms.

The large oak door suddenly swung open, and the group jumped and then giggled self-consciously at their nervousness. The woman standing in the open doorway was tall with long dark hair. She wore a black silk blouse over a purple velvet floor-length skirt, giving her the appearance that she belonged to a past era.

"Come in," Rachel said quietly, and stepped aside to admit the new arrivals for the night's séance. "Please place your cellphones in the basket on the table." She motioned to an oblong wicker basket atop a side table a few feet away. "We don't allow photography or videos of any kind."

Various looks of annoyance flashed across the guests' faces as they let go of their lifelines and placed them into the basket.

"Please sign the ledger next to the basket," Rachel said in her low monotone voice. After each had picked up the old-fashioned pen and signed a large ledger with their name and the date, Rachel led them to a small room, furnished only with three couches, a worn coffee table, and a standing lamp. The room smelled musky, as if the windows had not been opened in years.

No one spoke as they waited, perched upon the uncomfortable vintage couches. They adjusted their weight to avoid the springs threatening to pierce the threadbare needlepoint fabric at any moment. An elderly woman with snowy white hair coughed gently into a handkerchief and kept her eyes on her lap. Across from her sat a pretty blonde woman in her mid-forties. Next to her sat a man in his thirties. His eyes were moving about the faces of the group gathered there. They paused briefly on the blonde and then came to settle on the final member of the group—a harsh-looking man with a deep tan and a large nose. He was staring straight ahead of him at nothing in particular.

Several minutes passed. The sound of the crickets filtered into the room outside the closed windows. A car passed. Somewhere in the distance, a dog barked. Suddenly, a gong sounded from the hallway, and the group jumped.

"You can come in now," Rachel said from the doorway. The group was startled at her sudden appearance. She had made no sound. She simply morphed from the darkened hallway like a phantom.

The four strangers rose from the couches. The man in his thirties offered an arm to the elderly woman who was struggling to push up from the low-lying couch. She thanked him, got her bearings, and followed the others out into the hallway. She glanced down the long black-and-white tiled hall. The outline of several doors stood out in stark relief in the shadows before the hall was swallowed by darkness.

Rachel led the group into a large parlor. The overhead chandelier shed a warm glow from its tulip-shaped sconces. They looked quickly around the large fireplace, a few old-fashioned Queen Anne chairs, a footstool, a few potted plants, and some nondescript portraits hanging on the wall of old people sporting pointed white beards or lace bodices. In the middle of the room, beneath the chandelier, sat a round table draped in black. A large pillar candle commanded its center. To the right of the table, an enormous ornate mirror was leaning against a tall wrought iron easel. Five chairs surrounded the table.

"Please take a seat," Rachel said, "all but the high-backed chair at the head of the table. Madame Lorraine will join you shortly."

Rachel left the room quietly and disappeared into the dark corridor. The four guests chose their seats and settled in. The elderly woman coughed again and kept her eyes lowered. She clutched a small patent leather purse in her lap.

"Do we hold hands and sing Kumbaya?" the man in his thirties laughed. The blonde woman grinned, appreciative of the break in the oppressive atmosphere of the room. The tanned gentleman snorted.

"I'm Davis," the thirty-year-old continued. It was clear he was a man used to meetings and taking control. His eyes went to the blonde and paused.

"Oh, um, Brenda," she said, feeling pressured to speak. "Brenda Griffin."

"Dorothy Brindle," the elderly lady said softly without lifting her eyes from her handbag.

Davis and Brenda looked to the tanned gentleman, who folded his arms and looked perturbed. He lifted his eyebrows and shrugged. The group fell into an awkward silence. A clacking noise like bones rattling came from down the hallway. Brenda looked to the open doorway nervously.

"What is that?" she whispered nervously.

The noise came again, followed by a chuckling sound and twittering.

"It's just a bird," Davis said, smiling. "He probably plays a ghost later in the séance." No one laughed as a severe-looking woman in a flowing scarlet gown entered the room from the hall. Her dark hair was piled atop her head. She made her way to the head of the table without acknowledging the group seated there.

Dorothy Brindle finally lifted her eyes to study the woman who was setting a large deck of worn cards on the table. *Her face is paler than mine*, the elderly woman thought.

"I am Madame Lorraine," the woman said in flat tones. Her green eyes swept quickly over the four people seated around her. "If you follow instructions, we may be favored with answers from beyond the veil."

Davis fought to suppress a grin. The words were what he expected from a medium, but the woman's face was not. His image of a psychic conducting a séance had been one of purple eyeshadow, deep black eyeliner, overly rouged cheeks, and dangling gold earrings in the shape of planets. This woman's face was pallid, completely void of makeup, and she wore no jewelry. Her nose reminded him of a predatory bird. He found her features unpleasant to look at.

"Place your hands on the table, palms flat, hands spread, with your little fingers touching those of the person on your right and left. This forms the protective circle. You will by no means break the circle during the séance as events unfold," Madame Lorraine intoned, her inflection underscoring how many times she had repeated the words by rote.

Each of the guests placed their hands on the table and followed the instructions. Dorothy's small, veined hands were trembling as she pressed her pinkies to those of Brenda and Davis.

The lights went out, and Dorothy let out a small squeal. The blackness was complete after the sudden departure of the lights. Dorothy whimpered softly. Brenda resisted the urge to pat her hand, fearing breaking the circle.

"Jaziel!" Madame Lorraine cried out in the darkness. Brenda and Dorothy gasped. "Jaziel! Come to us. We are gathered. We invoke you to come from beyond the veil and speak to us. Please, Jaziel. Let me know you are here. Light the candle!"

A few seconds passed in the inky darkness. Brenda felt her heart throbbing in her neck. Then slowly, a small flame appeared in the middle of the table. It grew steadily until the faces around the table were highlighted in its orange glow. Their eyes darted about the table, gauging each other's reactions.

"Thank you, Jaziel!" Madame Lorraine called out, her head tipped back, and her eyes closed. "Do you have messages for the people gathered tonight? Are there souls who wish to come through?"

Dorothy bit her thin lips and watched the face of the medium. She wished she had not come here.

"I hear," Madame Lorraine said dramatically. "Yes, I hear. There is a woman here with us. She has passed. Tragically. A hurried death. A hurried funeral. She is smiling now. Hidden. Something is hidden. A plan thwarted."

Davis noticed the sudden change in the tanned man across from him. His eyes were open wide, and a look of fear crossed his face. His eyes met Davis's, and he quickly recovered his composure.

"I am one who was deceived," Madame Lorraine continued. "I am not at rest!"

A soft puff of air swept into the room from the left of the table. It came from a shadowed corner where there was no window. It was followed by a green mist emanating from the same direction. It floated into the room, undulating and growing as it neared the table. The group held their breath as the luminous miasma rose behind the medium's head and wafted toward the giant mirror leaning against the easel at her left elbow. It reached the mirror and spread out, covering the glass like iridescent spider threads, and then lifted toward the ceiling, where it dissipated and was gone.

Dorothy was simpering, little gasps coming from her lips. Her small, wrinkled face was scrunched up, and her eyelids pressed closed. Brenda suddenly screamed, and Dorothy's eyes flew open. Brenda was staring at the mirror, her hand to her throat. The others followed her frightened stare and gasped, the tanned gentleman slamming against the back of his chair. He recoiled from the mirror, sitting only a few feet from him. A woman's face was etched in green on the dark glass.

"That's enough!" he shouted. "What's going on here?" The muscles in his face were taut, and his grey eyes bulging. "What are you trying to pull?" he shouted angrily.

Davis studied him intently. It was obvious the man was frightened out of his skin.

Madame Lorraine opened her eyes. She lowered her head and took a deep breath. The face on the mirror slowly dissolved until the only image remaining was the reflection of the candle flame and the blurry faces of the group gathered about the table.

"The circle has been broken," Madame Lorraine said, her head still lowered, and her eyes closed. "But there was a message left for someone here. A man fought hard to get through, wanting his loved one to hear from him."

The medium raised her head and opened her eyes. She lowered them to the table and reached for a black bag lying there. The group registered its surprise as the bag had not been there at the beginning of the séance. Madame Lorraine picked up the soft velvet sack and opened it. She slid a small, folded sheet of parchment paper from inside and leaned with it toward the candle to read the scribbled words.

"My dearest Dot. All is well. You may proceed."

Dorothy cried out, her small frame trembling with sobs. "Charles!" she cried. "Oh my dearest Charlie. I miss you so much. I will take care of it. I promise. I love you!"

Madame Lorraine passed the paper to the elderly woman, who pressed it to her bosom and sobbed.

"Thank you," she said, in a shuddering breath. Those around her weren't sure if she was thanking Madame Lorraine or Charlie.

The chandelier suddenly blazed overhead, and everyone blinked in the sudden glare. The tanned man turned his head to stare at the mirror, but it only reflected the table and people seated around it. He was still angry as he turned his stare to the medium.

"I don't know what you're trying to pull here," he said hotly, "But you're messing with the wrong man."

Madame Lorraine leveled her green eyes at him and, with total calm in her voice, said, "I cannot control the spirits. If something here this evening has distressed you, you must look to your own conscience."

The man slammed his chair back, glowering at her. Davis feared he was going to strike her. Taking a few rattling breaths, he stepped away from the table and exited the room. The group heard him near the front door, ordering someone to "Get out of my way!" Then the door slammed.

"Would you like your cards read?" Madame Lorraine asked the remaining guests, who were still recovering from the man's outburst and the image in the mirror. Dorothy was still hugging the parchment to her chest, her eyes shut and tears streaming down her face.

"I think I got all I need," Davis said, a wry grin on his face. "Let's see…I will meet a tall, dark stranger, inherit a fortune, and move to Paris."

Madame Lorriane's eyes glittered as she fixed him with a menacing glare. He met it evenly, still smiling.

He rose, sliding back his chair. As he did so, Dorothy struggled to push hers back as well.

"Are you leaving?" he asked Dorothy, who looked up at him. She paused and then nodded. He helped pull back her chair, and she pushed up to a standing position, one hand gripping the table for support. Davis took her arm as she steadied herself and slipped the handle of her purse over a frail arm ensconced in an eyelet sweater sleeve. She looked back at the medium.

"Thank you," she whispered, and then allowed Davis to escort her from the room.

Madame Lorraine's eyes came to rest on the only remaining guest at the table. Brenda was having trouble controlling her heart rate. She kept glancing at the mirror, expecting to see another face appear.

"Do you wish a reading?" Madame Lorraine asked, picking up the cards. Brenda nodded.

The medium shuffled the cards with deft precession. She laid seven cards out on the table, side by side.

"You must think of a question and then choose," she said.

Brenda studied the cards with the odd symbols of planets and vine-wrapped edges and pointed to one. Madame Lorraine slowly flipped it over.

"The King of Spades," she said. "A man of secrets. Sometimes deceit. A card that signifies the need for careful interaction with a man in a powerful position, a controlling man. Missing clothes. Take action, or dire consequences can follow."

She watched Brenda's face as it changed from fear to concern. Her lips tightened as deep furrows formed in her forehead. She looked from the card to the medium and asked only one question.

"Can this man be stopped?"

****

"Did you put the notes in their pockets?" Madame Lorraine asked her sister as they settled into the Queen Anne chairs in the parlor with steaming cups of Rachel's mushroom tea. The guests had departed half an hour earlier.

"Of course," she said quietly, taking a long sip of the brew. "Well, pockets and purses, whatever was easier. I didn't plan on the mirror's face causing that man to react so violently. His name is Nathan Hennings, by the way."

"Yes," Madame Lorraine said in a low tone. "He was very upset."

Rachel glanced at the back of the large mirror leaning against the easel near the parlor table.

"It worked better than I thought it would," she said proudly. "Drawing the face with the reactor took the longest time. If we're going to use it again, I need to make more of the phosphorous smoke and the reactor."

"We won't use the mirror for a while," the medium said. "A magician never does the same trick twice, at least not until a little time has gone by. I am concerned about the list. Is she doing her due diligence when choosing our guests?"

"The only hiccup has been that David Wilcox," Rachel said.

Madame Lorraine looked at her quickly.

"Why was he here?" she asked, her face flushing. "How did he make it onto the list?"

Rachel set her empty cup onto its saucer and looked with intent at her sister.

"He didn't. The name for tonight was Dayton Wells. By the time I saw Davis's signature in the night's ledger, it was too late. You had already begun."

"Then who the hell is he?" Madame Lorraine spat, her face suddenly fearful.

"I'll talk to her," Rachel said sternly. "So far, everything has worked out. Dorothy Bridle paid her $1500 in cash to hear from her recently deceased husband. Even grumpy old Nathan Hennings paid fifteen hundred." She paused. "Why did you change the words?" Rachel asked, her eyes searching her sister's face. "You were supposed to tell him where his dead wife said something was hidden. That's why he was here. What was all the 'hurried death and a hurried funeral, and somebody not at rest' stuff?"

"Just giving the people what they want. Chills and thrills," she said.

"Well, you gave him more than that! I don't think he is going to go away quietly. He may want his money back. Especially after the way he reacted to the mirror image I drew from the internet picture you gave me."

"Leave it to me to handle him," the medium said, nonplussed. "Dorothy Brindle bought it hook, line, and sinker, though. I'm curious as to the meaning behind the note I handed her."

"I wrote the note from Charlie as instructed," Rachel said. "I didn't feel good about that one. She broke down. She really thinks it's from her dead husband." Rachel frowned and took a sip of tea.

Madame Lorraine sighed. "You will be the death of me," she said. "You can't be in this business and want to hold everyone's hand! Why don't you look at it this way? It made her happy to know she could still hear from dear old Charlie. Not a bad thing."

Madame Lorraine tasted her tea and cocked her head.

"What's in this?" she asked, wrinkling her nose. "It smells like seafood."

"It's Lion Mane mushroom tea," Rachel said. "I added a little ginger."

The medium took another tentative sip, shrugged, and took another. She turned her attention to the guests from the séance that night.

Rachel studied the amber liquid in her cup and chose her words carefully.

"Don't you worry that one of these times it will backfire? We don't know much about the people who come here. We're trusting our contact to supply us with their names and what you're supposed to say in their séance sessions. What if they're dangerous? What's to stop them from hurting us if something they hear in the séance hits too close to home? Or the police catching on to what we're doing?"

Madame Lorraine lowered her cup onto its saucer next to her with a loud clink. Rachel recoiled. She had gone too far. But it needed to be addressed.

"People pay us to hear from people who have passed or to have their cards read," Madame Lorraine said heatedly. That is not against the law. Haven't I always handled things?" the medium asked her, her voice laced with anger. "When Mark died, didn't I handle it?"

Rachel drew in her breath and looked at her sister with horror.

"Don't!" she said, her voice quivering. "You can't talk about him when you know I know what you did in your own marriage! Don't forget, I know your secrets. I know where the bodies are buried."

Madame Lorraine studied her younger sister for a few heartbeats. She thought back to the home they grew up in, filled with arguments, alcohol, and abuse. Their father departed on Christmas Eve when they were young, ruining the holiday for them forever. They grew up leaning on one another, especially after their mother succumbed to liver disease at forty-nine years old. She looked at Rachel now with interest. Would her sister ever really turn on her? She glanced over at her teacup with new suspicion. Then, smiling, she picked it up again and finished it off, the taste of earthy mushrooms in her mouth.

"It grows on you," she said smugly about the tea, running a tongue over her lips.

"Like a fungus?" Rachel asked.

7 THE WORD IS OUT

Friday morning, following the séance the night before, Davis Miles reread the opening to his article. The impact he wanted was lacking. He glanced at the yellow Post-It note attached to the top of his computer: *The first paragraph has to hook them*, it said. He muttered the phrase to himself for the millionth time in his career as a newspaper journalist. He hit the delete button and let it run backwards through the previous four sentences. Staring at the remaining blank section, he bit his lip, considered, and began again.

Mysterious Doings in the Big Easy

If you think voodoo is confined to the French Quarter and the Treme, think again. Just head over to the Garden District and knock at the door of the Stanton-Mills mansion. That's the home of the immutable Madame Lorraine, a third-generation psychic who will put you in touch with your dearly departed, read your fortune, and put on some pretty convincing parlor tricks. Price of admission? It depends.

The article went on to expound on the voodoo history of New Orleans, tracing its origins to enslaved Africans in the 1700s. It met its zenith under the rule of the celebrated priestess Marie Laveau, who was buried in St. Louis Cemetery No.1. Davis's keyboard clicked away as he hurried to meet his 2:00 PM deadline with the *New Orleans Tattler* newspaper. It was a boutique printing press, popular with locals looking for the latest gossip, slander, social events, and hot properties on the market.

"Got my tickets?" a male voice asked.

Davis looked up to see his friend Dayton Wells standing at his cubicle, one arm flung over the low partition. Dayton freelanced for the *New Orleans Tribune*, a job Davis coveted. Davis grinned and pulled open a drawer in his desk.

"Well worth it," Davis said, grinning, as he handed Dayton two tickets to the New Orleans Saints football game against the Carolina Panthers at Caesars Superdome.

Dayton studied the tickets, and his face lit up.

"How the hell did you score sideline club seats?" he exclaimed.

"Shhh!" Davis said, looking around him anxiously. "Calm down! Just take 'em and have a good time. I'm more a baseball fan anyway." He paused and leaned forward conspiratorially. "Last night was off the hook! That psychic is a whack job. But you know what? I think something else is going on there. I'd like to know how she did some of the special effects, like making a face appear on a mirror with green smoke. But you should have seen this guy blow up over it. This wasn't random."

Dayton grinned at his longtime friend.

"Glad it got you the piece you wanted," he said. "I only wrangled an invite because I was told there was a way to get Linda back. Dumb, I know, but this person said this Madame Lorraine worked miracles. I'm sure it's all bogus, but worth $25 for an entertaining night, and my cards read."

"Yeah," Davis said, staring off into space. "But I think there's more to it. I signed in with a fake last name. The background I did on her says she's a third-generation psychic, but I couldn't find out any of her other relatives' names or occupations. Her life before moving into that house is pretty blank."

"The bloodhound is on the hunt," Dayton grinned. "Thanks for the tixs, man. Go Saints!" He began walking off, slapping his tickets against his open palm.

"Hey Dayton!" Davis called, "The Superdome was built over a cemetery. It's supposed to be haunted."

"All of New Orleans is haunted," Dayton laughed and walked off.

Davis returned to his article. He glanced up at the large clock above the chief editor's office. 1:48. He gave it a quick polish, signed his name as the byline, and handed it to the runner. Leaning back in his swivel chair, he cupped his hands behind his head and stared at the dingy perforated ceiling tiles. He just wanted a shot at the *New Orleans Advocate* or the *Tribune*. He was tired of simpering fillers designed to titillate the old magnolias who read it with relish over their morning eggs and mimosas. His editor had asked him to do a Halloween piece on a side hustle in New Orleans geared to snaring tourists. When Dayton mentioned Madame Lorraine over oysters, Davis bribed him into letting him take his place at a bona fide séance. The football tickets had been given to him by a grateful restaurant owner needing some publicity.

Davis picked up his weathered brown leather satchel, flipped open the flap, and pushed his laptop down into it. He was done for the day, mission accomplished. But as he walked down the narrow hallway to the glass door leading out onto Canal Street, his mind was restless. Something odd was going on inside the Stanton-Mills mansion. It was worth looking into.

****

Detective Hilliard sat with elbows on his desk, peering down through bifocals at a report in front of him. It was the autopsy report from the Marjorie Harris case. His forehead melted into furrows as he read the gruesome details concerning the condition of her body. Just then, Lieutenant Calvo entered his office and plopped down into her customary chair across the desk from him. She slid over a stapled report.

"Tox report," she said.

Hilliard pulled it toward him with his forefinger. He scanned it, skipping over the medical jargon at the top. He released a soft whistle and settled back into his chair, the frame squeaking beneath his weight.

"Somebody really hated this lady," he said, pushing his glasses up higher onto his nose. "Pretty much pickled her alive."

"Traces of cyanide crystals were found in the bath water," Calvo said unnecessarily. "Looks like they were in the bath bomb. When cyanide interacts with hot water, the effects are felt within twenty to thirty minutes. Her skin was not only chemically burned, but the gas from the crystals had also shut down her oxygen supply. She suffocated. Hence, the petechiae they found."

Hilliard shook his head.

"They're sure it was in the bath bomb?" he asked.

"Yes. For a couple of reasons: They took samples from the bath water," Calvo said. "The rose smell was from a fragrance additive, but the rest was baking soda, citric acid, and cyanide crystals. The baking soda and citric acid are common components in bath bombs. On top of that, two of the remaining five that were in a tray on the tub ledge tested positive for the same cyanide recipe," Calvo said. "In my opinion, having three bombs in place on top upped the odds that she would choose one of them. The photo of the room showed that the silver tray had two bars of soap, a loofah sponge, and a large silver bowl of the bombs. The soap was tested. They were some luxury custom-made bars, no poison. Somebody concocted a lethal rose-scented killer."

"What about the candles? No cyanide in them?"

Calvo shook her head. "Just your garden variety $80 Passion Island candles." She smirked. "Anything on her phone?"

"It looks like it was possible that the music she had playing drained the battery from running all night," Hilliard said."She punched in some jazz at 11:00 that night, so we know she was alive then. Texts were mainly to her friend Stephanie that day about meeting at a gala.

There are several texts to one number in particular in the days prior. The contact name on her phone for those is "Sidebar."

"Sidebar? Sounds like a legal term," Calvo said. She jotted it down in her notebook.

Hilliard opened his desk drawer and pulled out a bag of black licorice. He opened the ziplock and offered the bag to Calvo. She grinned and declined the candy.

"I honestly didn't think you would ever give up those annoying hard caramels," she laughed. "At least the licorice is quiet."

Hilliard grinned and scooped three pieces into his mouth. "It took some getting used to," he said. "But I like them." He took a long swig of cola and wiped his mouth.

"I wouldn't overdo that," Calvo said, suddenly serious. "Licorice has caffeine."

Hilliard pushed the wad of licorice into his cheek with his tongue and leveled his eyes at her.

"First, you complain about the caramels all through the Broussard case, now you give me a substitute, and you're going to start up again? Why give them to me if you're not happy with them?" His voice had risen an octave.

"I'm just saying if you drink a lot of cola—which is heavy in caffeine—and then add licorice—which contains caffeine, you could get irregular heart rhythms, and....end up in the bathroom more often, if you get my drift."

Hilliard sighed, tossed the bag of candy back into the desk drawer, and slammed it.

"You're annoying!" he said, dully.

"I've been told," she said, grinning. "So, what do we think? Who wanted Majorie Harris dead? Obviously, the first person is the angry husband, *Colonel* Malcolm Harris," she said, emphasizing his preferred title.

"He has a very opportunistic alibi for the night she died," Hilliard said. "The CCTV footage from the hotel shows him entering an elevator with a man at 11:45 pm, and not coming out again until the following morning at 7:00. Desk clerk confirms he checked in at 6:30

pm for the conference dinner and speech. Other than in the bar later that night, he is not seen anywhere inside the hotel, outside in the parking lot, or anywhere else between those times. He didn't leave until the next morning. He has witnesses for that. Marjorie was using her phone to play jazz at 11:00 pm, so she was alive while he was in the bar having drinks. But you don't have to be there to have a bath bomb ready to go. We need to talk to that maid again. Find out Marjorie's routine. Did she have a nightly bath ritual? I mean, if it was Malcolm, he had to be sure she was going to take a bath that night while he had this iron-clad alibi of a conference in place. We need the maid's insight into what typically goes on in that house."

Calvo frowned. "By we, you mean me."

"Ja!" Hilliard said, grinning.

Calvo's mouth twisted sideways as she squinted at the man.

"No more Haitian Creole for you," she said. She shook her head and rose from the chair. "I'll take Camille. You tackle the Colonel."

Hilliard's grin disappeared. Calvo smiled as she walked to his office door. She stopped.

"I've been trying to get hold of Marjorie Harris' best friend, Stephanie Clemens, to set up a time to interview her. I finally got her on the phone, and let's just say you could chill your beer on this lady's attitude. She seemed surprised when I asked if she saw Marjorie the morning of the day she died. Remember, Colonel Harris said he thought Marjorie left at 9 am that morning to meet Stephanie about some Hampton emergency? Stephanie stumbled around a while when I asked her, and finally said, 'I'm really sorry she's dead. Truly. But I'm done covering for her. If you'll excuse me, I have a plane to catch.'"

Hilliard shook his head. "Sounds like the 'B' word," he said. "So by covering for her, she means Marjorie was sneaking around?"

"Possibly. There is a twenty-year age gap between her and Malcolm. I'll get hold of Stephanie when she gets back from the Hamptons."

She took another step out the door and turned around again.

"Did I tell you what Fallows said Malcolm answered when he

60

asked him about the whereabouts of the cat?" Hilliard's eyes narrowed. Undaunted, she continued, "He said, and I quote, 'How the hell do I know where the cat is? You guys probably let it out the door with all your coming and going.' Unquote."

Hilliard looked at her through hooded eyes, his face stoic.

"I need to ask Camille about the cat anyway," she said, smothering a smile. She exited quickly into the hallway as Hilliard let out a feigned shriek. Calvo was laughing when she nearly collided with Officer Patterson, a young man who had been with the force for a little over a year. He grinned.

"You two are like children," he laughed.

"Yeah. He throws the tantrums, I color on the walls," she said as she walked away down the hall.

****

Saturday morning, October 4th, Camille opened the front door upon hearing the shrill tone of the doorbell from the hallway where she was polishing the marble floor. She was surprised to see the kind police woman standing there who had talked to her two days ago on the morning she found her employer dead.

"Good morning, Camille," Lieutenant Calvo said, smiling. "I hope I'm not bothering you. I just have a couple of questions to ask you if you don't mind."

Camille hesitated. Calvo noticed the sudden tightness in her body.

"The Mister is not home," she said, her voice strained.

Calvo was surprised at the concern the maid seemed to feel in talking with her.

"We will be speaking with him again as well," Calvo said softly, still smiling. "It's only two questions, and I will hurry, tanpri souple."

The Haitian word for "please" seemed to soften the maid's agitation. She managed a small smile and stood aside to let Calvo enter. The hallway smelled of a lavender-scented floor polish. Camille led the officer into the same sunken parlor. The room was spotless, each couch pillow carefully arranged. Sunlight from the front window sparkled off a cut-glass vase of fresh white roses sitting in the middle of a gleaming marble coffee table.

Calvo claimed the same chair she had been seated in on the day of the murders. The maid took the chair next to her rather than mess up the couch. Calvo turned in her chair to face her and smiled again. Camille's hands were restless, smoothing her apron over and over in a self-soothing motion. Calvo had the impression Malcolm Harris had gotten to her.

"Camille, I didn't get your last name the other day. May I have that, please?" Calvo said, pulling out a small notebook from her pocket. She was afraid the tape recorder would worry the woman.

"Camille Augustin," she said meekly. Calvo jotted it down.

"That's a true Creole name," Calvo said, smiling. "You have a great ancestry." Camille didn't reply. "Um, ok, let's see," Calvo said, feeling her way delicately. "Marjorie, the Missus, did she take a bath every night?"

Camille's face flinched at the mention of her late employer's name, but she remained in control.

"Yes, the Missus liked her bath and her music and her candles," the maid said, beginning to sniffle. "I always have her robe laid out on her bed for her each night. She take it into the bathroom with her for her bath time."

"And her, um, bath products...the bath bombs, where did she get those?" Calvo asked carefully, studying the maid's face. There was no reaction to the question. She was sure Camille was not aware of what caused Marjorie's death.

"I buy them," Camille said simply. "She had special ones made for her at Christina's Boutique in town. Always same order. I just go and pick up."

Calvo jotted down the name of the store and paused. She didn't want to scare the woman off, but she felt she needed to hurry in case Malcom Harris suddenly came home.

"Were there always six in the order?" Calvo asked.

"Always six, yes," Camille said in broken English. "Same order always. The bill come in the mail."

Calvo thought over the information. The next question would have to be handled delicately.

"You are being so helpful, Camille. Almost done. The Mister, did he ever buy the Missus bath bombs?"

Camille's expression changed. Her guard was up.

"Why we talk about the bath things so much?" she asked, a touch of fear in her voice. "Something wrong with them?" She moved to the front of her chair.

"No, no," Calvo hurried. "It's just that the bathtub is where…well, you know. We are just checking anything in the room that may have been out of place. I assume the tray of soap and things on the tub ledge looked like they always did?"

Camille shut down. She pressed her lips tightly, and she looked on the verge of tears.

"It's alright, Camille," Calvo said, placing a hand on her knee. "No more bathroom questions, okay." Camille relaxed. "Will you stay on with the Mister?" Calvo asked pleasantly. "I'm sure he counts on you quite a bit. The house is so well cared for!"

Camille sniffed and smiled.

"He like the way I clean and cook," she said proudly. "I mainly spoke with the Missus about the housework, but Mister liked how I leave things alone in his office and bedroom. I make bed and clean his bathroom, but don't touch anything else."

"Oh, they had their own bedrooms?" Calvo asked innocently. "I've heard a lot of people have chosen to do that, and it seems to work for them." She smiled disarmingly.

Camille cocked her head and shrugged.

"Not like what I would choose, but…" She paused. "They used to share same room. A year ago, it change, maybe because of kitty, maybe not." She pressed her lips together again and stared at the floor.

"Was the Mister here earlier the day the Missus died?" Calvo asked softly.

"I do marketing on Thursdays, so he may be here or not be here. I fix them breakfast and then leave for the errands. He was preparing for big lecture that night, so I try to leave him alone."

"We need to speak with him again today," Calvo said. "Would you know where he is?"

"Mister is at funeral home. He picking out the flowers and the paper thing... how you say? The paper with the songs and things."

"The program," Calvo said. "I assume that's Faregate's Funeral Home? They seem to handle all the elite clientele in this parish."

Camille looked a bit confused at some of the Lieutenant's wording, but she slowly nodded her head. "Yes, Faregate's. I think that's what he said."

"Thank you for talking to me, Camille. Again, I'm so sorry for your Missus. I can tell she valued you a lot. Oh, by the way," Calvo said as she put her notebook away and stood. "Did the kitty come back?"

Camille broke into tears. "No, no kitty. The Missus and Richy are both gone!"

Calvo placed her hand on the woman's shuddering shoulder.

"Do you think Richy may have gotten outside and run away?" Calvo asked gently.

"No, never. Richy always stays in house. Even if door open, he never go outside. Attacked by bluejay once and now never go out."

Calvo made a mental note of the information.

"Does Richy have a collar with an address on it?" Calvo asked.

"Yes. Beautiful blue collar with gold tag," Camille said, wiping her nose with a tissue from her apron pocket.

Calvo took a step toward the hallway so that the next question would seem easier if it looked like she was leaving.

"Has the Mister called around, neighbors, shelters, that kind of thing to look for Richy?"

Camille rose to her feet, her face frustrated.

"The Mister leave kitty alone. I don't think he liked Richy very much. Missus usually try to keep Richy out of his way. When she go out that last night, she remind me to keep Richy in her room. I put kitty in there and finish up my chores. Mister was already gone to his lecture. I go to bed at 9:30 like always."

"Your bedroom is way at the back of the house," Calvo said. "Could you hear the Missus's music playing or the bath water running that night?"

"No. I am over behind the kitchen. I don't hear anything." She began to cry. "I wish I did."

"You said you put Richy in Missus' bedroom before you went to bed…who do you think let the cat out? I mean, if Richy sleeps in that room, and the Mister spent the night away that night…"

Camille's face looked confused. She blinked, trying to remember all the events of that evening.

"I don't know," she said, her voice shaking. "I know I put kitty in the Missus' room, close the door, finish cleaning, and go to bed. I did not even hear the Missus come home that night. I just find her in the morning…" Her face reddened as she tried to hold back the tears.

"Camille, if you have a picture of Richy, I will look for him, okay? I know this has been a lot for you."

Camille's face brightened. She darted into the hallway and disappeared. She returned holding a small photograph of a beautiful Persian cat with long white fur and blue eyes. He was seated on a fancy cat bed.

"Where is the cat bed usually kept?" Calvo asked, studying the photo.

"By the Missus's bed," Camille said, sniffling again. "Part of reason the Mister has his own bedroom, I think. I comb Richy every day. He has a lot of long fur, and it get tangled if you not brush it."

"He's a beautiful cat, and I will do all I can to find him," Calvo said, placing a hand on the woman's arm. "May I borrow this photograph so I can ask around if anyone has seen Richy?"

"Oh, yes, plz," Camille said, slipping into her native tongue. "I pray he come home. I also pray for Missus in heaven."

"So do I, Camille. So do I. It may be better if you don't tell the Mister I was here today." Camille looked relieved to comply. She walked Calvo to the door.

8 DOROTHY

Dorothy Brindle took a deep breath and looked about her at the manicured lawn and groundskeeper busily trimming azalea bushes near the driveway. The Gothic Revival mansion loomed before her, ornate columns of white granite glistening in the morning sunlight. She adjusted her paisley dress, pulled her white eyelet sweater tighter onto her shoulders, and pressed her purse against her side. Finally, she reached out a lace-gloved hand and pressed the doorbell.

A full minute passed before a young man wearing khaki shorts and a blue polo shirt with a sailfish logo opened the door. His face registered surprise at seeing the elderly woman standing there. He sputtered something incoherent before exclaiming, "Dorothy! For Pete's sake, this is a surprise!"

Dorothy managed a stiff smile and tried to calm the trembling she felt inside. It would not be good for him to see her nervousness.

"It's nice to see you, Everett," she said, the words sounding insincere to her ears.

An awkward silence followed until the young man caved to the tension.

"Uh, well, do come in," he said, stepping to one side.

Dorothy entered the cluttered foyer, her eyes swiveling to take in the avalanche of expensive décor. Abstract art in garish colors covered the walls. A cheetah rug with the head still attached sprawled out before her on the travertine marble floor. Gothic masks in various stages of tortured countenances lined a side table. Packing boxes were stacked everywhere. She fought to hide her disgust.

"Here," Everett said, motioning toward a room to his right. "Come on in, have a seat. Pardon the boxes, I'm still unpacking."

Dorothy flinched at his words. She looked about at dozens of moving boxes with the words DEN and KITCHEN scribbled in black marker.

"I uh, don't play the host that great," Everett said, running a hand through his tangle of dark brown hair. "I have water and beer," he said, chuckling. "Oh, yeah, uh, sit down. Here, let me move that."

He picked up a stack of books from a chair, and Dorothy sat down, perched on the edge of the club chair with her back straight. She clutched her purse handle with both hands. When she didn't respond to his invitation for a drink, he said awkwardly. "I don't suppose you drink beer."

She finally looked up at him, her blue eyes dimmed by cataracts and small gold-framed glasses.

"A beer will be fine," she said.

He looked surprised but nodded, grinning, and left the room.

Dorothy looked about her. Her eyes came to rest on a few framed photographs lining the mantle top. They were all the same girl in various forms of undress and exotic locations. She shook her head and glanced down at the open box near her feet. Packing paper spilled from it, revealing various drinking glasses.

Everett returned, carrying two long-neck bottles of IPAs. As he went to hand Dorothy one, he paused, laughing.

"Told you I'm not good at this," he said. "I should have asked if you wanted a glass. I never use one."

"A bottle is fine," Dorothy said.

"Right!" he said, cracking the bottle cap with an opener. He set the bottle of craft beer on a small table next to her and walked to a desk chair across the room. He plopped into it. "The desk is coming today," he said, trying to make conversation. He took a long swig of his beer.

"Quite a change from your other home," Dorothy said, taking a tentative sip of her beer. It had a bitter taste, and she set the bottle back onto the table.

"Yeah," Everett said, his voice tight. "Funny how life can throw you a big gift like that." He tipped the bottle back and swallowed.

"Indeed," Dorothy said, her mouth stomach roiling. She smoothed her skirt and chose her words carefully.

"As you know, I was attending to my sister in Florida when poor Charlie passed." She watched his face. "I haven't been able to face talking about it until now. People keep telling me that I should be rallying by now, as if one month is enough time to adjust to losing a man you shared your life with for fifty years."

Everett wasn't sure how to respond. Deep sentiments were not his strong suit. He merely nodded, hoping his face looked sympathetic.

"I understand that you were helpful the day Charlie collapsed," she said. "You were there at the house. I'm sure having you around was a comfort, as you are his only remaining living relative, well, aside from me, that is."

Everett shifted in his chair. His fingers tightened on his beer bottle.

"I am ready now to hear what happened," Dorothy said, her voice small. "Not the coroner's antiseptic telling of it, but Charlie's last moments. Did he suffer?"

Everett's face tightened. His tan covered any reddening of his cheeks, but there was a change to the lines around his eyes and mouth.

"I, uh, well, you know I wasn't there when he, uh, fell. I made him a sandwich. We watched a ball game together in the den. With you away, I thought he could use the company. After you called him, I told him I would head out, but call if he needed anything. I split. He was fine. So, I don't know if he suffered." He took another drink, draining the bottle.

Dorothy gripped her purse handle harder and tried to steady her nerves.

"When I heard he was found dead, lying by the recliner where I left him," Everett continued, sensing that she needed more information, "I thought he might have gotten up to go to the bathroom or something, and lost his footing or something happened to his heart." He paused and looked longingly at his empty bottle.

"Mind if I get another one?" he asked, but he was already on his feet and headed for the foyer. He returned in a few minutes, his movements manic. He was already drinking from the bottle by the time he fell into the desk chair. He didn't notice Dorothy's labored breathing or her purse now sitting on the floor beside her.

"Last one," he said. "Gotta hit the store. Oh, you're not drinking yours. Not your cup of tea?"

"No, no! It makes me dizzy, and I can't afford that at my age. Charlie and I always just had a small sherry before bed." A slight shudder ran through her small body. "So, it was a heart attack, then?" she asked, her voice husky.

A few moments of silence ensued. Everett took another drink.

"Yeah, I mean, that's what they said, didn't they? I heard they worked on him there in the room, but finally loaded him into an ambulance. They told me later he was DOA before he got to the hospital."

Dorothy gasped. The crudeness of his stark statement came as a shock.

"Oh, sorry!" Everett said hurriedly. "Damn! Sorry! Like I said, hosting isn't my thing. I'm really sorry. Look, I can imagine how hard all this is, but Grandfather left you pretty well off, right? I mean, you won't have to worry about money and stuff."

Dorothy fought the temptation to launch at him. It was only her frailty that kept her from doing so.

"You didn't do so badly yourself," she said tersely. "From living in a friend's garage to this." She swept her hand about her.

Everett's efforts at feigned hospitality vanished. His face became stonelike, his dark brown eyes becoming almost black.

"If that's all," he said, standing, "I have a lot of unpacking to do."

Dorothy remained seated, staring up at him, her face a mask.

Finally, she pressed a hand to the chair arm and struggled to stand. He didn't offer to assist her. Her knees protested as she finally stood unsteadily.

"Thank you for seeing me," she said.

Everett walked out into the foyer and waited for her at the front door. He opened it without further comment. Dorothy stepped out in the heat and turned around to look at him.

"Interestingly, you contacted Mr. Layton about the will before the funeral was barely over," she said. She turned and stepped carefully down the steps past an urn of flowers. "Your geraniums need watering," she said, and walked toward her Cadillac. The mansion's front door slammed behind her.

Dorothy Brindle slid slowly into the driver's seat of her 1984 baby-blue Cadillac that she and Charlie purchased when his first business sold. She laid her patent leather purse on the seat next to her, the clasp standing open. Sunlight through the windshield glinted off a bottle whose neck was protruding from one corner of the open purse. Dorothy started the car and glanced over at the empty beer bottle, a thin smile smoothing her wrinkled lips.

****

Lieutenant Calvo stepped into the boutique that sat next to a few dress stores in the French Quarter. She was immediately bombarded with the fragrances of multiple bath products and lotions. The store was a blend of upscale display cases and whimsical bath décor, mainly in gold and silver plating. The pale blue walls and cream-colored moldings gave the space a feeling of calm, as did the soft meditation music playing overhead.

A young woman with perfectly coiffed hair and a tailored suit approached Calvo, beaming a smile of unnaturally white teeth. The Lieutenant was wearing her New Orleans sweatshirt and a pair of jeans. Her dark braids were piled atop her head and held in place by a large blue clip. A few ladies attired in expensive dresses cast surreptitious looks in her direction.

"May I be of service?" the young woman asked. There was a slight note of credulity in her voice.

"Yes, please," Calvo said, ignoring the raised eyebrows around her. "I'm here in search of bath bombs." She smiled disarmingly. "I have an Aunt's birthday coming up, and the woman cannot live without them. She's pretty picky, which is why I'm here."

The young woman's frozen smile remained in place.

"Of course," she said. "Let me show you our gift selections." She turned and walked past several displays to a low table draped in ivory. Multiple baskets of bath bombs were seated in various arrangements on a tiered platform. The aromas coming from them were intoxicating. In front of each collection was a gold gilt card with the number of items included, the array of fragrances, and the price. Calvo swallowed over the latter.

"Does your Aunt have a favorite fragrance?" the girl asked.

"Uh, yes. She's very fond of roses," Calvo said.

"A popular choice," the sales lady said mechanically. "We have several selections. This one contains twelve variations, all rose-scented. We make our own blend of soothing salts."

Calvo looked past the large basket the young woman was indicating, obviously hoping to make a $250 sale. A basket of six was perched upon a gift box on the top tier. It was priced at $125.

"If she likes these, and I'm sure she will," Calvo said pleasantly, "can she have a standing order? That way, I won't have to choose each time."

The clerk's face lit up. "Oh, we can do better than that! We have a subscription service. Your Aunt can join that, and we will deliver her preferred items monthly, right to her door. She can choose from our other products at the same time. We have custom lotions, foaming bath products, embroidered towels, loofahs…"

Calvo interrupted her. "I don't mind picking them up," she said. "I work just down the street."

The clerk's enthusiasm disappeared.

"Well, it's available should she change her mind," she said solemnly. "Do you see something you'd like?" she asked, glancing over Calvo's shoulder at more promising customers.

"You say these are your own special blends," Calvo said, ignoring her question. "Do they vary from batch to batch? Can a customer request something special to be added?"

The young store clerk pulled her gaze from a large woman dripping in diamonds and sighed. "We have a large line of products in the bath bomb inventory, as you can see. Whatever your skin routine, I'm sure we can accommodate it. We don't do special requests other than some packaging options. May I ring one of these up for you?"

"Let me think about it," Calvo said sweetly. "I need to make sure I have Auntie's favorite scent down for sure."

The clerk's chest rose as her lips pressed together. She walked off toward the large woman, the beaming smile in place before she reached her.

Calvo studied the basket of six red-colored bath bombs. They looked the same, except for some white marbling. She could smell the rose fragrance even through the cellophane gift arrangement. The police lab had the remaining bath bombs. There was no need to drop $125 on the package. She glanced at the clerk, who was happily showing the customer a table laden with large gift baskets that included champagne and two crystal glasses. "There's a day's wages," Calvo muttered to herself and walked to the counter at the back, where a terrifying woman stood in black silk, heavy makeup, and straight black hair. Her eyes ran over Calvo's attire in one swift glance.

"I need to find out about an order," Calvo said, ignoring the look of conceit on the woman's face. "It's a standing order for Marjorie Harris."

The woman remained in place, nothing in her facial expression changing. After a few seconds, she said, "Are you Miss Harris?" Her tone made it clear she thought that an impossibility.

Calvo smiled. "I am not. I am here in an official capacity. Miss Harris is the victim of a homicide."

Calvo took pleasure in seeing the woman's countenance dissolve into one of shock. The Lieutenant pulled her badge from her jeans' pocket and laid it on the table. The clerk's eyes stared at it momentarily and then looked at the strange woman in the New Orleans sweatshirt and braided hair.

"I don't see what this has to do with Christina's," she said sternly, but there was an underlying quiver in her voice.

"Miss Harris has a standing order here for bath products," Calvo said. "I'm particularly interested in her orders for bath bombs. As I've been informed, it is a repeat order. I'm assuming you keep a record of that."

The woman paused.

"Perhaps I should speak to the owner," Calvo said, nonplussed.

"I am the owner," she said, pushing her shoulders back, her face coloring. "Christina Orray. This business has been here for fifteen years, and we've never had a whiff of scandal!"

Calvo resisted the urge to make a sarcastic remark about "whiffs" inside a heavily perfumed store.

"It's a simple request," Calvo said. "No one is denigrating your store. It's routine. Can you show me her order data, please?"

Christina bit her lip and reached down beneath the gold onyx countertop. She retrieved a large, spiral-bound ledger and flipped it open. She hastily went through the pages until she reached the names ending in 'H.' Reluctantly, she turned the ledger to face the Lieutenant.

Calvo leaned over the book. It was obvious that Marjorie ordered products from the store regularly. Lotions, towels, perfumed gels, and bath bombs. At the top of the page was the date of her last order. It read: Six-pack rose variety bath bombs. The total was listed. Next to that was a signature. It was that of Camille Augustin. The date was two days before the murder. Calvo pulled out her cell phone and took a photo of the page before the clerk could object.

"I didn't say you could do that!" Christina shrieked. A woman in leather slacks, peering over bath beads, glanced in her direction. The clerk's face colored. "Are you satisfied?" she asked in a hushed voice.

"Not quite," Calvo said, enjoying the snobby clerk's discomfort. "I understand you have a subscription service. With Mrs. Harris ordering so regularly, I'm curious as to why she didn't avail herself of that and have it delivered rather than send her maid to pick up the items?"

The clerk's eyes narrowed into slits. "I have no idea," she said, icily. "Mrs. Harris could certainly afford the service. I guess asking her now is out of the question."

Calvo's face flamed. She resisted the urge to climb over the counter and strangle the woman. Instead, she took a calming breath and picked up her badge, taking her time replacing it in her pocket.

"I'll study this photograph," Calvo said, flipping over the page to make sure she had all of Marjorie Harris's orders for the past six months. "I'd appreciate your discretion in this matter. It's an ongoing investigation."

"Oh, I'll be sure not to advertise your visit today," Christina said acidly and slammed the ledger cover closed.

"Preciate it," Calvo said. "Great customer service." The clerk gave her a hateful stare.

She walked out of the store, grateful to leave the heady fragrances and inhale the mouthwatering smell of zesty crawfish coming from the open door of Olde Nola Cookery. Calvo threaded her way through the tourists to her parked car. A man who was passing her, going in the opposite direction, rolled down his window.

"You leavin'?" he called.

Calvo nodded and slid into her driver's seat, revved up the engine of her old Mustang, and pulled out. The man pulled a U-turn and slammed into her vacated spot. As she drove to the precinct, she rolled down the window to rid the car of the overwhelming smell of lavender clinging to her sweatshirt.

"Let's hope this trip was worth it," she sighed.

9 THE SET-UP

Hilliard entered his office on Monday morning, blowing on a steaming cup of coffee. Calvo looked up and hurriedly placed a hand over her tablet.

"Porn?" Hilliard asked, grinning, as he rounded the desk and set the coffee mug on the table. He sank into his worn leather desk chair, the frame squealing in protestation.

Calvo eyed the mug and said, "Please tell me that's decaf."

Hilliard's nostrils flared.

"Am I to anticipate an inquisition over every beverage choice I make?" he asked acidly.

"Only the ones with caffeine," Calvo said.

He sighed and picked up the mug, slurping loudly.

Calvo quickly filled him in on her conversation with Camille and her trip to the "hoity-toity" bath shop. The two detectives had an appointment with the funeral director at Faregate's Funeral Home at 2:00 that afternoon. Calvo had omitted her discussion with the maid about the missing cat.

"Soooo," Hilliard said, "What are you hiding under your hand?"

She removed her hand from the face of her tablet and looked at her partner determinedly.

"If you must know, it's a list of cat shelters," she said shortly, her facial expression firm. "Richy is missing. I realize you don't put any merit in that, but I find it suspicious that the cat goes missing on the day of the murder. Might mean something, might not. Camille did give me the impression that Malcolm was not fond of the cat. Plus, and I do think this is important, Camille said she shut Richy up in Marjorie's bedroom because Marjorie asked her to keep it out of Malcolm's way while she was at the gala. She must have thought Malcolm was coming home after his lecture, or why bother if he was going to be sleeping overnight at the hotel? Doesn't that sound like he kept that little tidbit from her? And, if Richy is shut up in the room, who let him out? Marjorie wouldn't, not if she was getting ready for bed and the cat sleeps by her bed. Camille went to bed."

Hilliard slurped again and took his time answering her.

"The cat could have slipped out when Marjorie got home from the gala, and she was too tired to go get it. Maybe it had to poop. This is a waste of time! Somebody probably left the back door open..."

"Camillie said the cat won't go outside. I guess it was attacked by a bird once or something."

"I'm trying to humor you here," Hilliard said, setting the cup down. "What the hell does a missing cat have to do with a bathtub murder?"

Calvo leaned forward and fixed him with the stare he knew all too well.

"Marjorie loved that cat. It slept by her bed. She'd had it for two years. Why, on the day of her murder, is the cat suddenly gone? Unless...UNLESS Malcolm knew Marjorie wouldn't be around anymore and he got rid of it."

Hilliard chewed on his lower lip and considered it.

"Kind of careless, don't you think?" he asked. "To risk doing something that obvious on the very day she died?"

"Not to a man like the Colonel," Calvo said. "He probably thought Camille would assume the cat ran away. She said Malcolm didn't bother with the cat. He probably didn't even know that Richy wouldn't go outside. It isn't something that would come up in a murder investigation's questioning."

"You're right there," Hilliard said, grinning. "I got the only partner in New Orleans Parish that notices a cat food bowl."

Calvo snatched up her laptop angrily. "I'm going to lunch," she said. "I'll be back in time to go to the funeral parlor. You are a jackass! This is why you're divorced!" she yelled as she marched out into the hallway.

"This is why you're single!" Hilliard yelled back.

Calvo's face was red as she passed two female police officers walking past her in the opposite direction, struggling without success to suppress their laughter. She shoved open the door to the front desk area. Her eyes fell on a small, elderly woman seated in one of the waiting-area chairs, clutching a large paper bag and a purse. Calvo was about to push on the outside door's security bar to leave, but something made her pause. She turned to the woman who seemed nervous.

"Are you being helped?" Calvo asked her kindly.

Dorothy Brindle looked up at the mocha-skinned woman, her eyes taking in her uniform and name badge.

"I'm not sure," Dorothy said, meekly, and clutched the paper sack tighter.

"She's waiting for Pimperton," the desk clerk said. "He's at lunch. She says she has a murder to report." The female clerk arched an eyebrow and grinned.

Calvo returned her attention to the woman who was nibbling her thin lips.

"A murder?" Calvo asked. "Which parish did it occur in?"

"This one," Dorothy said, her voice rising. "It's my husband's murder! We live over on Lafayette."

Calvo struggled to hide her surprised expression. The woman may be dealing with dementia, she thought. Her eyes drifted to the paper sack the old lady was clutching, hoping there wasn't an old man's head inside. She glanced over at Officer Grifton next to the X-ray scanner and nodded surreptitiously to the old woman's paper bag. He grinned and nodded, meaning it had been checked.

"Well, it just so happens that I deal with homicide," Calvo said, relieved. "Why don't you follow me back, and you can tell me all about it?"

Hilliard looked up in shock as Calvo reentered the office with a petite old lady in tow.

"This is Ms. Brindle," Calvo said.

"Missus," Dorothy corrected her and settled softly into Calvo's vacated chair.

"Missus," Calvo corrected, grabbing an uncomfortable steel-framed chair from against the back wall. She placed it next to Dorothy and sat down. When the woman remained silent, Calvo began the conversation.

"You said you had some information about a murder?" Calvo asked, her eyes dropping to the brown paper bag clutched in Dorothy's fingers. If the bag hadn't been cleared by security in the entry, she might feel nervous.

Dorothy studied her white-laced, gloved hands for a moment and then inhaled deeply.

"My husband passed last month," she said, her voice catching. She raised her eyes to Detective Hilliard, ignoring the female Lieutenant next to her. Calvo understood. Mrs. Brindle was from a generation that deferred to the male species. "I was away in Jacksonville…Florida…helping my younger sister. She had a knee replacement. Charlie and I spoke by phone a few times a day while I was away. On the night he died, we spoke around 7:00 because Charlie usually goes to bed by 8:00. I could hear the television on in the background, so I knew he was in the den. It sounded like sports. He doesn't usually watch sports. He watches history documentaries. He's especially fond of the Civil War series."

Dorothy stopped speaking and blushed.

"I'm sorry," she said meekly. "I realize I'm speaking of Charlie in the present tense. I'm not batty. I just haven't gotten used to him being gone."

Hilliard managed a semi-sympathetic smile. Inwardly, he was cursing Calvo for letting this woman follow her in her like a stray cat.

"You were saying about a murder…?" he pressed gently.

"Yes. You see, I asked him what he was watching, and he said, 'We are watching sports.' I asked, 'Who's we?' He said his grandson, Everett, had dropped by. I don't care for Everett, but I was relieved that Charlie had someone there with him. He's not used to doing without me. I told him not to stay up too late, and I would be home late the next day."

Hilliard absently tapped the eraser end of a pencil until he caught Calvo's look of disapproval. He laid the pencil down.

Dorothy read the detective's impatience. She placed the brown paper bag on his desk within his reach.

"I found this," she said, and waited.

Hilliard shot a look at Calvo and then gingerly unfolded the flap of the bag that was creased over. He hooked a finger inside and bent the open bag toward him. Lifting his chin and leaning forward, he peered inside.

"Uh, there's an empty beer bottle in there," he said, trying unsuccessfully to hide his reservations.

"Yes," Dorothy said, her voice taking on a sterner tone. "Don't touch it without gloves. It may have fingerprints."

Calvo smothered a grin as Hilliard's face flushed. He jerked open the desk drawer to his right and yanked a pair of purple latex gloves from the pop-up box. His jaw muscle jumping, he shoved his massive hands into the sausage-like casings. He made a point of snapping the wrist elastic loudly against his skin. He pulled the bag closer to him and carefully lifted out the beer bottle by its lip. He set it on the desk where the dark amber glass glowed beneath the fluorescent overhead light. Hilliard's eye pivoted back to the small, blue rheumy eyes watching his every move.

"Charlie doesn't drink beer," she said, as if this bit of information was self-evident. "Everett drinks beer. Everett always brings his favorite beer when he comes over because he knows we won't have any to offer him," she nodded toward the dark bottle with an IPA local label affixed to it. Hilliard didn't recognize the brand, but there were hundreds of craft breweries working out of their garages in Louisiana. The beer logo sported an African tribesman holding a spear against a burnt orange background. Hopped Up in the Big Easy was the brand name encircling the logo. IPA was stamped beneath it.

Hilliard waited, but he had to admit, the woman didn't seem like a ding dong, and he was becoming interested in her story.

"When I returned home from my sister's, Charlie had died and was already taken away." She lowered her head, swallowed, and pulled a small lace handkerchief from her purse. Taking several breaths, she jerked her chin up, a look of determination on her face. "One of our wonderful neighbors had come over to bring Charlie a casserole, knowing I was away. She had waited until his company left. Charlie didn't answer the door. Our neighbors all look out for each other because we're all retired. We keep an eye on each other's houses when we're away. Things like that. Well, Charlie didn't answer the door, and Julia didn't want to just leave the casserole on the porch to cool off, or an animal get it, so she tried the door, knowing we wouldn't mind if she placed it inside. The door was locked, so she got the spare key from the hiding place where we keep a key so she can bring in our packages and water the plants while we're gone."

Dorothy paused again, and her chin trembled. Calvo fetched her a bottled water from the mini fridge. She unscrewed it for her, and Dorothy took a long drink. It seemed to steady her.

"Julia found Charlie lying on the floor next to his recliner," she said quickly, wanting to get it over with. "She called the police. She stayed as they checked Charlie at the scene, but she told me later she was sure he was gone. They put him in a...a..."

"That's alright, Dorothy, we know the rest of the procedure," Calvo said gently. "Tell us about the bottle."

"Julia said she and a few of the other neighbors heard that Charlie died of a heart attack. No police came back to the house, so they assumed it was okay to clean up, so I wouldn't come home to a mess. Charlie doesn't do dishes or housekeeping, you see. I left him meals in disposable microwave bowls so there wouldn't be many dishes. When I got home, the house was tidy. A few glasses were draining in the sink drainer. I found some freshly washed dish towels and bath towels in the dryer. I emptied some old food from the refrigerator into a trash bag, took it to the garage, and threw it in the trash. The women had cleaned up, but no one had taken the cans to the curb."

"That's where you got this bottle?" Hilliard asked. "In the trash can?"

Dorothy shook her head. "No. One of Charlie's house slippers had been placed neatly by his favorite recliner, but the other one was missing. I bent over and peeked beneath the recliner. The matching one was there... and so was that bottle, lying on its side like it rolled under there," she said, her color rising on her pale cheeks. "We have a glass of sherry in little sherry glasses at bedtime, and that's all. The only time Charlie has a beer is when Everett comes over. I think Charlie was holding that bottle when he collapsed, and it rolled under the chair where no one noticed it."

Hilliard looked with renewed interest at the bottle. He leaned over and sniffed the remaining dried contents. He straightened and looked at Calvo to gauge her response to the whole thing. She merely cocked her head.

"Smells like beer, alright," Hilliard said, leaning back and sighing. "What were the results of the medical examiner's report? I'm assuming there was an autopsy. There usually is with a sudden death."

Dorothy sniffed, and her face tightened, readying for the response she had gotten from the police when she first told them her suspicions about Charlie's death.

"It said 'heart attack.' Charlie didn't have heart problems. I'll tell you what he did have! An ingrate for a grandson eager to get his hands on his inheritance. I know Everett did this. The only times he visited were when he needed money. Go to his house! You'll see this is the same brand of beer he drinks. Dust this bottle for prints!"

Hilliard bit his bottom lip and sighed.

"Mrs. Brindle, I can understand your distress, and I'm really sorry about your husband's passing. But finding Everett's fingerprints on a beer bottle that you admitted he probably brought to the house when he visits proves nothing."

"Unless there is something in the bottle that shouldn't be there," she said defiantly. "If there's something in that bottle that would cause

Charlie's death, then I need to know! There's another thing! Where are the other bottles? I've been around Everett. He never stops at one beer, especially when he's watching a long sports game like he claims he was with Charlie. That bottle is the only one in the house. And it was under the recliner where Everett probably missed it. I went back out to the garbage can and looked. There were no empty bottles of beer. None in the kitchen garbage can. Are you going to tell me that lazy grandson of Charlie's was thoughtful enough to carry the empties home with him? No one does that. They just throw them away."

Hilliard looked to Calvo for help.

"I asked Julia if she or any of the neighbors threw away any beer bottles. She said she didn't see any. Guess what else wasn't there? Any sign that Everett made Charlie a sandwich. He said he made my husband a sandwich. Out of what? I made all the meals for the time I would be away and froze them for Charlie. There wasn't any sandwich meat or anything to make a sandwich with, only bread. I knew Charlie wouldn't fix himself anything. Just warm up what I made him. Are you going to sit there and tell me not only did Everett bring his own sandwich makings, but he carried out the empty beer bottles as well?"

Her voice had risen an octave. "I don't think he ever made Charlie a sandwich or even stayed for the whole game. I think he brought in a few beers, poisoned the one he gave Charlie, hung around drinking while he watched to see if the poison was taking effect. When Charlie started to show signs of impairment and finally collapsed on the floor, Everett scooped up the empty bottles and left, not seeing the one that rolled under the chair. He just wanted people to think Charlie died of a heart attack, so he removed any traces of the beer drinking. He had to admit he was there because Charlie told me he was there when I called to check on him and heard the game on in the background. Everett was probably furious that I happened to call at that exact moment, or he would have denied even being there at all."

"Dorothy," Calvo said, placing a hand on the woman's small, gloved fingers. "Tell you what, we'll have the bottle tested. There may be enough dried liquid in the bottom to show some results. If... and I underscore IF, they find something that shouldn't be there, then you will have to face a very difficult decision." Calvo watched the pale face to see if the elderly woman was tracking. When Dorothy's face remained stoic, Calvo continued. "Dorothy, to be sure, they may want to…to…"

"Dig him out of the vault!" Dorothy spat. Calvo rocked backwards. "Then we'll do it!"

"An exhumation is not that easy," Calvo said, trying to regain her composure. "It requires a court order, and it's expensive."

"I have money! And now, so does Everett! A great deal of money! Blood money! He didn't even bother to come to the funeral, but he was at our lawyers' two days after the burial to ask about his inheritance. He said he got the time wrong for the funeral, and that's why he wasn't there. Hogwash! I sent him one of these myself."

Dorothy pulled a rumpled memorial service program from her purse. She handed it to Calvo. There was a picture of a distinguished gray-haired man in his later years, a wreath of roses surrounding the image. Centered were the words:

Charles Brindle
1943-2025

"He's very handsome," Calvo said kindly. She flipped the cover open and scanned the short page inside. It was a list of songs, speakers, the names of the pallbearers, and a scripture. The service ran from 1:30 – 3:30 pm. A note at the bottom listed the name of the cemetery and the time of the vault burial that same day. "Food and a short memorial will be held at Charlie and Dorothy Everett's home at 413 Lafayette Street following the vault closure," was in pale blue text at the bottom.

"Notice Everett's name is down as one of the pallbearers," Dorothy said, her voice seething with anger. "We had to pull a cousin from the guests to fill in for him."

Hilliard reached out his hand for the program, and Calvo passed it to him. He scanned it and laid it down. Taking up a pen, he grabbed a small pad of yellow-lined paper.

"What's your grandson's last name and address?" Hilliard asked.

"He's not *my* grandson. He's Charlie's from a former marriage. It's Everett Brindle. He just bought a *castle* in the Garden District. Here, here's that address. He's dating some chippy, so she may be there as well."

She picked a crumpled piece of paper from her purse with Everett's address on it and handed it to Hilliard. A small, pale purple folded notecard fluttered to the floor. Her eyes opened wide, and she hurriedly retrieved it, stuffing it down into her purse. Her eyes darted between the two detectives. She lifted her chin, regaining her composure.

Calvo looked at the small woman in the pale blue dress and matching jacket with renewed interest. There was more to this. She just couldn't figure out what.

****

Calvo and Hilliard arrived at Faregate's Funeral Home ten minutes before 2:00. The building was like all funeral homes: one-story with an A-frame roof, brown shingles, and a porte cochere for the funeral hearse and other cars. Tastefully arranged potted urns flanked the front entrance, where a red runner with gold trim ran from the curb to the double glass doors. Faregate's was scrolled in italic gold gilt lettering across the glass face to the left.

The two detectives entered the foyer where four large wing-backed chairs were clustered around a polished mahogany coffee table. A box of tissues sat off to one side, while a few brochures were neatly spread across the center. There was a faint smell of lilies in the air that Calvo found depressing.

No one greeted them, so they seated themselves in two of the chairs. Hilliard glanced up at the clock. They were still two minutes early.

"Guess funeral homes don't have a bell you ding?" Hilliard asked.

Calvo shook her head and sighed. "This isn't a hotel," she said. "How did your wife ever take you anywhere?"

Hilliard grimaced but answered her, "She liked polishing my

rough edges…at least for a while."

Calvo regretted her snide remark. Sarcasm was one thing; cruelty was another. She grabbed up a small leather-bound photo album and busied herself looking at it. Inside were recommendations for local florists, vocalists, stationery shops, and caterers. She glanced at the selections with mild interest until something caught her eye. Beneath a scrolling title from a stationary store called Scripted! in New Orleans were five samples of fancy funeral programs. The third one was the same color palette and wreath of roses that were on Charlie's Brindle's program.

"Look," Calvo said, pointing it out to Hilliard. "Same as Charlie's."

Hilliard shrugged. "So? This funeral home handles most of the well-heeled deaths in the parish. Dorothy was probably shown this same book to look at to pick out a printer for the programs. No big deal."

Just then, a rotund man with large owl-like glasses appeared from around a hallway. He wore a three-piece charcoal gray suit with a purple paisley tie. His combover was unconvincing, and his cologne smelled expensive.

"Harlow Fargate," he said, extending a pudgy hand sporting an immaculate manicure. "How can I help? I believe I told you in our phone conversation that the coroner usually deals with law enforcement, not me."

He clasped his hands in front of his large waist and waited.

"We are looking into the recent murder of Marjorie Harris," Hilliard said, evenly, rising to his full six-foot-six-inch stature. Mr. Faregate flashed an amused grin as if to say, 'I'm not intimidated.' "You are handling her service, are you not?"

"We are," he said, the grin still in place. "Is that a crime?"

"No," Hilliard replied. "I need to ask, and this is strictly confidential, when did Mr. Harris approach you about looking into setting up a funeral service for his wife?"

The arrogant grin disappeared from the funeral director's face. He hesitated before answering.

"I can check, but I believe Mr. Harris called me the day after his wife's passing. He came in the day after that. He requested a closed casket, chose some rather expensive floral arrangements, and said a vocalist wouldn't be necessary. He did ask for the business card of our preferred caterer and requested that the reception be held here in our hall. It's one of the services we offer," he said proudly.

"So, pretty routine," Hilliard said. "Nothing unusual?"

"Well, no. But for some reason, he said he wasn't happy with the printing company that does the vast majority of our orders for the service programs. When I suggested them, he said he had used them in the past for invitations to a conference and was not happy with the results. He took a business card for a different store."

Calvo flipped open the leather-bound book of recommended vendors that she had looked at on the table.

"By any chance, was it this one that he ended up choosing?" She pointed a finger at the store with a sample mirroring Charlie Brindle's program.

"Why, no. That was the one he had been *unhappy* with," he said with a new tone of confusion. "He took the card for the printing service above that one. May I ask just exactly what you're looking for?"

"We'll know it when we see it," Calvo said sweetly, taking a business card from Scripted!, the printers Malcom passed on. "When is Marjorie Harris' funeral to be?"

"This coming Saturday," Mr. Faregate said. "I believe it was scheduled to accommodate out-of-town guests. Plus, there is the issue of preparing the body…" He paused and coughed delicately.

"Yes, I'm sure Mrs. Harris 'condition' presents some challenges. Thank you for your time," Calvo said.

The two left a concerned-looking funeral director staring after them as they exited the building. Calvo held up the business card and read it aloud:

"Scripted! It's over on Magazine Street."

10 WHAT'S GOING ON HERE?

Detective Hillard backed his Ford Explorer into a parallel parking space and cut the engine. The stationary store sat in a forgotten strip of shops outside of the main tourist hub. To its left was a vacant store with soaped-over windows. To its right was a bakery with a sandwich sign out front advertising specials. The front window display case spotlighted various cakes and floral arrangements. The logo Flowers and Flour was splashed across the window in bright pink paint.

Hilliard leaned over Calvo to stare at the print shop window. Scripted! was spelled out in a tasteful font of ivory lettering upon a sparkling window front. Also in the window were posters highlighting the wide range of printed items available to customers. Two overflowing baskets of flowers hung from black wrought iron hooks beneath a gold and cream striped canopy. It, along with the colorful bakery next door, looked incongruous in the eclectic marketplace that seemed to be reinventing itself.

The two detectives alighted from the car. As Calvo shut her door, a man exited the bakery, carefully cradling a birthday cake and a large bouquet of red roses. When Hilliard rounded the car to join her, she grinned.

"One stop shopping for the husband who forgot his wife's birthday?" she said glibly. "Everything but the toaster."

Hilliard shot her a look and shook his head.

"What?" Calvo exclaimed quietly. "You never gave your wife a romantic toaster for a gift?"

Hilliard's response was to step up onto the sidewalk and ignore her, but his facial expression showed he was pissed off. Calvo followed him to the door, chuckling softly. The smell of Caribbean Cuban Steak wafted on the breeze from The Rum House across the street and a few doors down. Hilliard's stomach rumbled in appreciation. He was starving.

The shop bell tinkled as Hilliard and Calvo entered the small store. Shelves of brochures, menus, invitations, monogrammed stationery, and programs for everything from school events to funerals dominated the pastel-gold walls of the shop. Calvo looked about her with appreciation at the elegance portrayed in such a small space. A small table sat in the middle of the room, draped in a gold lace cloth. Propped up on picture easels were the store's seasonal trends.

A young woman in a simple floral dress came from behind a desk at the back. She smiled and extended her hand.

"Good afternoon," she said brightly. Calvo was in street clothes, so the woman saw only two promising customers, although they seemed like an odd pairing. "My name is Beverly. What can I assist you with?"

Hilliard, feeling out of his element amidst all the fancy papers, took a step back, leaving Calvo closest to the woman.

"I have a niece's wedding coming up," Calvo said pleasantly. "She's marrying into money, so obviously I'd like the invitations to be elegant and tasteful. No neon floral if you know what I mean."

Beverly's face brightened.

"Oh, of course!" she said. "We have a wonderful selection of wedding invitations in our Monarch series. If you'd like to have a seat at my desk, I can show them to you. Will your niece be coming in to approve your selection?" she asked as she led them to the rear of the store.

"Uh, yes, but she sent me ahead to see what you offered. She's in Baton Rouge and scouting out shops there, but I have heard wonderful things about your store, so I told her I'd drop by and relay to her what I find."

Calvo noticed the clerk's enthusiasm wane slightly at the mention of Baton Rouge. It was hard to compete with the capital city's offerings. She came around to her side of the desk, and the two detectives sank into two gold tufted armchairs opposite her. Beverly reached to her side, where a stack of photo albums was piled on a side table.

"Here we are," she said, and placed a maroon leather binder before Calvo. She opened the cover and flipped to the middle.

"These are our Monarch custom wedding invitations. Aren't they lovely? Understated with just the right amount of embossing and scrollwork. These," she said, pointing to an image on the next page, "have gold foil. It's extra, as is the layered filigree invitations."

Hilliard's eyes raised, and he coughed when he saw the prices beneath each collection. Calvo kicked him in the shin as she leaned forward to study the book.

"I do like the filigree," she said, choosing the most expensive option. "Do your more, how should I say this, elite customers choose this for their weddings? I'm single, so this is new to me." She smiled disarmingly.

"Oh yes!" Beverly gushed. "Mrs. Williams-Helbert ordered this very style for her daughter's wedding last year. It was the social event of the season! This style includes wax seals, lined envelopes, and save-the-date cards. How many are on the guest list?" she asked.

Calvo glanced down at the invitation in question and noticed the price was for 250 invitations.

"I believe she said around 250 people, but you know how it is. That usually grows as soon as you remember your cousins twice removed."

Beverly laughed, clearly enjoying an upcoming sale of their most expensive item.

"You can tell your niece that we do ask for half down at the time of the order. In this case, the base price would be $7,500, without extras like the gold foil or layered filigree. And of course, tax, etc. She will need to come in and choose her font style, color palette, etc. We do require a one-month notice. You're lucky it's our off-season for weddings," she said, smiling.

Hilliard blanched at the deposit price, and Calvo kicked him again. While the clerk was adding up numbers in her head, the Lieutenant got to the real reason for their visit.

"I must tell Dorothy Brindle how much I appreciate her referring you," Calvo said innocently. "I can see why she used you for her late husband's funeral service."

The smile melted on the clerk's face, and a look of fear flashed across it.

"Dorothy Brindle?" Beverly asked in a hushed tone.

"Yes," Calvo said. "She's a friend of my landlady," she lied. "She went on and on about how much you helped her in her time of grief."

This time, there was no mistaking the change in Beverly's face and posture. She leaned back and struggled to compose herself.

"That's kind of her to say," Beverly said simply.

Calvo was confused at the clerk's sudden agitation concerning a simple funeral program. She decided to push a little.

"I imagine you deal with a lot of people who are grappling with the overwhelming decisions made around funerals. It's hard enough to be in a state of shock at losing a loved one, especially if their passing was sudden, as in Dorothy's case. Or like poor Marjorie Harris. Such an awful thing. Will you be handling her funeral's program?"

At that, Beverly pulled the binder toward her and flipped to the back, where there was a plastic holder. She plucked a sample of the Monarch invitation Calvo had chosen and handed it to her.

"Please give this to your niece," she said, trying unsuccessfully to sound enthusiastic. "As I said, we do need a month's notice. Our busy summer season is over, but Fall is popular in Louisiana due to the cooler temperatures."

Beverly rose and came around the desk, already walking toward the front door before the two detectives were fully out of their chairs.

"We close at four," she said, glancing up at a round wall clock near the door, the hands pointing at 3:57. Please don't hesitate to call if I can be of further assistance." She produced a business card from her dress's side pocket and held it out. Calvo took it and thanked her.

As the two stepped out into the weak afternoon sunlight, Hilliard laughed.

"Here's your hat, what's your hurry?" he said snidely. "That may be the most polite bum rush I've dealt with."

Once inside the car, Calvo looked down at the invitation for a few seconds.

"She was scared," Calvo said finally. "Why? The minute I mentioned Dorothy Brindle's name, her whole attitude changed. It went into overdrive when I dropped Marjorie Harris' name. What's going on here?" she asked, looking at Hilliard for his reaction.

Hilliard leaned forward and shifted around, trying to arrange his tall frame into the seat. He shook his head and started the engine. As they angled out into the meager traffic, a man came out of Flowers and Flour trying to hold both the cake and the floral bouquet in one hand as he fished his keys from his pocket with the other. Calvo allowed herself a moment of amusement.

The two detectives arrived back at the station. Calvo carried the invitation and business card with her as they walked into their shared office. She laid them on the cluttered desk and sat down. Hilliard took his seat opposite her and immediately opened his desk drawer, pulling a handful of black licorice from the bag there. He popped all six pieces into his mouth.

"You're going to ruin your dinner," Calvo said disapprovingly.

"It's hard to ruin stale pizza," he said.

Just then, Officer Clement appeared in the doorway.

"Got your rush job on the tox report for the beer bottle," he said. "The prints are still being processed. Running them through the database." He handed the stapled report to Calvo and walked off down the hallway.

The Lieutenant scanned the typical medical jargon at the top and ran her eyes down to the boxes she was interested in. Her eyes opened wide, and she whistled.

"What?" Hilliard asked, his speech garbled. He swallowed a wad of the chewed licorice and leaned forward.

"There *was* poison in the beer!" Calvo said, her voice an octave higher. "Thallium to be exact."

"Thallium?" Hilliard said, shocked. "Thallium was banned in the 1980s. It was once used as a rodent killer. You can't even find that stuff anymore. High five to Jennings in the lab. You normally have to run a special test to locate it."

"I'm guessing they didn't run that test during Charlie's death," she said slowly. "Just another old man with a bad heart."

"Thallium can cause a heart attack," Hilliard said, "among a slew of other symptoms. It depends on how high a dose he got of it. It can mimic one as well."

Calvo handed the report to Hilliard, who studied it. She leaned back in her chair and laced her hands behind her braids. As her mind whirled, she looked at the clock, watching the sweep hand move as though the world was predictable and contained in neat little seconds.

"Ok," she said finally. "Here are our choices. A. The grandson *did* poison his grandfather for the money. B. Dorothy added poison to the remaining beer in the bottle after she returned from Florida to set up the grandson whom she hates. If he goes to prison for killing Charlie, he can't inherit."

"The Slayer Rule," Hilliard said. "Yeah, I saw Knives Out too. Problem is, if Dorothy is telling the truth, and the beer was brought in from Everett's place, then his prints *should* be on it. Or, it means he did leave a bottle behind, and she put Thallium in it to frame him. I'm not buying that this guy is dumb enough to miss a bottle if he just poisoned someone. Wouldn't he notice he's leaving with one less than he brought in with him? Which means Dorothy would have had to get a bottle from his house if his prints show up on it. Is that little old lady capable of coming up with a scheme like this?"

"Ever heard of Miss Marple?" Calvo asked smugly. "I don't see it. She just told us she wants us to open his casket and check for poison. I know darn well she didn't kill her husband, so she must be sure

Everett poisoned him with doctored beer."

"We have two deaths we're dealing with," Hilliard said, ignoring her. "We know that Marjorie Harris' bath water held traces of cyanide, tied directly to the bath bombs. Obviously, the Colonel is the main suspect, except we can't tie him to the bath bombs. You said Marjorie had a standing order at the shop, and the maid always picked up her order. Malcolm has an iron-clad alibi that he was at a lecture and stayed the night at a hotel with a friend, returning home the next morning after Marjorie was long gone. The bath bombs had to have been placed there the day Marjorie died, or she would have been broiled alive the night *before* the lecture. You said she took a bath every night."

"Yeah, I looked over her standing order at the store for the bombs. It equals averaging one a night. Camille said she never missed her bath, candles, and music. The last order was two days before her murder. Three had cyanide in them, and they were the top ones in the tray, guaranteeing she picked a deadly one. You know, Camille said she was out running errands that day. It would be pretty easy for Malcolm to just go into Marjorie's bathroom while she's downstairs or out and switch the bath bombs. It would take two minutes. I think we're making this too hard."

"How fond was the maid of her?" Hilliard asked, peering at his partner over the top of his bifocals. Her reaction was what he expected.

"Are you nuts?" Calvo asked hotly. "That poor woman is destroyed. She had nothing to do with it. And what would it benefit her? She is well paid, let me tell you! Marjorie depended on her."

"If we can't put the bath bomb in Malcolm's hand, we've got a long climb ahead," Hilliard said, sighing.

"We still have one hope of incriminating him," Calvo said, grinning.

"What?" Hilliard asked.

"Kitty, kitty, kitty," Calvo cooed.

11 A CHANGE IS IN THE AIR

Rachel knelt in the damp grass and drove a spade into the flower border, turning the soil. The sound of birds and insects churring swirled around her as she prepared the side yard's foliage for a change of seasons. Now and then, the scent of fetid pond water wafted to her on a welcoming breeze from the small body of water behind her. It was rimmed with paving stones. A few wild water plants grew along its muddy banks. Her mind had been racing all morning, but working here in the rich soil calmed her. She inhaled deeply of the flowering Sasanqua bush next to her, its vibrant burgundy, red, pink, and white blossoms perfuming the air.

"What are you doing?" came a shrill voice from the back kitchen stairs landing.

Rachel sighed, her shoulders slumping. She rocked back onto her heels and knocked mud from her gardening gloves.

"I'm getting the garden ready for fall," she said. "The camellias are just starting, along with the Encore Azaleas and the Sweet Olives. You can feel the change in the air. It's October."

She turned her head to see her sister tilt her face to the sky, closing her eyes. The temperature and humidity were finally livable, and she enjoyed a moment of the sun caressing her face.

"The Golden Wonder Tree isn't looking too good," Rachel said, peering up at it near the wrought iron fence. It struggled last year."

Madame Lorraine, bored with the flora and fauna report, got down to business.

"Come inside," she said. "I got an upsetting call concerning one of our guests."

Rachel sighed and stood, her knees stiff from kneeling, and began peeling off her dirty gloves. Her sister's face looked strained. *Another lovely morning spoiled*, she thought, and walked toward the house.

The medium was already seated at the kitchen table, nursing a cup of coffee, when Rachel entered and laid her gloves on a paper towel near the sink. She grabbed a china cup and poured her second cup of tea of the morning. Bracing herself for what was coming next, she settled slowly into a chair across from her sister.

"Dorothy Brindle's name has come up," Madame Lorraine said, getting straight to the point.

"Dorothy? What happened?"

"Our 'friend' saw her coming out of the police department yesterday around lunchtime. Of course, she recognized Dorothy."

"Why would she be going to the police?" Rachel asked, abandoning her tea. She watched the taut tendon in her sister's neck tighten further.

"Well, isn't that just the question of the day?" the medium barked.

"If you're that upset, until we find out, cancel the séance for tonight. Although I don't see why you think Dorothy would go to the police about us. All you did was give her a message from her dead husband. She was so happy to hear from him. Ruby, you need to take a breath," Rachel said, and then put a hand over her mouth. "I'm sorry... Lorraine. I meant to say Lorraine."

"Dammit! One of these times, you are going to slip up!"

"I'm sorry," Rachel repeated. "It's hard to forget a lifetime of calling you that. But let's take a breath, okay? We don't know why Dorothy went to see them. Maybe she was robbed. Elderly people are prime targets for break-ins in this town. If you want, we can cancel tonight, or you can do a reading. No séance stuff."

Madame Lorraine leveled her eyes at her sister.

"Geraldine Montez is on the list for tonight! We'll lose her if I just give her a reading. She is richer than God and in a bitter divorce battle for all the marbles. It's already been set up. It's perfect, and she already paid for a séance, not a reading. She's planning a European trip to get away from the messy headlines, so it has to be tonight."

Madame Lorraine drained her cup and slammed it down so hard that Rachel was surprised the china saucer didn't shatter. After a few seconds, she seemed to calm down.

"We'll go ahead with the séance, but you make sure to double-check the names for tonight! We can't afford another Davis Wilcox showing up! Make sure they are all vetted!"

"I will," Rachel promised. "Let's just try and keep our heads."

"The guillotine has never been used in America despite our French ancestry," her sister said sarcastically and rose from the table. "I need to go study my notes if I'm going to pull this off tonight."

"Should I reach out to Dorothy?" Rachel asked, fearing an eruption. "You know, kind of a courtesy check to make sure she was happy with our service."

Madame Lorraine turned to stare down at her sister seated at the table with a look that frightened Rachel.

"Our service was to give her a seance," the medium said. "Talk to her dead husband and then hand her a note from him. Am I missing something?"

Rachel swallowed and forced a smile.

"Of course not! I could ask her if the $1500 she spent on the séance was well worth it to talk to Charlie. You know, a kind follow-up."

The medium continued to stare at her sister. There was something off, Madame Lorraine thought. Rachel seemed nervous. The twitching nerve near her right eye gave her away every time.

"I'll call her," Madame Lorraine said finally, picking up her empty coffee cup. "I'll keep it light. If she sounds nervous speaking to me, we may be in trouble."

Rachel watched her sister as she crossed the kitchen. Ruby never offered to call the guests. Ever. She didn't want her phone number to ever show up in a guest's phone logs. Something felt wrong. Rachel stood, carrying her cup and saucer to the sink, where she rinsed them and placed them in a drainer. She took her sister's coffee mug from the countertop and washed it as well. The medium walked away toward the hallway and then stopped, turning to face Rachel.

"How is Socrates doing? Is he getting the voice right?"

"He's got the words down, but he hasn't quite got the voice perfect. It's a little high. I'll work with him some more today," Rachel said.

"That bird has to be perfect!" Madame Lorraine yelled as she stormed from the kitchen. Her heels echoed from the hallway, followed by a slamming door.

"Oh, oh!" Socrates squawked from the room down the hall. "Trouble is coming!"

****

Malcolm Harris crossed his arms and stared belligerently at the detective across the desk. Calvo placed a bottled water in front of him and squatted on the hard steel chair.

"We appreciate you coming in," Hilliard said, gauging the man's hostile body language. "I know this is a busy time with the funeral plans and all."

"Yes!" the Colonel exploded. "Let's talk about that, shall we? I understand you spoke to the funeral director yesterday concerning me! Why would my preparations for Marjorie's service be of interest in a murder investigation?"

Hilliard chose his words carefully.

"Mr. Harris," he said, deliberately omitting the man's chosen title of Colonel. Harris' nostrils flared. "I'm sure you can appreciate that we are doing all we can to find out what happened to your wife. We often talk to funeral homes, in the off chance someone has shown interest in the funeral, like a suspect," he lied. "You know it is very common for a killer to attend the service."

Malcom considered the information for a moment. His shoulders seemed to relax, but he kept his arms tightly crossed.

"And what did you find out?" he asked, sounding unconvinced.

"Nothing of value, I'm afraid," Hilliard said, avoiding looking in Calvo's direction.

"Well, do you have *any* leads?" Malcolm asked impatiently. "Anything you can tell me?"

"Only that the coroner's and toxicology reports confirm she was killed from cyanide poisoning, and it came from a bath bomb. There was cyanide in two of the remaining bath bombs in your wife's bathroom on the ledge of the tub. Someone, someone who knew her routine, had to have put them there. Can you think of anyone who would want your wife dead? And in such a brutal fashion?"

Calvo noticed the same muscle jumping near the Colonel's jawline that she had seen the day they questioned him in his home.

"No, of course not!" he said. "You'd have to practically be a chemist to make a thing like that."

"You'd be surprised what's online," Calvo said quietly. He gave her an angry look and continued.

"Marjorie had a few jealous girlfriends. She flaunted her wealth a lot. She was not averse to dressing down a store clerk, that sort of thing, but nothing that would warrant this."

"And Camillie?" Hilliard asked. He could feel Calvo's hateful glare without looking at her.

"The maid? Hell, no!" Malcolm barked. "She hasn't stopped crying for three days. No. I really don't know who could have done this."

"You realize this person would have had to gain access to your house," Hilliard pressed. "Who has a key?"

He could feel the wheels turning in the man's head. A slight blush of color crossed Malcolm's face.

"No one," he answered bluntly. "Outside of myself and my wife, just the maid. You can appreciate that there are a lot of expensive items in my home. I don't pass out keys like candy."

"We looked at the CCTV security camera footage from around

your house that day and the day before," Hilliard said. "The only people who come and go from the house are you, your wife, and the maid. There is a landscaper there for about three hours the day of the murder. Other than that, only a meter reader who checked the box at the side of your house and left. That's a problem. No one else is seen entering your home."

"There is a blind spot in the back by the kitchen entrance," he said. "Marjorie was after me about it, and I had planned to install a camera there. Now I wish I had. Let me know what you find out," he said. "The maid told me she sleeps with one of my golf clubs next to her bed. As you say, someone got into the house. I'd appreciate it if you do your job and find out who."

Calvo resisted mentioning that the footage didn't show the cat being outside as well. She'd keep that card up her sleeve for now.

"We also checked the CCTV footage of the Roosevelt Hotel for the night you gave the lecture and stayed over. Your alibi holds up. You did not leave the hotel all night."

Malcolm Harris leaned back, gloating. "Well, imagine that," he said, haughtily. "I guess you can stop wasting your time investigating me and find out who killed my wife!" He began to rise from his chair.

"One last question in that department," Hilliard said. Harris sighed and dropped back into the chair. "The hotel footage shows you exiting the elevator at 7:00 am the morning after your wife's murder. You entered your house and found us there at 8:30. The hotel is only a fifteen-minute drive from your house, so let's say 7:15-ish to get home. What took you another hour and fifteen-ish to get home?"

Harris clenched his teeth. His breathing became erratic.

"I stopped for breakfast," he said. "I hate hotel food. The breakfast buffets are always crowded and the same old stuff."

"The Roosevelt has the 'same old stuff?'" Hilliard asked doubtfully. He picked up a pen. "Where did you eat breakfast?" His pen was poised over a notepad.

Once again, Harris grimaced.

"I don't know," he yelled. "Some place in the area. I don't recall."

The Colonel rose, taking control of ending the meeting. He pushed the chair out of his way.

"The maid knows more about what went on that day than I do," he said. "I had an important lecture on my mind!"

He strode to the door, opened it, and exited the room.

"I hate that he keeps calling her 'the maid,'" Calvo said, "as if she weren't worthy of being called by her name." She turned her attention to Hilliard and raised an eyebrow. "What if he asks the funeral director if we were there, asking about suspicious persons looking into Marjorie's service? We didn't do that."

Hilliard shrugged. "You can't trust a funeral director's memory," he said. "They inhale a great deal of formaldehyde."

Calvo stared at him as if he had sprouted moose antlers.

"You're certifiable," she said.

"Probably," Hilliard said absently. He was playing with an idea. "Did you notice his reaction when I asked him who all had a key to his house? Definitely awkward. I think our good Colonel has a secret. Get Gleason to check into the breakfast joints between the hotel and Harris' home."

"I don't see why it matters," Calvo said. "Marjorie was already long dead. We still have to look at Dorothy's husband's death. She is not going to stop pestering us until we do."

"No, she isn't," he said softly. "She's proved there was poison in the bottle, but exhuming Charlie is a big deal. If his tissues show the same poison, it doesn't prove his grandson put it in the bottle. We have only Dorothy's word for the bottle being under the recliner in the first place. We have to wait until we get the print results back. And with that in mind, we'll need a set of Everett's prints to compare them to. I think maybe we see if we can pay a friendly visit to Everett Brindle and see what we can find without a search warrant."

"Friendly visit?" Calvo said. "You *are* optimistic."

The two left the office and stopped at the front desk. One of the desk sergeants was waving a phone message at Calvo.

"I was just about to give you this," she said, sliding the phone message across the counter beneath the plexiglass partition. Calvo picked it up.

"Well, the fox has come to the trap," she said, "Everett Brindle wants to talk to us." She looked over at Hilliard, who was studying a newspaper from the stack of them on a waiting area table. He seemed frozen. Calvo's grin faded as she stepped over to him. "What's up?" she asked. She looked over his elbow at an article on the front page of the *New Orleans Tattler*. It carried a subtle Halloween border. She read the headline: **Mysterious Doings in the Big Easy**.

"The Stanton-Mills mansion?" she asked her partner, confused. "So what? They pull out the local psychics every time this year as filler for the gossip rags. Madame Lorraine's name is always one of them. What's got your attention?"

Hilliard looked down at her with a queer expression. He reached into his side pants pocket and pulled out a pale purple business card. He held it out to Calvo, who took it. It was simple and uncomplicated. It merely had the name Madame Lorraine embossed across the face in gold. Beneath her name in small script was the address of the Stanton-Mills mansion. There was one final sentence in an italic font. It read, *By Appointment Only*.

Calvo looked up at him, confused. "Where did you get this?"

"From the private desk of Colonel Malcolm Harris," Hilliard said.

Calvo was about to retort, but something was tugging at her memory. She had seen this exact color of cardstock before. It had been a pale purple notecard that fell out of Dorothy Brindle's purse when she visited their office the day she brought in the beer bottle.

12 PUZZLE PIECES

"You took a psychic's card from Malcolm Harris' desk?" Calvo sputtered. "When did you do that, pray tell?"

"When we were there. You went in to tell the maid goodbye, and I backed into his study while no one was looking. I just wanted a quick peek. This card was sticking out from under his desk calendar. The purple color caught my attention, and I, well, borrowed it."

Calvo looked up into her partner's face, which took on the innocent, crooked smile that melted the knees of many Ben Affleck groupies.

"Don't give me that little boy grin," she hissed, leaning in, aware that the desk clerks were nearby. "You can't just take things without a warrant! That's what you were stuffing in your pocket!"

"I didn't take it," Hilliard said meekly. "I picked it up and forgot to put it back down. I'm also going to keep this newspaper," he said. He waved it in the air, turning toward the two officers behind the desk. "I am stealing this newspaper!" he called out. The two looked amused and shook their heads, grinning. Hilliard hit the security bar on the front door with his hip and exited with Calvo right behind him.

"Slow down," she yelled as the much taller detective strode to the

Ford Explorer. "One of your strides matches four of mine."

"Not my problem," he said, opening the driver's side door.

Calvo slid into the passenger seat and slammed her door. "Taking things without a warrant is *your* problem!" she spat. "Don't you get me in trouble with this kind of crap!"

"You're scrappy for a short person," Hilliard said, starting the engine. "It doesn't strike you odd that a stiff-necked narcissist like Colonel Malcolm Harris would have a psychic's calling card? Come on! You're the one with the insatiable curiosity! It's damn odd."

"Let me see it again," Calvo said, still sounding miffed. Hilliard pulled the business card from his pocket and handed it to her. He pulled out of the police station parking lot and headed for the nearest gas station. Calvo studied the card. Her brow furrowed. "It says 'By Appointment Only,'" she read.

"Yeah? So?"

"There's no phone number. How are you supposed to make an appointment? You don't go there, I assume, unless you've made an appointment, so how does one do that?"

"Website?" Hilliard offered.

Calvo pulled out her phone and googled Madame Lorraine's name. There were only newspaper articles listed from past releases, usually around Halloween. No website. Calvo entered New Orleans psychics in the search browser and whistled.

"Well, the Big Easy is well represented in the realm of the palm readers," she said. "But, no Madame Lorraine. Oooh! Here's one for you! She's a love specialist!"

Hilliard sniffed loudly, pulled into a gas station, and up to a pump, killing the engine.

"Just for that, you pump," he said, and leaned back into his seat.

"Fine, but you didn't answer me."

"I don't know," he said grumpily. "He glanced down at the newspaper lying folded on the console. "There! Ask the guy who wrote the article about her. I'm assuming he interviewed people who went to her. He mentions pretty specific parlor tricks. Get hold of him."

"There is something else," Calvo said, still staring at Madame Lorraine's card. "This is the exact same purple color that was on a folded note that fell out of Dorothy's purse when she handed you Everett's address. It's a pretty distinctive color."

Hilliard thought it over for a few moments. "So, you think there's a connection between Malcolm Harris and Dorothy Brindle?"

"I'm saying it seems like a really strange coincidence. We have two people who have lost their spouses under mysterious circumstances."

"I say interview that reporter, see what he knows. Here ya go."

He handed Calvo a department fleet credit card. "Unleaded," he said, and picked up the newspaper to read the article again. She slammed the car door behind her.

****

Rachel set the plate of sandwiches and fresh tomato slices on the kitchen table and refilled her sister's glass of iced tea. She was tiptoeing around her. *The New Orleans Tattler's* front page lay between them on the small table. Madame Lorraine's face had taken on the hue of an eggplant.

"It's that asinine young man from the séance!" she choked. "I told you he would be trouble. That's why he was there that night. To get a damned story for his paper!"

Rachel helped herself to a sliced ham sandwich with mayonnaise and bean sprouts. She slid her fork under a tomato slice and placed it beneath the top slice of bread. Her hand trembled as she tried to pour tea into her glass from the heavy glass pitcher.

"Maybe it's not a bad thing," she offered timidly. "It could bring in more business."

"You don't get it!" her sister yelled. "There's good publicity and bad publicity. We don't need the spotlight on us. AT ALL!"

Rachel withered and picked pieces of bread from her sandwich like a bird. She chewed them daintily and tried to think of something to diffuse the situation.

"We are a full house tonight," she said, forcing a positive tone into her words. "Two more joined, so there are now six. Two for a séance and four for readings."

Madame Lorraine ran the numbers in her head for the night's monetary total. It mollified her temporarily. She took a bite of the sandwich and a long drink of tea before giving her sister her full attention. Her face was still flushed, but she was calming down.

"We'll do the Crystal Skull and the Automatic Writing tonight," Madame Lorraine said. "Do you remember the clues for the Crystal Skull?"

"Of course, I do," Rachel said. "If you mention a flower, it turns green. If you mention an animal, it turns red."

"Yes," the medium said. "Everything's ready. I studied the notes, and I think we can give the vastly wealthy Geraldine Montez something she will never forget!"

Madame Lorraine's mood changed again as she glanced down at the byline on the newspaper article spotlighting her.

"Davis Miles," she said heatedly. "Didn't he sign the book, Davis Wilcox? So he lied about his name!" Her head jerked up, and she looked at Rachel with bulging eyes. "Wait a minute! He kept helping Dorothy Brindle that night at the seance! Remember? Even walked her out to her car. Now, she's seen at the police station, and he's writing an article about us. This is not good. Something is going on."

****

Six people entered the candlelit parlor of Madame Lorraine—four were strangers. It was 7:00 PM. It had been dark since 5:30. A brisk October wind was scattering leaves and debris outside; white plastic bags rising on the current to dart like ghosts among leaf-bereft trees. The Stanton-Mills mansion stood in stark relief against a waning moon. No one else seemed to be out in the wind. An owl hooted from a Spanish Oak across the street.

The small group paused just inside the shadowed room resembling a parlor. They waited for further instructions from the tall woman who had asked them to sign into a ledger in the hallway.

"You may take your seats," she said evenly, all but the large chair at the head of the table. Please remain quiet and seated."

With that, she turned and left the room. Geraldine Montez chose the seat closest to where the medium would be seated. Another woman, in her thirties, sat next to her, jockeying her chair into position as close as she could to the table. A woman, in her mid-fifties, took her seat next to her. The only male in the group paused uncertainly and took the chair farthest from them across the table, putting him to the left of the medium. Calvo and a young woman in her twenties took the remaining two seats.

A few people coughed lightly as the silence settled in. Calvo studied the group and the surroundings with the methodical calculations of a seasoned police officer. The large room felt like a movie set. It had all the accouterments of a haunted séance parlor. The portraits of long-dead people from the 1700s were especially unnerving. She felt their eyes on her as she adjusted her chair.

Most of the party was staring at a large crystal skull seated next to the only light source in the dark room, a pillar candle whose orange and gold flame waved back and forth languidly on some unknown current of air. Also lying on the black lace tablecloth was a sheaf of white paper with several pencils resting beside it.

The young man in the group shifted restlessly in his chair. He kept glancing at his luminous watch dial. Calvo took it all in. The oldest woman in the group, maybe sixty, wore expensively tailored clothing with a silk scarf tied in a fashionable Parisian Loop. It was clear from across the table that the gold bracelet and necklace were the real thing. *Funny how expensive gold can even look heavy*, Calvo thought.

Just then, Madame Lorraine made her entrance. All eyes turned to her as she slowly rounded the table and slid soundlessly into the high-backed chair nearest the fireplace. She adjusted her black lace neckline and finally turned her attention to the group, sizing them up one at a time.

"Good evening," she said, her voice rich with nuance. "I am hopeful the night will bear fruit for you all. It is the season of witches and nocturnal things, is it not?"

106

A shudder ran through Geraldine Montez. She couldn't take her eyes off the pale face next to her, the medium's nose birdlike in her profile. A faint smell of incense emanated from her black, brocade dress. Geraldine's heart rate had increased, and she began to second-guess her coming here tonight.

"You will each place your hands on the table, palms down, fingers spread until your little fingers are touching those of the person to your right and left."

There were a few awkward moments as the party tried to follow instructions. When their fingers were touching, Madame Lorraine nodded. Calvo noticed how the candlelight gave the medium's pale countenance an ethereal glow. It was like a light was lit from behind her skin.

"Some of you have paid for a séance entreaty," Madame Lorraine intoned, "others are wanting a spirit reading for which we will use the skull this evening. We will conduct the two séance entreaties first. You will remain quiet, no matter what happens. Do not try to address the spirits yourself. Do not break the circle. We will begin."

Geraldine felt a breath of air touch the back of her neck. Her short blonde hair was above her scarf, exposing her neck. It rippled in gooseflesh as the current swept past her. She wanted to place her hand over it, but dared not move her fingers. An odd smell came from behind her that she did not recognize. It was a musty smell, like that of a closed room needing to be aired out, and an acrid odor of something chemical.

Madame Lorraine, head back and eyes closed, suddenly called out, "Jaziel! We are gathered. Will you come to us?"

At that exact moment, a green fog entered the room from behind Geraldine. It wafted and spread out behind the medium, climbing higher and higher, separating into spiderweb threads as it crested about the young man's head, seated next to the medium, and rose into the impenetrable blackness above. Geraldine felt the same small breath of air on her neck again, and then it was gone.

Calvo's eyes widened as she studied the darkness overhead for the green miasma to return.

"Jaziel is here!" Madame Lorraine called out, a note of pleasure in her voice. "Speak to us, dear spirit! Do you have a message for Geraldine Montez, who is seated here tonight?"

Geraldine felt her breathing shorten and her nerves pulsing in her neck. She suddenly felt cold, despite her layered fall clothing. Her eyes were fixated on Madame Lorraine, whose head was bobbing slowly back and forth as if to find the right wavelength to the afterworld.

"Yes," the medium sighed with a throaty rattle. "I see a cabin. There is a man, not yet seventy years old. I see flames. Smoke rising. I see…"

The medium stopped suddenly. The group sat in tense silence. Geraldine Montez tasted blood and realized she had bitten her lower lip. She ran her tongue over it and glanced nervously around the table at the eyes that were all watching her. She flushed and returned her gaze to the medium. *Was she finished with her reading?* she worried.

Madame Lorraine sighed and said, "The spirit has gone. I can say only to stay clear of a cabin or small house where there are woods and isolation. There is death waiting there."

Geraldine's face lost all color. She tried to swallow, but her mouth was too dry. She felt dizzy and put her head down.

After a few moments, Madame Lorraine lifted her head again and took several deep breaths. The woman seated next to Geraldine felt near panic. She had also paid to have a spirit visit during a séance. She had been assured the $1,500 payment would be worth it. But now, after hearing the woman's message next to her, she was reluctant to hear what the future would bring to her.

"You are Marsha Jennings?" Madame Lorraine asked her.

"Yes. Marsha Jennings," she answered, her voice barely audible. She tossed her head to throw her long brown hair over her shoulders and waited.

"Jaziel," Madame Lorraine whispered, "is there another who wishes to speak? Is there a dearly departed or some future event for our visitor here tonight, Marsha Jennings? Will you share your sight with her?"

Marsha's hands felt as if they had plunged into ice water. She waited, her breath coming in short pants.

"A husband?" Madame Lorraine breathed. "Yes. Swords above his head. Hidden messages. Codes. A sting. Darkness."

All eyes turned to stare at Marsha for her reaction. Calvo found her own heart racing after such an ominous message. The woman sat stonelike, only her blinking gave her the look of someone still breathing. Geraldine had managed to raise her head and was also watching the woman seated next to her.

"Jaziel has gone!" Madam Lorraine called out dramatically, and the young man jumped. "Such dire things this evening," the medium said, sounding empathic. "Take them to heart. The spirits are never wrong. Take precautions." She looked at Marsha. "The swords in Tarot readings mean betrayal, or it could mean the actual weapon."

She paused and withdrew her hands from the table. "Continue to leave your hands on the table," she said. "We will now invoke the spirits outside Jaziel's realm for our readings. These are the spirits who dwell amongst us and know things we cannot see. They are not of Jaziel's deeper rooms, but are helpful, all the same. We will start with you," she said, speaking to the young man next to her. "Do you wish to talk to the skull or to the pencil and paper?"

He waited, uncertain what the correct answer would be.

"I don't know," he said, laughing self-consciously. "Uh, I just want to know if I'm going to get the job promotion, so which is better for that?"

Madame Lorraine looked displeased.

"Never tell me your intent," she said. "The spirits already know what your heart requests. You must not try and control the outcome. If it is a Yes or No answer, then the skull can answer you."

"Oh! Uh, sorry!" he said, his cheeks coloring. "I guess the skull thing."

Madame Lorraine leaned closer to the table, lowered her chin, and stared into the glass eyes of the large skull in the center of the table. She had both hands placed on the table before her, palms down.

"What is your name?" the medium asked, without taking her eyes from the skull.

"My name? Uh, Brett...Johnson."

"Do you have a message for Brett?" she whispered. "Come to us like a bird on the wing!"

All eyes watched the large skull whose faceted edges glowed eerily in the candle's flame, which had begun to flicker. The tension around the table was palpable. Eyes bulged as the skull began to glow green.

"Excellent," Madame Lorraine said. "He has come with something of which he wishes to know the outcome. If it is favorable to him, please show us. Come swiftly, like a sparrow. If not, we await your wisdom."

Seconds passed, and the skull glowed green. Brett looked anxiously at the medium.

"Is that a yes?" he asked hopefully.

"It is," she said. "You have been favored."

"Sweet!" he said loudly, and then flinched. "Sorry. But thank you!"

Brett continued to smile idiotically as Madame Lorraine turned her attention to the woman seated next to Marsha.

"Your name?"

"Wanda Mileau," she said simply.

Calvo noticed the sudden intensity with which the medium looked at the fifty-year-old woman.

"Mileau?" she asked, her green eyes practically glowing.

"Yes. M-I-L-E-A-U," Wanda spelled, obviously used to doing so.

The corners of the medium's lips twitched in amusement.

"No need to spell for the spirits," she said lightly. "They know all about you. Your name is only for my benefit. Is your reason for being here tonight something that can be answered with a Yes or No?"

"No," Wanda said.

"Very well, we will use automatic writing to convey your message from the spirit world. This is not as powerful as a séance, you understand, but many have found it useful. What is your question?"

Wanda looked around herself self-consciously at the others. She would have preferred a private meeting but was informed that those were reserved for people with follow-up needs after an initial séance or reading.

"I would like to speak to someone who has passed," she said, carefully, not wanting to give too much away. "Can you ask where I should look? The person who has passed will know what I mean."

"This type of question is usually one meant for a séance, but I will allow it," Madame Lorraine said. She picked up a sharpened pencil and pulled the large candle closer to her. Selecting a sheet of paper from the several to her left, she placed the pencil tip against the paper and closed her eyes. Her breathing became deeper, and her body rigid. The pencil began to move in a large swirling motion across the paper.

Calvo leaned to her side to get a better look at the paper. The candle was blocking her view. The young woman who had accompanied her was completely mesmerized by the process.

The pencil went on, picking up speed, digging into the paper's surface until it was flung to the floor. The pencil tip continued on to the next sheet of paper, drawing large, concentric circles, and then smaller ones, each overlapping the other. Madame Lorraine's breathing was labored; each minute that passed was an exertion on her strength.

The pencil flung away another sheet and attacked the third pristine white page. After only a few swirls, it became centered, writing out something hard to decipher in the candlelight. Calvo squinted at the writing that was upside down from her position at the table. She could make out a capital P. The rest was a maze of scribbled letters. With a flourish, Madame Lorraine's hand flung the pencil from her. It hit the floor and rolled a short distance. Her head dropped dramatically, exhaling loudly.

After several seconds, she lifted her head, breathing deeply.

"The spirits have answered you," she said, her breath erratic. "Here."

She passed the paper to Wanda, who took it with trembling hands. Her eyes widened in surprise. She looked at the medium in shock. When she sensed the others staring at her and trying to get a peek at her message, she folded it and placed it in her lap.

Not much of a poker face, Calvo thought, wishing she could read the message herself. Knowing it would be her and Carol's turn next, she steadied herself and hoped it would work.

Madame Lorraine's breathing was finally under control. She turned her attention to Calvo just as the young man blurted out, "Hey, is it okay if I cut out now?"

The look he received from the medium ended his retreat, and he slumped into the back of his chair, grimacing, still maintaining his finger positions on the table.

"Your name?" Madame Lorraine asked Calvo.

"I'm just here with my niece," Calvo said. She had signed the register as Elena Beauford. "She didn't want to come alone. You'll be reading for her." Calvo smiled disarmingly, but her heart was thudding against her ribs. The medium's green eyes were unnerving. "Her name is Michelle Hadley, soon to be Duprie," Calvo said, beaming.

Madame Lorraine looked between the two women for a moment, and then her eyes settled on the younger one.

"You wish to know your future," she said, a satisfied smile on her face. "I see a new life with a new man. A good life. You wish to know if it will last?"

Carol feigned surprise and nodded eagerly.

Madame Lorraine leaned forward toward the skull, her stare boring into its hollow eye sockets.

"Will Michelle Hadley be happily married? Will it last? Will the doves of love descend from the heavens to bless her union?" the medium rasped.

Seconds passed. Everyone at the table, even Brett, held their breath for the response.

An eerie green glow began at the base of the skull and grew until it had infused the glass head with an otherworldly light.

Carol, aka Michelle, clapped her hands with delight and grabbed Calvo's wrist enthusiastically.

"I will not even admonish you for breaking the circle," the medium said, allowing herself a stiff smile. "We are concluded for the evening."

Calvo's "niece" hugged her happily. The women congratulated her, but without much enthusiasm. They looked stressed and haggard. Brett popped from his chair and made a beeline for the door. He burst into the hallway and grabbed his phone from the basket. He was already punching in his friend's number to tell him his good news when Rachel opened the door for him. He exited with his phone pressed to his ear.

There was no conversation as everyone left the parlor, the skull still growing green, and stepped into the long hallway. Rachel held out the basket of phones and thanked them for coming. She waited until they were all stationed at the front door. Moving slowly behind them, she reached around and opened it for them.

"Thank you for coming, and have a pleasant night," she said, her voice colorless.

Calvo and Carol hurried to the Lieutenant's Mustang. They waited until they were inside and the doors closed before bursting into laughter.

"How did I do?" Carol asked, her eyes sparkling.

"Well, *Michelle*, you did fantastic!" Calvo said, underscoring the fake name. "Makes me wish you really were my niece!"

"Did you get what you wanted?" Carol asked.

"Oh, yes," Calvo said, pulling a small recorder from her pocket and clicking it off. "I think I'm beginning to understand how part of it works."

13 MYSTERIOUS DEATHS

The air near the lake was crisp, alleviating the constant Louisiana heat that Saturday afternoon. Waylan Montez took advantage of the change in the weather and tackled the avalanche of leaves scattered about the lawn behind his cabin. The purple of the Chinese Pistachio leaves lay incongruously amidst those of the typical oranges, golds, and reds of the Sugar Maple, Oak, and Sweetgum trees. Smoke curled lazily from his burn pile a few feet away. He raked the small broken branches and brittle leaves into clusters and carried them to the small fire.

Inside the house, Geraldine Montez and her sister Emily were cutting up salad greens and slicing cucumbers. The mouthwatering smell of baked lasagna was coming from the oven. Emily paused and took another sip of her Merlot.

"I can't thank you enough for inviting me this weekend," she said. "It's been a rough year. Your timing couldn't be better."

Geraldine continued with the salad preparations, lost in thought. She slid the knife blade through a ripe tomato and finally gave her sister her attention.

"Oh, well, it's fine," she said self-consciously. "I know we don't see much of each other. I'm sorry for the last-minute notice, but the divorce mess took over my life."

"I can imagine. It has to be hard having the papers reporting on it. You must wish it was already over. It was a nice surprise to get your invitation," Emily said gently, not wanting to tempt fate. Geraldine could erupt on a dime. When her sister didn't answer, she walked to the sliding glass door that led out onto a wooden back porch with two steps leading down to the yard, where Waylan was bent over gathering an armload of fall foliage.

"He is hard at it," Emily said, smiling. "You'd never know he was 69. He's in better shape than most men ten years younger."

"He hits the gym five times a week," Geraldine said, "but he's had heart issues in the past. Telling him to take it easy is a waste of time."

Geraldine joined her sister at the glass door. She watched as her husband tossed another load of leaves onto the fire. The smoke billowed into the sky. He wiped his eyes and backed away as the wind blew it into his face. He ran a hand under his running nose and returned to his rake.

"I know you said he was here to go over who gets what from the cabin," Emily said, treading lightly. "You two seem to be handling it ok now." She looked out past Waylan at the sparkling lake, lying only a few feet from where he was raking leaves. A waterski boat was moored to the private dock. "Did you guys use the lake much?"

"Yes. The boat is about to be put up for the winter, but the kids come some summers and bring the grandkids. I can't remember the last time I went out on the boat. I'd rather watch and have a margarita. He gets the cabin in the divorce settlement. I imagine this will be my last time here."

Emily nodded uncomfortably. She couldn't remember ever feeling totally at ease around her older sister. Their lives were so different. She was divorced three times and living paycheck to paycheck, while Geraldine was richer than anyone they knew. Emily could only live through the postcards Geraldine sent her from Paris, Venice, Germany, and Egypt. She kept them on the refrigerator door, held in place with magnets that looked like lemons and limes.

"Do me a favor," Geraldine said, backing away from the porch door. "There should be a big salad bowl in the cabinet over there, above the coffee station. Would you get it down?"

"Sure. I can set the table too if you like. Just tell me which plates."

"Oh, any will do," Geraldine said, glancing past her out the glass doors at her husband.

Emily walked to the coffee station, shaking her head at the expensive cappuccino maker, bowls of specialty coffee pods, and a second coffee-making contraption with more dials than an airplane cockpit. She reached up to the cabinet and opened it, her mouth dropping at the collection of expensive-looking serving bowls.

"Williams and Sonoma must be sold out," she said, laughing. Geraldine didn't respond. Emily chose a beautiful bowl with an acanthus leaf border and pulled it down. She carried it to the country-style wood table that sat near the sliding glass door and set it down. She would look for plates to match. She had a feeling there were matching sets for everything.

As she turned from the table, she stopped and gasped. Smoke was billowing up through the air, undulating like a snake on the fickle breeze. Waylan was stumbling through it toward the house, his shoulders slumped forward and one hand gripping his shirt near his heart.

"Geraldine!" Emily yelled and slid open the glass door. She ran out onto the porch just as Waylan collapsed, face down into the stiff grass.

Geraldine came running and stopped on the porch, frozen, her eyes bulging.

"What happened?" she cried.

"Call 911!" Emily cried, turning the man over and beginning compressions on his chest. "I think he's having a heart attack!"

Geraldine ran back into the kitchen and grabbed the landline receiver. She paused, holding it in mid-air. She watched through the glass as Emily worked furiously to save Waylan's life. He was unresponsive. Geraldine picked up her glass of wine and took a long drink. She gave it a couple of more minutes until she saw Emily drop her hands from Waylan's chest and burst into tears. Finally, she dialed the three numbers and began taking deep, shuddering breaths.

"911, where is your emergency?" the dispatcher asked in a rehearsed tone.

"This is Geraldine Montez," Geraldine wailed into the phone. "We're at 102 Hillshore Drive. I think my husband may be having a heart attack. My sister is administering CPR, but he's not coming around. Please hurry!" She broke into sobs.

"Is he breathing?" the operator asked.

"I don't know. I don't think so. Oh my God! Please hurry!"

"They're on their way, ma'am," she said. "What was he doing just prior to this happening? Does he have a history of heart problems?"

"What?" Geraldine cried. Her attention had turned to her sister, who had resumed trying CPR on Waylan, refusing to give up. Geraldine watched her anxiously.

"I asked if he has a history of heart issues?"

"Uh, yes. Yes, he does. Irregular heart rhythm, high blood pressure, that kind of thing. He's been hospitalized before.:

"How old is he?"

"He's 69. He would have been 70 in two months," Gerladine cried. She broke into fresh sobs.

"Hang in there," the dispatcher said. "They're almost there. I asked what he was doing just before this happened. Was he exerting himself?"

"He was raking leaves. He's been at it for about an hour. I guess it was too much. Are they here yet?" she bawled, her eyes fixed on her sister, who had finally given up. Waylan lay motionless in the grass. Thin tendrils of smoke laced the treetops as the breeze pushed them out over the lake. Somewhere in the distance, a siren wailed.

****

"I don't see why we need to start decorating for Thanksgiving when Halloween isn't even here yet," Nick Jennings complained.

"Because it's my year to host and I need to figure out what all I have," his wife, Marsha, said. She was standing at the kitchen island counter where a stack of cookbooks lay open to various recipes. "The dishes need to match. There's a box of them in the garage. It says "Holiday dishes" on it. All I'm asking is for you to count how many plates there are in it. You don't even have to carry it up yet."

Nick sighed. He knew by now, after three years of marriage, not to argue with her. Sighing loudly, he left and went into the hallway, where he opened the door to the garage and started down the two cement steps, stomping as he went.

Marsha glanced down at his phone, which he had left on the kitchen counter. She picked it up and looked at his phone calls. There were two that morning for someone whose contact name was 'Breeze.' Her face hardened, and she slipped the phone into a drawer under a stack of kitchen washcloths. She walked softly to the hallway and listened to the garage door. Her heart was pounding as she strained to hear his movements. Something toppled over, and he swore. Minutes passed with only the sound of boxes being dragged across the cement floor. Marsha leaned against the door, barely daring to breathe.

****

Calvo sat with her young friend in Carol's cluttered studio apartment near downtown New Orleans. The intoxicating aroma of barbecue and a mixture of other cooking smells wafted in through the open window from the restaurants dotting Bourbon Street. The two women enjoyed mint juleps as they sat in frumpy overstuffed chairs turned to face a small television and stereo system.

"Do you know just when she slipped this into your pocket?" Calvo asked the young woman.

"It must have been when she was taking her time opening the front door to let us out," Carol said. "She walked behind us, and I thought it was odd as she could have just opened it from our left instead of going around. I only found it this morning when I was looking for my lip balm in my purse. What do you think it means?"

Calvo studied the spidery handwriting on the purple notecard she was holding in her right hand. It read:

The Spirits say the conditions are favorable for a union. There are obstacles, but the magic arts can overcome them. With help, you will enjoy a long, happy marriage.

Calvo's mouth twisted to the side as she reread the words.

"I think what's going on here is setting you up to have to come back and spend money for 'magic arts' to help you make sure it's a good marriage. Obviously, the tall lady is the accomplice to the psychic, and she listened in on the séance, heard that you are getting married, and nervous about it. She scribbles this note in the next room and puts it in your purse on the way out."

"Wow! Quite a racket," Carol said, sucking on her mint leaf. "I guess the good news is that they bought I was your niece and getting married, or they wouldn't have gone through with the note. You still haven't told me what's going on, though. Is this an investigation you're looking into? The Murder of the Reluctant Bridegroom, kind of thing." She smiled wickedly at her neighbor, whom she had known for a year. Although there was a good ten years difference in their ages, she liked the police officer. They often went out for drinks.

"I can't go into it right now," Calvo said. "I know that's sucky when you just helped me, but it's only a theory I'm working on for the moment. I promise to let you know all the juicy details when I figure it out. You were brilliant, and I owe you one."

"Wellll," Carol said, grinning. "You could watch Oscar for me next weekend. I'm going to Natchez for a friend's real wedding."

Calvo laughed. "That's the least I can do. Just give me Oscar's preferred food. He wouldn't touch Finster's last time I watched him."

"That's cuz you give that cat the boring dry stuff. Oscar will only eat wet food."

"Then pour water on the dry stuff," Calvo said haughtily and finished off her drink. "Gotta meet Hilliard. Thanks again. Text me the deets on your trip, and you can bring over his royal highness the night before you go. Hey, did you ever board Oscar in a cat shelter when you took trips before?"

"Yeah, twice. I don't like leaving him there, no matter how nice they are. Cat guilt! Are you looking for somewhere to leave Finster?"

"No...no, no," Calvo hurried to assure her. "Which shelters have you tried?"

"Same one both times. It's the nicest. It's a bit pricey, but it lowers my guilt for leaving him behind. It's called "Caviar and Claws.""

"Oh, good grief!" Calvo exclaimed. "Ok. Sounds like what I'm looking for. Thanks." She walked to the door.

"I'll watch Finster if you need me," Carol said, getting up. "That place will set you back a few hundred a night."

"Thanks," Calvo said again, and hurried out into the small hallway.

****

Rachel spent the afternoon in her greenhouse. The smell of damp earth, herbs, and flowers centered her. There was a tension in her stomach and nerves that never seemed to subside lately. She reassured herself that it was her imagination. The seances had gone well. The money was coming in. No one seemed to be onto them. But Lorraine's behavior was off. She couldn't put her finger on it. She disappeared several times a week without telling her where she was going.

She pruned a rose bush and dropped the clippings into a tall barrel that would later be tossed into a compost pile. Everything seemed to be thriving as the liquid gold of the autumn sun poured in through the glass ceiling and walls. She checked on a clustering of mushrooms and was turning to go to the next aisle when her eyes fell on the oleander sapling she was raising from a pot. It was already nine feet tall. She walked to it and bent to study its stalk. Several branches were missing There were fresh cut marks near where they had been attached to the trunk..

****

Nick Jennings pulled the large, tall box over to him, heaving beneath the weight. 'Holiday Dishes' was written on the side in black marker. He ripped the old brown paper tape, barely securing the folds of the box, and opened it. Pushing packing paper aside, he looked down at a stack of white ivory plates with gold filigree edges. Sighing, he lifted the first two and tried to see to the bottom of the stack. He ran his hand down the edge of the plates, hoping to count them by feeling their edges instead of having to pull them all out.

Something stung his hand, and he yelled, yanking it from the box. A small puncture wound was evident on the side of his hand. Within seconds, it had turned red and was swelling. Nick abandoned the box and headed for the garage stairs. His hand was already cramping.

"Marsha!" he yelled as he began climbing the stairs. He looked down in horror to see the red area spreading and a blister forming. A small green dot sat in the middle of the wound. "Marsha!" he screamed again.

By the time he stepped out onto the landing in the hallway, his head was feeling dizzy, and he was perspiring. He walked clumsily to the kitchen and saw only the pile of cookbooks. Holding onto the counters, he made it to the sink and ran cold water over the wound, which looked like it had doubled in size. A black area was also forming. Panicking, he turned to the counter for his cell phone. It was gone.

"Marsha!" he screamed, as his legs gave out from under him and he fell onto the floor, his breathing labored and failing.

The tall box of holiday dishes lay abandoned in the garage. A small shiny black spider with a red hourglass shape on its abdomen crawled from the box's packing paper and scurried down its side.

****

Rachel sat in her dark bedroom, watching the bare tree limbs outside her window thrash in the autumn wind. It had always been her favorite time of the year until that night. Now, the moment the first chill marked summer's retreat, she felt anxious. It was subliminal, tucked away in her subconscious, always surprising her when she finally paused to assess why she was feeling off-balance. And then it

121

would hit her. It was October…almost the 17th. It was the day that changed her life forever.

She listened as her sister finally settled in her bedroom next door. She knew Ruby's routine as well as she knew her own. There was the faint sound of the bed springs creaking and the even softer sound of the chain on the lamp beside the bed being pulled. Rachel waited another fifteen minutes, the glow of her luminous clock dial staining her bedspread in red.

When all was quiet, she tiptoed to her closet and reached up to the top shelf. She moved several items of seasonal clothing out of the way until her fingers felt the smooth leather top of the scrapbook hidden there. She pulled it out and carried it to her bed. Taking a flashlight from her bedside table drawer, she climbed into bed and pulled the scrapbook beneath the blanket. Ducking her head beneath the canopy of fabric, she turned on the flashlight and opened the cover.

Each time, Rachel felt prepared to look at the old newspaper articles. And each time she was surprised to feel the same visceral collapse of her stomach. Her breath caught as the focused beam of light played across the brittle pages and garish black headlines.

Day Six of the Search for the Little Bridger Boy Shows No New Findings. Authorities are Baffled.

Centered in each article was the ubiquitous photo of Timothy Bridger. It was the photo that she had seen plastered all over town in Missing Person flyers stapled to trees and fences, and taped to shop windows. The headshot showed a smiling, freckled-faced boy with large brown eyes, a tassel of brown hair peeking from beneath a red ball cap, and a plaid shirt. She read the words beneath the photo with silent lips that mouthed the words she had memorized.

Last seen delivering newspapers near the Layton Lane area on Sunday morning, October 17th, 2007, around 5:30 am. He was riding a red-and-white Huffy bike with a bent back fender. The bike was located half a mile from Layton Lane, the same day he

disappeared. The baseball cap is red with a black oil stain on the right-hand side. Timothy Bridger is 11 years old.

Rachel turned her attention to page A-4 of the same paper and read the small insert, practically buried in the news about sports, the surge in global gas prices, and the wildfires in California. In less than a quarter of a column, a story concerning the disappearance of a local banker who had been missing for almost a week was tucked in. Leads were drying up, it said, and the local sentiment was that he ran away from some questionable business practices. Rachel stared at his name, her heart welling up in a small panic attack: Ronald T. Harrington.

The house moaned around her. She lifted her head from the covers and felt the sweat matting her hair. Eighteen years ago. Eighteen years! Ruby had held her husband's death over her head with emotional blackmail. But Mark had fallen down the main staircase. It was reported as an accident. Not like what happened to Ruby's husband, Ronald. Yet, Ruby had kept Rachel tethered to her all these years, using veiled threats and guilt about their horrific childhood.

A gust of wind rattled the shutters outside her window, and she cringed. The ancient wood groaned beneath the force of the gale. The weather could turn on a dime when the Mississippi or the Gulf reared their heads. This time, it would not be a hurricane that threatened the house's exterior. It would be something churning from within the walls.

14 SUSPICIOUS MINDS

Faregate's funeral parlor parking lot was filled. A long line of mourners filed inside in subdued reverence. Many of Marjorie's closest friends had tossed the typical etiquette of wearing black to the wind, and instead, used the occasion to be seen in the latest fashions. Ever conscious of where the news cameras were focused, they angled so that they were framed in their favorite profile. The Harris murder was still making headlines, and the reporters were out in force. One of them was courtesy of the New Orleans Police Department.

Malcolm Harris stood in the receiving line next to an expensive mahogany casket. An ornate spray of white lilies and ferns adorned the top and cascaded down the sides.

"I'm not surprised it's a closed casket," one of the female mourners whispered to another as they neared the widower. The other woman nodded knowingly and then pressed a handkerchief to her dry eyes as she reached Malcolm.

"You are holding up so well," she gushed, holding his hand a little too long. She angled her body so that he could take full advantage of her scooped decolletage. Malcolm Harris was now a very wealthy free man.

Malcolm accepted the typical canned offerings of "This too shall pass" and "I'm so sorry for your loss," with a calm demeanor. There was no show of emotion.

The mourners took their seats in the large chapel area and perused the memorial service program. Calvo was doing just that when Malcolm entered to take his seat in the front row. He stopped when he saw the Lieutenant, his face hardening. Calvo looked up and gave him a look of sympathy, which seemed to agitate him all the more.

As he continued down the aisle to the front of the chapel, Calvo noticed his body language change and his hands clench. He was looking to his left at a young man in an expensive three-piece Italian suit seated in the second pew. The man looked straight ahead, ignoring Malcolm's hateful stare. The Colonel regained his composure, and walking stiffly, he moved to the front pew and sat down, his back ramrod straight.

Calvo had watched with interest and wondered who the handsome young man in the blue suit was. Her attention was diverted by the sound of sniffling coming from across from her and slightly behind. She looked over to see Camille sobbing into a sodden handkerchief. Calvo's heart broke for her. *She's the only one here who even gave a damn about Marjorie*, Calvo thought about the maid, turning her head to stare at the military-style haircut on the back of Malcolm's head. The pastor took the podium, and the cookie-cutter memorial service began.

****

The smell of scented soaps assailed Calvo's nostrils as she entered the posh waiting area of Caviar and Claws at the conclusion of Marjorie Harris's funeral. It was not what she expected. Most cat shelters had an antiseptic smell mingled with various animal odors. She looked about her at the sage green walls with ivory trim, gold-framed photos of a variety of pedigree cats, plush chairs, a coffee table spread with cat magazines, and a display case hosting bottles of pet shampoos, collars, customizable food bowls, and clothing. She had rarely seen a spa catering to humans that would rival the ostentatiousness of this boarding house for felines. She stepped up to the tall counter where a woman was busily typing into a laptop.

"May I help you?" she asked, making a point of glancing at the wall clock.

"Yes, please," Calvo said. "I have lost my cat, and I thought I would check here to see if anyone turned it in. I have a picture here of him. His name is Richy."

Calvo produced the color photo of Majorie Harris' missing cat that Camille had given her, and waited.

The woman picked up the photo and laid it back down, pushing it with one finger toward the Lieutenant.

"I'm afraid you've confused us with a cat shelter," she said. "We pamper our clients. Owners bring them in to be groomed, spoiled..."

"Yes, but you also board them, correct?" Calvo asked, interrupting her.

"Yes, but you said your cat is missing. We don't handle that kind of thing."

Calvo regrouped and said, "As you can see, Richy is an expensive cat. He's Persian. Has a cat that looks like Richy come in within the last week? Maybe someone found him and, not knowing who he belonged to, decided to keep him, and brought him in to be groomed?"

The woman's arched eyebrow told Calvo she was not entirely convinced by her story. Sighing, she disappeared into a back office and returned within a few minutes.

"No Persians," she said. "Sorry."

"That's alright. Thank you for your time," Calvo said. She left. Once inside her car, she crossed off the fancy cat spa and looked over the remaining list. There were only two pet shelters in the area. It was too late at night now to go there. She would tackle it on Monday.

****

Detective Hilliard walked the perimeter of the large Harris mansion. His eyes scanned the eaves for the security cameras and took note of each placement. He came into the side yard and began looking through the manicured bushes and gardens there. He noticed there was not a single cat paw imprint or the usual signs a cat had been anywhere, digging in the dirt.

"Damn that woman and her cat theory," he muttered to himself.

"You say something, boss?" Officer Clements asked as he pulled his head from a large yew hedge.

"No, and stop calling me 'Boss'!" Hilliard brushed dirt from his hands and turned to say something to the officer. His eyes fell on the electrical box attached to the side of the house. This was where he had seen the meter reader in the CCTV footage. *Nothing unusual about that*, he thought.

"Let's check out the back of the house, where Harris said there is a blind spot with the security cameras," Hilliard said, and strode off in that direction. He followed a flagstone pathway to the rear, where a small gardening shed was located. Placing a hand above his eyes to shield them from the sun's glare, he peered up at the eaves. He cocked his head and stepped over a few inches, still staring at a certain spot high up beneath the gutter.

"Clements," he said, as the officer caught up with him. "Look up there," Hilliard said, pointing. "What do you see?"

Clements shielded his eyes as well and leaned forward, his head craned all the way back. "Looks like some holes," he said.

"Yeah, that's what I see," Hilliard said. He walked away and rounded the corner of the house. Striding to the front door entrance, he looked up at the security camera positioned there. Making a mental note of its size and the position of the anchoring screws, he walked back to where Clements was still waiting. Hilliard looked up again at the holes and smiled. "Somebody removed the camera from back here. Isn't that interesting?"

Hilliard glanced over at the garden shed. He walked to the small metal building and opened the unlocked door. Inside was a lawn mower, some pots for planting, rakes, shovels, and two portable gasoline containers. A folded tarp lay atop a box of garden spikes. He looked behind him to see where Clements was, and then whispered into the small building, "Kitty, kitty, kitty."

Embarrassed that he had even tried to find the cat, he backed out of the shed after a minute and shut the door.

The two men walked back to the front of the house and entered the front door, armed with a search warrant and a key Malcolm Harris had been reluctant to part with. The house was as immaculate as it always was. The pervasive smell of roses gave it a funereal feeling, as did the dozens of fancy bouquets sitting on every available surface. Notes of condolences were nestled atop florist picks.

"What exactly are we looking for?" Clements asked.

"The warrant is for Harris's laptop, Mrs. Harris's purse, her bathrobe, and anything we find that relates to the bath bombs," Hilliard said, making a beeline for Harris's private office. "Let's get this done while he and the maid are still at the funeral reception. You take the master bedroom with the bathroom where Marjorie Harris died. Look for anything that seems odd. Oh, and, uh, see if the cat bed is still there. It's usually next to her bed."

Clements shot him a dubious look but headed for the curved staircase, snapping latex gloves onto his hands. Hilliard pulled on his own gloves and entered the private domain of the master of the house. War medals and propaganda token photos were everywhere. A bookcase looked like it housed every book on every major war in history. While the room was tidy, it didn't carry the same pristine feeling as the rest of the house. This room was off limits to the maid, he remembered.

Hilliard looked over the desk top, taking in the bronze paperweight, cup of expensive writing pens, notepaper, and a desk calendar. He leaned over the calendar and noticed October 2nd was circled in red. Penciled into the square was the word LECTURE.

"I guess writing down MURDER MY WIFE would have been a little too obvious," he muttered to himself. Other dates were those of luncheons, golf games, and an occasional "dinner with Marjorie."

He straightened and looked toward the bookcase where something caught his eye. It was a faintly blinking green light. His stomach clinched, and he swore under his breath. *Of course, there would be a camera watching his every move,* he thought angrily. So far, he had done nothing suspicious. Hadn't even opened a drawer. He looked down, trying to think of his next move, when he noticed a gold trash can filled with discarded papers. He rubbed his nose while taking another surreptitious look at the blinking light. The garbage can was behind the desk and not within the camera's viewpoint.

Hilliard pulled his phone from his pocket and pretended to check something. He dropped it and cursed, bending to pick it up. He quickly moved aside a few of the crumpled papers in the can. There, torn into two halves was a pale purple notecard. He grabbed it and stood up, pretending to check his phone for damage from the fall while turning his side to the camera and stuffing the notecards into his pocket. He stretched languidly. Turning to the laptop, he unplugged it and tucked it along with the cord under his arm. Taking one more look around, he left the room.

He was now on alert for cameras inside the house. They were probably everywhere. He would keep it casual but still go about his mission. He opened the coat closet near the front door and did a cursory search. He looked into the sunken living room, glanced casually into the dining room, and entered the kitchen. The first thing he noticed was that the cat food bowls were gone. He walked into the large pantry, seeing only food items. Again, no sign of a cat....no cat food or litter bag.

He heard Clements above him, moving about the master bedroom. He hoped he didn't do anything that would compromise their search. You had to be specific about what items could be seized in a search warrant. Hilliard opened the door to the garage and stepped down the two stairs into the spotless 4-car bay. Two Range Rovers were parked side-by-side. Next to them was a vintage Jaguar. A space showed where Malcolm's car usually sat.

Hilliard poked around, peering into golf bags, moving flammable liquids lined up on a workbench. He studied these, looking for anything that might contain cyanide. A medium-sized box with some white crystals caught his attention until he realized it was rock salt for the driveway on the rare occasions they received snow. He lifted the lids to the four garbage cans. One can contained a white kitchen garbage bag with some used coffee grounds, empty containers, and soiled napkins inside. Some empty boxes were in the recycling can. He looked beneath the workbench and into a few tall storage cabinets. There was no cat carrier, no bags of litter, no cat food, nothing to show a cat had ever been here. *There should be cat toys somewhere*, he thought, once again cursing Calvo's name for haunting him with the whole cat theory thing.

He entered the house and was coming down the hallway when Clements reached the bottom of the stairs. He was carrying two brown evidence bags, taped shut with police tape.

"I didn't see anything that caught my attention, sir," he said. "It's pretty spotless. The only things in the bathroom are clean towels, brand new bars of soap still in their wrappers, and a vase of white roses. That's it. I've got the purse and the robe."

"None of her things, like perfume bottles or jewelry, are sitting out?" Hilliard asked.

Clements shook his head and shrugged. "Looks like a guest bath would look to me," he said. "Nothing personal at all. Oh, and no cat bed. And I looked under the bed and in the closets, the other rooms.... There isn't one."

Hilliard placed the laptop into an evidence bag and stood with his hands on his hips, staring up the stairwell to the balcony above. The anger flowed through him like water through a drain. It was a familiar feeling. He got it when he was dealing with someone who thought they had gotten away with murder.

15 WHO'S PLAYING WHO?

Everett Brindle opened his door to find the two detectives standing on his front door mat. They were five minutes early. His eyes traveled up to meet those of the male officer who towered over him. They then looked down at the petite woman with mocha-colored skin and a profusion of black braids.

"The odd couple has arrived," Everett said sardonically, and opened the door wider to allow them in. "Thanks for coming on a Sunday."

"It's what we live for," Hilliard said sarcastically.

Calvo and Hilliard entered a broad foyer. They were greeted by a large cheetah rug, arms spread and teeth bared. Everett seemed to delight in their reaction to his trophy.

"You don't see these very often," he bragged. "Not cheetahs."

"That's probably because they run too fast to catch them," Hilliard said with a sour expression. "You called us about wanting to talk about your late grandfather?"

"Uh, yeah, yeah I did," he said, looking as if he regretted it already. "Come on in here."

He took the two detectives into the same room he had led Dorothy into on the day she visited. The packing boxes were gone. A massive mahogany desk sat before the front-facing window. Calvo glanced toward the fireplace at the row of pictures of a scantily clad young woman in various frames. The 'chippy,' she thought and grinned. Hilliard and Calvo sat down on two armchairs that flanked the back of a giant cherry wood desk. Everett strode to the other side and eased into a tall-backed leather chair as if he were conducting a cooperate meeting. He readied himself, squared his shoulders, and began.

"So, uh, I have a bad feeling about my grandmother," he said, his eyes landing on anything but the faces of the two officers before him. "She came over about a month after Grandpa's funeral and pretty much accused me of doing something to him."

He paused and waited for their reaction. An awkward silence followed, so Calvo egged him on.

"Just what did she say to make you think Charlie died of anything other than natural causes?"

"Oh, so you're familiar with who I'm talking about," he said, surprised. He looked a little thrown off balance, but continued, "She asked a bunch of questions about what happened that day I was over there…like how did he die, kind of stuff," Everett said, his hands clasping and unclasping each other.

"That's normal, don't you think?" Calvo asked. "You were the last to see him, and she just wanted to know what happened."

Again, the surprised look. His eyes darted across the room. Then, in a flash, his expression changed. Everett leaned forward, his anger showing.

"That's just the point!" he said. "We don't know that I was the last one to see him. We don't know anything really. I told Dorothy…that's my grandmother, but I guess you know that too…I told Dorothy that when I left, he was alive and sitting in his recliner. I was doing a good thing to go and look after him while she was away. I made him some lunch, watched a ball game with him… Now look at what I get for my efforts. He goes and dies right after I leave, and I'm in the crosshairs!"

Calvo looked to Hilliard to gauge his reaction to the sudden outburst. They let Everett twist in the wind for a few moments before Hilliard picked up the conversation.

"I'm a bit confused at your apparent angst over this," Hilliard said evenly, enjoying the fear that had crept into the young man's face. "Has anyone come out to question you? No, I don't think so. Has anyone accused you of killing Charlie? Dorothy Brindle is understandably upset to return home from a trip and find her husband dead. Do you find that unusual that she would want to know what happened?"

Everett was furiously chewing on his lower lip, his nostrils flaring.

"She accused me!" he shouted. "She did! She kept bringing up how much money I got out of Grandpa's passing. I can't help it if I was his only living relative, other than that old...other than Dorothy."

Hilliard shifted in his chair as his hands gripped the arms. It was a sign that Calvo recognized that he was about to lose it.

"Mr. Brindle," Calvo said in soothing tones. "It would help us clear this whole thing up if I could just ask you to go over your actions the day Charlie died. Let's start with how you came to be there. Did Charlie invite you over, or did you initiate the invitation?"

She could see the wheels turning in Everett's head as he considered his answer.

"I called to check on him," he said, his tone more subdued. "I knew Dorothy was away, and so I called him. So what?"

"I'm sure he appreciated the gesture," Calvo said, smiling. "What did you say to him?"

Again, Everett paused. The lip chewing resumed.

"I, uh, asked if he had eaten lunch and if he would like me to come over for a few, make him a sandwich, and watch some TV. You know, keep him company."

"What time would that call have been?" Calvo asked.

This time, Everett's face registered alarm. His eyes darted along the top of his desk as he struggled for an answer.

"Don't really remember exactly, but probably somewhere around one o'clock, maybe a little later."

"Well, we can check your phone for the exact time," Calvo said.

There was no mistaking the sudden shift in Everett's demeanor. His face took on a sheen of perspiration.

"I don't see why you need any of this stuff!" he said, his anger back in place. "Jeez! All I did was visit him for a few hours."

"So, you called around one," Calvo said, hurrying on before he could shut down. "What time did you arrive?"

"I...not totally sure, but I guess around four. I had to run an errand first."

Hilliard began to say something, but Calvo hurried on.

"Did you bring him something to eat or drink?" Calvo asked, picking up the pace.

"No! I told you. I made him a sandwich there."

"What kind of sandwich?" Calvo asked. "What was in it?" Dorothy had told them there was no lunch makings in the house, so the Lieutenant was eager to see what Everett said.

"Seriously? I don't remember. This was a month ago. Just whatever was there," he said, swallowing. He picked up a ballpoint pen and absentmindedly drummed it against the desk.

"But bread and some kind of meat, or peanut butter and jelly?" Calvo asked, sounding like it was just a throwaway question.

"Yeah! It was peanut butter and jelly. I'm no gourmet in the kitchen," he said, chuckling awkwardly.

"Fine," Calvo said, smiling disarmingly. "What did he have to drink?"

Everett hesitated, the hunted look returning to his face.

"Just water," he said, and glanced away.

"And you? Did you join him for lunch? Have a sandwich, a glass of water?"

"Yep, sure did," Everett said, feeling his feet back under him. "That was it. No big deal. He doesn't eat much anymore..." He caught himself, and his face flushed. "I mean, he didn't...wasn't... You know, before he died.

Calvo nodded. She studied the young man before her, taking in his tightened body language and shiny face.

"What game did you watch?" she asked.

134

This time, Everett practically rose from his seat. She feared he was going to conclude the conversation or ask for an attorney. Instead, he sat back against the chair and swallowed again.

"The LSU Tigers game," he said, his mind racing.

"Really?" Hilliard asked, finally joining in. Sports were his wheelhouse. "There are no baseball games in September. The Tigers stop play in May."

Calvo cringed, fearing the confrontation would be the last straw for Everett.

"No!" he said, blushing, "I meant the Saints. Duh!" he laughed, and ran a hand across his forehead. Hilliard stared at him. Everett rolled the pen against the desk.

"I think we're about finished here," Calvo said, and saw him visibly relax. "So, it seems pretty up front. You came over to keep him company, made him a peanut butter and jelly sandwich, watched the Saints game, and left about what time?"

Everett went on alert again, leaning forward, and his head bobbed.

"Let's see, that would have been about…oh…seven o'clock, I think. Yeah, seven. I told him goodbye and to call if he needed anything. Dorothy called while I was there and said she would be home the next day, so I thought everything was cool. Bad luck that he passed away an hour later."

Everett missed the twinkle in Calvo's eyes or Hilliard's shifting again in his chair.

"Yes," Calvo said, her voice lowered. "Bad luck. Well, thank you for speaking to us," she said.

"Uh, I have a question," Hilliard said, leaning in. "You said you arrived around four o'clock in the afternoon? Kinda late for lunch."

Everett's nostrils flared, but he returned the Detective's stare.

"I was going to go at lunch, but my errands ran long. Dinner is just as good. It was mainly to keep him company."

Hilliard's mouth curled. Calvo rose quickly and thanked the young man again for speaking with them.

"That's it?" Everett asked. "Are you going to tell Dorothy she is just imagining things? I mean, she's just a batty old woman who's mad at me for getting some of Charlie's money. It's not like she didn't get plenty."

Hilliard took a deep breath and moved to the front of his chair. Calvo placed a hand on his shoulder.

"We'll talk with Dorothy," she said lightly. She extended her hand to shake his. "We appreciate your time, and we're sorry for your loss. I hear Charlie was a good man."

Everett flinched and shook the proffered hand. Calvo wiped his sweaty grip from her hand along her pant leg as Everett came around to the front of his desk. He looked anxious to have them gone.

"May I use your bathroom before we go?" she asked meekly. "We have several more stops to make."

Everett hesitated but said, "Yeah, sure. It's down there by the kitchen." He waved a hand in that direction.

"Thank you so much," Calvo said sweetly and walked off down the hallway, leaving a decidedly uncomfortable Hilliard alone with Everett.

"So cheetah rugs are hard to come by, huh?" Hilliard asked, standing inches from the giant feline's open mouth. He forced a conversational tone when all he wanted to do was kick the hell out of the guy. He glanced to see Calvo enter a door several feet away on the right.

Calvo stood in the neat but sparse bathroom for a few seconds. There was no toilet paper and no soap. It looked as if no one had used it. She guessed the 'chippy' used the upstairs digs. She turned on the faucet. Carefully opening the door, Calvo peered out. Hilliard saw her and jockeyed around to block Everett's view of her.

"So just how big do these cats get?" Hilliard asked.

Calvo slipped hurriedly into the hall and dashed for the kitchen. She opened the refrigerator and looked inside. There were several beer bottles of the same IPA brand as the one Dorothy brought to them. She took a quick photo of them with her phone and closed the refrigerator door. Calvo peered down the hallway to see Hilliard's broad back. Scurrying to the bathroom, she stepped inside, turned off the faucets, took a breath, and came out just as Everett was wondering what had happened to her.

"All set," she said lightly, and gave Hilliard a quick look. He smothered a grin as the two headed for the front door.

Everett was staring at Calvo's dry hands.

"I keep forgetting to put paper and towels in there," he said, eyeing her closely.

"No problem," she said, wiping her hands along her pants leg. "I grew up with brothers."

His eyes narrowed and he glanced between the two detectives.

"So, you'll call off Dorothy?" Everett asked as he opened the front door for them.

"You have my word that Dorothy will be the next person we call," Calvo said, smiling.

The two left a nervous and suspicious Everett Brindle staring after them as they walked to their squad car.

"Same beer," Calvo said, as they slid into the car.

"Nicely done," Hilliard said, and pulled a glossy photograph of Everett standing next to a downed cheetah somewhere in the wild.

"Where did you get that?" Calvo asked.

"He pulled out a batch while he was bragging about the cat. He actually gave me this one, like it was a birthday present or something. Just to brag! Nothing shows a good fingerprint like a glossy photograph."

Calvo shook her head and laughed. "He handed you the fingerprint we needed!"

"Tells me he thought he had nothing to fear. Maybe he really didn't know that one of the bottles had rolled under Charlie's chair. What an ass!" Hilliard continued.

"Or," Calvo said slowly, "it could be he is innocent and doesn't know what's going on."

Hilliard waved his hand to dismiss the notion and continued.

"Changes all this talk about wanting to bring Charlie lunch to now, oh yeah, it was dinner. I think Dorothy's right. I'm beginning to think he never made him lunch or dinner or anything else. He went there to kill him," he said, shaking his head as he backed down the driveway.

"I tend to agree," Calvo said." I'm just playing devil's advocate. By the way, did you catch what he said? He said, 'Bad luck that he passed away an hour later.' How did he know what time Charlie died? We need to check to see if that tidbit made the papers."

"Like I keep telling you," Hilliard said. "Go see the reporter guy who put out the article about Madame Lorraine."

"Ok, ok! I will. Hey, all this beer talk has made me want one. Pub time?"

Hilliard smiled. "Pub time," he said. "We're off the clock now anyway. Nice going on checking for the beer brand. I was running out of cheetah trivia facts."

Calvo laughed and looked out the window as the pastel sunset colors stained the ancient oaks and historical buildings. She couldn't picture herself living anywhere else.

****

The following morning, Lieutenant Adelaide Calvo parked in front of the small dingy building with the name *New Orleans Tattler* embossed on a wooden plaque in the front window. She entered the small reception room where several peeling faux leather chairs lined the walls. A low, worn wooden coffee table held various editions of the newspaper and multiple coffee mug stains. A bored-looking teenager looked up from her laptop as Calvo approached the desk.

"Yes?" she asked in a soft southern drawl.

"I have an appointment with Davis Miles," Calvo said.

The young woman scanned Calvo from top to toe in the uncomfortable manner women use to size up the competition. The officer was wearing blue jeans, a plaid top, and a baseball cap.

"Sure," she said, sounding none too pleased. "Through that door. His cubicle is at the back. You know what he looks like, right?" she asked, watching Calvo intently.

"No, actually, I don't," Calvo said.

This seemed to allay the young woman's concerns that Calvo was here on something other than business.

"Dark brown hair, cute smile, and there's a bobblehead doll of Marilyn Monroe on his desk."

Calvo smothered a grin and thanked her. She went through the open door to the smell of ink and stale coffee. It was a small open area with six cubicles spaced evenly on each side of an aisle. A few people tapping away on laptops glanced up at her as she walked by, their faces mirroring the unhappiness of being back to work on a Monday. At the rear of the aisle on the left, she spotted a Marilyn Monroe bobblehead and stopped. A young man had his back to her, intently reading something on his laptop screen. Seeing her reflection in the screen, he wheeled around in his chair to face her.

"Addie?" he said, flashing a smile that went beyond the 'cute' description the receptionist had given it.

"Adelaide," Calvo corrected, suddenly feeling out of her depth.

"Cop a squat," Davis said, pulling a folding chair from the wall to his side.

Calvo sat down on the wobbly chair and placed her leather-bound folder in front of her, her arms wrapped around it protectively. Davis glanced at it and smiled again. Calvo wished he would stop doing that.

"What can I do for you?" he asked. "You said on the phone that you were interested in an article I wrote. Did I smear someone near and dear to you, or leak that night you were found coming out of a drug dealer's back storeroom?"

Calvo's eyes bulged before she realized he was teasing her. The back of her neck felt hot.

"No, I…I wanted to talk to you about this," she said, embarrassed at her sudden lack of composure. She pulled the newspaper with the front page article about Madame Lorraine from her ledger. Davis leaned forward and took it from her.

"Yeah. Typical Halloween fodder," he said, grinning. "What's of interest to you?"

"You mention Madame Lorraine in it," Calvo began carefully. "The article reads as if you knew her, or had attended something of hers. I was curious about it."

Davis leaned back and laced his fingers behind his thick brown hair. He studied the young woman before him, whom he guessed was about his age.

"Can I ask what your interest is?" he said, slipping into his journalistic persona.

Calvo considered his question and made a decision. It was going to take too long to pussy foot around it like this. She reached into her back pocket and pulled out her badge. She held it up.

Davis's eyes widened in surprise, and the smile returned.

"Did not see that comin'," he said, amused. "Did I do something wrong?"

"No, we have an interest in Madame Lorraine, and I would just like to know if you did indeed attend one of her….events."

"Yeah. I went to one. I took a friend of mine's place because I wanted to see what goes on in these seances. It was for the article."

"What did you think?" Calvo asked, relaxing into the conversation. "Do you think something is going on there? Most psychics have a rep for cheating people."

Davis took his time answering. He was doing his own background research into the medium. He leaned back again into the ergonomic chair and threw his feet up onto a counter, crossing them at the ankles.

"Tell you what, Addie," he said, confidently. "What say you and me share information? I scratch your back, you scratch mine."

Calvo resisted the urge to smile.

"And just how much scratching do you foresee happening?" she asked, her eyes sparkling.

"Oh, I'm a pretty itchy guy," Davis said. "We both keep it confidential. I don't let on that you're here asking questions. I share what I find, you share what you find."

"And what's to keep you from putting what I give you into your paper and blowing all my hard work?" Calvo asked.

"Pinky swear," Davis said, holding up his little finger. "Nothin' goes in that you give me unless you say so. Now, that doesn't stop me from printing my own findings. But I'm not stupid. I don't want the pigeon to fly the coop either. I'll keep a tight lid on it until we're ready."

"We?" Calvo asked, grinning.

"I think we'd make a good team," Davis said, his smile causing butterflies in the Lieutenant's stomach.

"I bet you do," she said, smugly. "Ok. But if you burn me…"

"Yeah, like I'm going to hack off a police officer. I do have some integrity," he said, "despite public opinion. So, you obviously are here because you think something is going on at the Stanton-Mills mansion. So do I. So does this little old lady named Dorothy Brindle. I met her the night I was there for a séance. She's why I'm suspicious. She got a message from her dead husband, Charles. I looked Charles up, read his obit. Untimely death, but natural causes. Dorothy doesn't think so. She came to me when the autopsy report said heart attack, and no one would listen to her."

"I listened to her," Calvo said. "I'm working on it. By any chance, did you get the names of the others there that night you were there?"

"Sure. That's how my mind works. Never miss a thing." He grinned. "There was me, Dorothy, some woman named Brenda, and a mean, tanned guy who wouldn't say his name. He got really upset when Madame Lorraine said a woman was 'coming through,' hinting that she was murdered and that something was hidden. Then, and I got to give her props, a face appeared on this big mirror next to the guy. He erupted! Pretty much ended it. I helped Dorothy up, and we left."

Calvo's pulse quickened. "You didn't get his name?"

"He was not the sharing type," Davis said, making a face.

"What did he look like?"

Davis grinned. "Short silver hair, broad shoulders, straight posture, military-like. Really tan. Enormous nose! Probably mid-50s. He was not happy to be there."

Calvo tried to hide her disappointment. It was the exact description of Malcolm Harris, except for the age and the nose.

"Are you sure he wasn't older? Like in his 70s?" she asked.

"Nah. He wasn't that old."

"Can you remember exactly what the spirit said?" she asked, leaning forward.

"Oh…uh…she said, 'I'm not at rest, something hidden, hurried death, hurried funeral, a plan thwarted,' something like that. The face in the mirror was a lot younger than this guy, so maybe it was his daughter or something."

"And Dorothy's message?"

"Short and sweet. Actually, hers was on a piece of paper that was in a little bag. Madame Lorraine read it, and then I saw it when Madame Lorraine gave it to her, just before Dorothy pressed it against her. It said, 'Dot. All is well. You may proceed.'"

"You may proceed?" Calvo repeated, blinking. "How odd."

"Oh, it gets better," Davis grinned. "I've been studying the local obits. I think a few of these might interest you."

16 DEARLY DEPARTED

Lieutenant Calvo sat elbow to elbow with Davis Miles as they hunched over his laptop. The subtle scent from his cologne and his closeness were causing her palpitations. He deftly scrolled through the recent local obituaries, stopping at the first one on his list.

"Ok, so after I learned a little more about Dorothy and that she was suspicious that her husband did not die of natural causes, it got me thinking. You either believe the spirits at the séance wrote her a note from dearly departed Charles, or something fishy is going on over there. I'm pretty much the kind who leans towards 'fishy.' So, I started looking at any odd deaths that have happened recently. I started out with newspaper articles, and then matched them to the obits. Turns out, our little hamlet seems to be replete with people going bump in the night."

He pulled up a newspaper article describing the sad accident of a local New Orleans man who fell overboard while fishing and was presumed dead after an alligator entered the water after him. His body was never found.

"Yes," Calvo said, "there was a lot of talk about it at the time. But his friend witnessed it and said it was an accident. Some of our people handled it."

"Moving on," Davis said, ignoring her. His fingers tapped again in the search engine and brought up the obituary for Roger Landry. "This is the guy who went overboard. He was loaded. I mean, 'Move Over Bill Gates' loaded. The surviving widow—Abegail Landry."

Calvo scanned the obituary, noting the lack of other relatives who stood to inherit.

"Granted, that kind of money is always a motive, but his friend saw him fall into the water. The wife wasn't around."

"Moving on," Davis said again. He brought up the other local obituaries and moved through them, finally stopping at one. "Nick Jennings," he said. "Young guy, about my age, dies of a spider bite." He turned to Calvo with raised eyebrows. "A spider bite! Really?"

Before Calvo could respond, he scrolled down to the names under the letter M.

"Waylan Montez. Sixty-nine. Died at his cabin from a heart attack. Surviving widow, Geraldine Montez."

Calvo gasped. Davis turned his head to look at her.

"You okay?" he asked.

"She was at the séance I attended!" Calvo said. "Geraldine! Madame Lorraine told her to stay away from a cabin. That there would be death. There was something about fire or smoke… did the cabin burn down?"

"It doesn't say, and I couldn't find any articles about it. My friend writes for the *Tribune*, and he checked too. If he died of a heart attack, it isn't going to fill a lot of columns in the papers unless he's famous or something."

"Wait!" Calvo said. "You said Jennings. There was a Marsha Jennings at the same séance as Geraldine. I recorded it! Go back to Nick Jenning's obit. Is he survived by a wife? Marsha Jennings?"

Davis's fingers flew across the keyboard. He paused, leaned toward the screen, and smiled.

"Survived by his loving wife, Marsha Jennings, a younger brother, and his mother."

"Oh my gosh!" Calvo said, her head spinning. "Her séance reading mentioned 'a sting'! And he dies of a spider bite. What the hell?"

144

"Can I hear the recording?" Davis asked.

"I didn't bring it, but sure, you can hear it," Calvo said. She felt like the floor had disappeared.

"Any other deaths you are finding?" Calvo asked. She could feel her pulse pounding in her neck.

"The usual. Car crashes. Older people. These were the ones that caught my eye because they seemed odd. I mean, how many heart attacks can there be in one month?"

Calvo snatched a sheet of paper from his printer and scribbled down the names.

"Was there anyone else at your séance that stood out?" she asked.

"There was a pretty blonde lady," Davis said. "But I didn't hear hers. Dorothy was upset, and I'd seen enough for my article, so I helped Dorothy out to her car and left. The blonde's name was Brenda Griffin."

"You certainly have a good memory," Calvo said, acidly.

"It's my job," he said, missing the sudden shift in her behavior.

"Have you typed in her name, other than on a dating site?" Calvo asked.

He shot her a surprised look and chuckled.

"Good idea…the obits, not the dating thing. She was a little too old for me."

He typed in the name Griffin under the local obituaries.

"Nope. No Griffin. Happy now?"

"We need to get a look at the sign-in book at the good Madame's house," Calvo said, ignoring him. "I can't do it. She would recognize me from being there, pretending to be there for my niece."

"That leaves me out, too," Davis said. "Plus, odds are she's seen my article, and I'm not on her Christmas card list. But you're thinking what I'm thinking, right? There's a link to these people attending seances and their loved ones turning up their toes."

Calvo grimaced at the crude phrase, but she nodded.

"If these names of mysterious deaths turn up people close to them who are attending the seances, then yes, there's a connection. But what? How do you bring in a spirit for questioning?"

****

The doorbell shrilled, echoing down the long hallway. Madame Lorraine, who was seated with Rachel at the kitchen table, looked up from her reading material in surprise.

"Are we expecting someone?" she asked.

Rachel shook her head and stood up. "I'll see who it is," she said.

She walked past the library where Socrates was squawking about visitors, and opened the front door. She was surprised to see a tall man standing there with an above-average height female.

"May I help you?" she asked dubiously.

"Yes," the female said, smiling. "We would like a reading."

Rachel paused. The woman brushed a strand of hair from her face. Her large diamond ring glinted in the sunlight. She was dressed in an expensive three-piece linen suit. The man was in a blue pin-striped shirt, a dark blazer, and tan slacks.

"I'm afraid we only do readings by appointment," she said.

"Oh, well, do you have an opening today, by any chance?" the woman smiled again. She flashed the enormous diamond with emerald settings again as she pushed her long brown hair from her shoulders.

"One moment," Rachel said. She closed the door, leaving them standing outside. Detective Hilliard and his sister Emma waited.

"There is a man and a woman outside," Rachel said in hushed tones when she reached the kitchen. "They want a reading. She's wearing a diamond the size of a walnut!"

"Were they sent?" Madame Lorraine asked. "Have they been vetted?"

"I don't think so. We would have been told, and an appointment set up. They seem to have just come on a whim. That newspaper article is probably behind it. I imagine we'll get more uninvited people. What do you want me to do?"

"Show them in," Madame Lorraine said, her curiosity getting the better of her. "I'll handle them."

Rachel walked hurriedly down the hallway and opened the door.

146

Her manner was more gracious, and she smiled apologetically.

"You are in luck," she said. "We do have an opening now if you'd care to come in."

"Oh, how wonderful," Hilliard's sister said. "Thank you so much!" she cooed, her southern accent drawing out the word 'so.'

The two followed Rachel into the hallway.

"You will need to sign in," Rachel said, waving a hand toward an open ledger on a nearby hall table.

This is what Hilliard had hoped for. Calvo had told him that everyone had signed in before the séance began the night she attended. Hilliard flashed a meaningful look at his sister, and she stepped up to the book and signed Emma Taunton, along with the date, as indicated. She stepped aside, and Hilliard picked up the pen.

"Your home is so lovely," Emma gushed, stepping to block Rachel's view of the ledger. "Is the wallpaper original? You don't see flocked wallpaper like this anymore."

Rachel beamed. "Well, it was banned when there were fears of poisoning concerning the flocking. Back in the late 1800s, emerald green became the popular color, and it began showing up in everything, including flocked wallpaper. Women, who had their ballgowns dyed in the color, were dropping dead. You see, you needed arsenic mixed with copper to make the color. The gowns would get sweaty on the dance floor, and the poor women's skin absorbed the dye, which killed them. The same problem with the wallpaper. The flocking could flake off and be inhaled."

Emma's eyes opened wide.

"Goodness! Y'all sure do know a lot about it," she said, genuinely impressed.

"I have a working knowledge of such things," Rachel said modestly, missing the clicking sound coming from Hilliard's direction. "Let's go in," she said, just as Hilliard stepped away from the ledger.

They followed Rachel into a parlor with a large fireplace, worn, but comfortable-looking chairs, and a round table with six chairs around it. It was draped in black with a large pillar candle seated in the middle atop a black onyx slab.

"Please be seated, and Madame Lorraine will be right with you," she said and left the room.

Hilliard took the opportunity to study the room. There were a few portraits of grim people sporting pointed beards and top hats. A glass dome housed a stand of dried flowers, reminiscent of the William Morris era in the 1800s. A faint musky smell of tired fabric permeated the room. Minutes later, Madame Lorraine walked in. She wore a simple dark blue dress that reached her ankles. Her black and silver-threaded hair was piled in a bun. Hilliard's first impression was that of repulsion. Her pale face looked as if it hadn't seen sunlight in a year.

"Good morning," she said, without warmth. She took her seat at the head of the table and folded her long hands together. "I don't usually do this," she said, her tone as one bestowing a gift. "I had an opening. What can I do for you?"

Hilliard noticed her eyes go to Emma's diamond ring. His sister had made sure to place her hand on the table where it was in full view.

"My sister here saw something about you in the paper and has been bugging me to come with her to get her tea leaves read, or her palm looked at, or whatever it is you do," he said.

Madame Lorraine's eyes narrowed, but she remained in control.

"No tea leaves. No palms," she said evenly. "I can offer you a quick reading. If you want to attend a séance, those are held in the evenings and are more involved. A reading is $50," she said, elevating the price from the usual $25, "and a personal séance begins at $1,500."

Emma remained composed and took over before her brother could sabotage the entire thing.

"I would just love a reading now," she gushed, "and then please put me down for a séance! How thrilling!"

Madame Lorraine studied her for a moment and then reached behind her to a small tea table where some paraphernalia sat. She selected a deck of Tarot cards and passed them to Emma.

"Shuffle them," she said. When Emma had done so, Madame Lorraine continued. "Now press them between your palms while thinking of the question you wish them to address. Your energy will pass into the cards. Focus on only one question."

Emma did as she was told, continuing to play the part of an enthusiastic guest. She pressed them between her palms and squeezed her eyes closed. After a few moments, she opened them and smiled.

"Ok!" she said. "I have my question."

Madame Lorraine took the cards from her and, with her left hand, laid out ten cards in the cross position and four up the side. She began with the two overlapping cards in the middle and turned them over.

"Two of pentacles," she said. "The King of Pentacles below that." She continued turning the cards in order, surrounding the two middle cards, and stopped. "My, you have several cards showing pentacles and fortuitous sword cards."

The medium next turned over the four cards running alongside the cross-section. When she got to the last card, she said, "This is the overall outcome of the reading." She turned the card over and read it. "The Wheel of Fortune," she said. "In the upright position. That means a positive turn of the wheel. According to the cards, there is great wealth and positive outcomes for beginning a business venture or benefiting from an inheritance or windfall."

Emma clapped her hands like a small child.

"Oh my! That is exactly what I wanted to know!" she exclaimed. "I want to start a publishing business," she lied, "and I was worried about taking on investors. My Uncle Perry is not expected to live much longer, and I'm in his will. My share of the inheritance will be substantial. I mean, I have a lot of money of my own, but that would set me up to follow my dreams! Oh, thank you so much!"

Madame Lorraine managed a thin smile.

"The cards are never wrong," she said. "I do think a séance would benefit you based on what you just said. It might give you insight into how soon that inheritance might be forthcoming."

Hilliard's forehead wrinkled, but he kept quiet.

"Yes! Yes, please!" Emma gushed. "When may I come back?"

"I will have Rachel schedule your appointment," she said. "I don't deal with the business end. It disrupts my connection to spirit."

She rose, and Hilliard stood up. Emma stood up as well. Madame

Lorraine stood still near her chair and looked back and forth between them.

"Such a tall family," she said, her voice low. "How tall are you, my dear?"

"I'm 5'11", Emma said. "It was awful in Junior High, but I love being tall now."

"I'm sure," Madame Lorraine said. "Well, we'll be in touch. You can pay Rachel on your way out."

She walked from the room and disappeared into the hallway. Rachel appeared at the same time.

"That will be $50," she said. "I do hope you found your reading satisfactory. I would appreciate it if you don't announce your meeting here today. We have strict rules about our services being available only by appointment. I wouldn't want others to feel they can just come to the door."

"Oh, of course not!" Emma said, feeling the sting of the rebuff. She pulled out her wallet and made a show of fingering through a row of hundred-dollar bills until she came to a fifty. She plucked it out and handed it to Rachel with a smile.

"Please write your phone number down here," Rachel said, offering a small pale purple card and a pen. Emma did so and handed it back. "That's fine. I'll be in touch to schedule your seance."

Rachel walked them to the door, nodded, and shut the door behind them without further engagement.

When the two reached the blue Lexus, they got in with Emma behind the wheel. She started the engine, and they didn't speak until they were out on the street and heading toward town. Hilliard resisted the urge to stare at the windows to see if the two women were watching them through the lace sheers.

"You did perfect!" Hilliard said to his sister as she navigated past a stream of tourists on a walking tour. "She didn't notice me taking pics of the ledger pages with my phone, right?"

"No! She was all caught up in telling me about poisoned green wallpaper and dresses. I heard your phone camera clicking, but I don't think she did. She was too busy talking."

"Well, I owe you one. Something is going on there, that's for sure. They wouldn't have let us in if it weren't for that ring, I can tell you that right now."

"Speaking of the ring," Emma said shyly. "Can I keep it?"

"Sure," Hilliard laughed. "It's just $45 worth of glass. I wouldn't wear it out in public, though. Someone might mug you, thinking it's real. I do want the thousand in cash from your wallet. I gotta give it back to the burglary division. And the Lexus is due back to the rental company by 3:30."

Inside the Stanton-Mills mansion, Madame Lorraine and Rachel stood in the kitchen. There was a weighty feeling to the atmosphere.

"What names did they sign in with?" Madame Lorraine asked, a tension showing in her shoulders.

"Emma Taunton and Bill Arndt," Rachel said.

"Look them up," Madame Lorraine said. "We have to be very careful. They didn't come here through proper channels. If they're legitimate, she's an easy target for a big payoff."

"It's been pretty quiet out there," Rachel said. "I think Dorothy may have given up. We should be okay now."

The headlines spanning the front page of the *New Orleans Tattler* shocked the Garden District the following morning:

"DIG HIM UP!"

Dorothy Brindle, the widow of the late philanthropist Charles Brindle of New Orleans, has given the directive to have her late husband exhumed due to her suspicions of foul play. This comes after a month of behind-the-scenes investigative work, bolstered by Mrs. Brindle. Judge William T. Humphrey yesterday approved the court order. Details will follow as to the date the exhumation will take place.

The byline read Davis Miles.

17 SMOKE AND MIRRORS

Lieutenant Calvo placed her coffee mug on Hilliard's desk and plopped into the chair across from him. She laid her leather folder on the desk as well and took a sip of her coffee. Hilliard was grinning at her.

"What?" Calvo asked, looking at him through the steam rising from her mug.

"You had to buy a mug with dancing kittens?" he asked, shaking his head.

"A. I didn't buy it. My friend made it for me, and B. they are grown cats, not kittens. I should have gone with the boring, generic, tarnished, metal mug you have, but I actually have a personality, and I don't mind showing it. If we're through dissecting my mugware, I have some news. I checked two cat shelters and a fancy boarding cat palace. No Richy."

She waited for a response but got none.

"I also went to see the reporter. We had an interesting convo. His name is Davis Miles, as you may recall from his name on all these articles."

"Perfect," Hilliard said, reaching for a manila file. "I've got some stuff from the meeting with the voodoo woman."

Calvo laughed and opened her folder. She pulled out the notes she had made when she and Davis went over the obituaries.

"You go first," she said. "I'm dying to know what happened."

"Well, she is a piece of work," Hilliard began. "She could have made her living as a ghoul in a horror flick. I'm not kidding. That woman is bloodless. I've never seen such pale skin. Then, when you add these green eyes that look like they're backlit, it's intimidating. Then there's her nose…if an eagle and a ghost had a baby, that would be Madame Lorraine."

Calvo was laughing.

"You forget I've already seen her. I was at one of her séance's remember?" Calvo said.

"Well, am I wrong?"

"No. You're not wrong. What did you find out?"

"I took some pictures of the two pages of signatures that look like they are from the past two months. There weren't as many as I would have guessed. Her seances seem to run only about one or two a week."

He pulled a printout of the camera shots from his file folder and turned it around so that it faced Calvo. She ran an eye down the lined ledger pages, taking in the dates, and shook her head. This confirmed it.

"Some of these names match the ones that Davis and I pulled up of mysterious deaths in the past month or so," Calvo said.

She handed Hilliard her notes. As he read over the names of Montez, Jennings, and Landry, he let out a loud whistle.

"Something is rotten in Nawlins," he said, using his pet name for the city. "She was trying to set up my sister Emma to come back for more after she got a look at the fake diamond and money she had on her. I get the whole money sting thing, but murder? That's a whole nother ball game."

"All we have to do is look at Dorothy Brindle," Calvo said. "She goes to a séance, gets some weird message from her husband Charlie, "to proceed" with something. She puts us on the trail of Everett and a poisoned beer. If Everett's prints match both the poisoned beer bottle and the photograph he handed you at his house, it's Bingo. I had my doubts, but I don't know. Besides, if Dorothy had anything to do with it, why would she consent to an exhumation? She must be sure Charlie was poisoned, and if thallium is found in his tissues, then it's case closed. There is no way to explain Everett's prints on the poisoned beer bottle she found under the chair."

Hilliard chewed on it for a minute.

"Ok," he said slowly, "but how does Madame Lorraine benefit from that? She gets a cool $1,500 for the séance and Charlie giving his wife a message, but then what? There has to be more. Plus, I got the impression from the lady who opened the door that we were not welcome, that is, until she got a look at Emma's rock."

"Told you," Calvo said smugly. "There's no phone number on the business card, yet it says by Appointment Only. There has to be a third party involved—someone who vets the people sent over for a reading. Meanwhile, we need the autopsy reports for the names of the deceased who are on both of our lists."

"I'll get Peterson on it," Hilliard said, making a note. "Let's check these other names from the good Madame's guest book while we're at it. There may be more bodies in the graveyard than we know. And," he added, "we may be closing in on Harris. This was in the trash can in his office when we searched." He pulled the torn fragments of the purple notecard from his file. "Ready for this?"

Hilliard placed the two torn fragments of the notecard on the desk and pieced them together. In the same italic handwriting that Calvo had seen on Carol's notecard, it read:

PRODUCT AND INSTRUCTIONS WILL BE DELIVERED ON OCTOBER 2. SIDE YARD. 1:30 PM.

"Oh my God!" she said. "The product has to be the bath bombs, right?"

"Hold your horses," he said. "We still need proof. He could claim it was something for his lecture that night. Maybe a PowerPoint thumb drive."

"Delivered to the side yard?" Calvo asked incredulously. "And the message is on the same purple notecards as Dorothy's and Carol's?"

"I'm just saying, it's not enough. But we're getting there."

She placed her notes from her meeting with Davis next to the photocopies of the names in Madame Lorraine's ledger. "Let's half these," she said. "We need to figure this out before the body count rises."

****

Rachel wiped her sweating forehead and crammed the pruned branches from plants in her greenhouse down into a trash can. She wiped her face with the back of her hand and looked about her with satisfaction. The fall pruning was done. She wetted a finger on her tongue and ran it along a trickling of blood running down her wrist from where a thorn had pierced her skin. Hefting the large garbage can of clippings, she walked to the side glass door and elbowed the lever. The fall air fanned her sweating face as she walked out into the back yard and along the sidewalk toward the front of the house.

Just as Rachel rounded a bush, struggling to keep her arms wrapped about the large plastic can of clippings, she stopped. A man with a black vest with orange stripes is walking away, rounding the corner of the house, and disappearing from view. The back of his vest read Meter Reader.

Rachel set the can down and walked to the area from where he had been walking away. Nothing seemed out of place. *What was he doing here?* she wondered. *The meter box was on the other side of the house.* She turned to leave and saw something brown stuffed behind a large azalea bush next to a stone statue. She walked over to it and pulled a large paper bag out of hiding. The neck of the sack was folded over. She opened it and looked inside.

The world seemed to stop. There, in neat packets of hundred-dollar bills, wrapped in rubber bands, was more money than Rachel had seen in one place. She was about to lift out some of the packets to count them when a scream came from inside the house.

Rachel quickly crammed the bag of money down behind the bush and ran for the steps to the kitchen door, forgetting the trash can of clippings. Climbing them quickly, she flung open the door and found her sister just entering the kitchen from the hallway, a newspaper clutched like a rag doll in her hand. A blood-red tinge of color flooded her pale complexion. Her chest was heaving.

"For goodness' sake, Ruby," Rachel cried. "What is it?"

The green eyes that turned on her caught her breath. The hatred shining from them was palpable.

"Look at this!" her sister screamed, slapping the crumpled newspaper down on the kitchen table. Whatever was there in the black ink had been enough to ignore Rachel's slip of the tongue.

Rachel walked over to the kitchen table and smoothed out the heavily creased paper. Her breath caught when she saw the headlines on the front page in bold black ink.

"DIG HIM UP!"

****

Officer Peterson rounded a corner in the police department hallway and collided with Detective Hilliard, who was balancing a box of documents.

"Sorry," Peterson said. "I just came from your office. Got those autopsy reports and the prints analysis you wanted." He smiled and walked off, a cloud of Drakkar cologne following him. Hilliard wrinkled his nose and continued, following the cloud of cologne to his office door.

"I hope that guy never commits a murder," Hilliard said, plopping the cardboard box down onto his desk. "That cologne would lead the police straight to him. I think he has a thing for you," he said, grinning at Calvo, who was reading a report.

"Ok," she said without preamble, and her eyes were dancing. "Take a guess, any guess…" She was waving a lab report.

"Santa Claus is really Donald Trump?"

She shot him a baleful look.

"Not even you can ruin this moment for me," she said happily. "The print analysis from the beer bottle and photograph Everett gave you is back. They match. It's Everett Brindle's prints on both!"

Hilliard lit up. "Merry frickin' Christmas!" he said. "I get to put the cuffs on him!"

"We have to get an arrest warrant first, but ok, you get to give him the bracelets. But wait, there's more…I've got Nick Jenning's autopsy report here," she said. "It looks like he died from a black widow spider bite on his left hand." She paused and continued reading. "The poor guy was only in his thirties. Is that normal?"

Hilliard slid into his chair and snatched the file from Calvo's hands. She sighed and waited as he read over the details.

"No," he said, still reading. "Normally, they are more deadly to older people or kids. Unless…." His eyes ran down the page. He flipped over the stapled pages until he came to what he was looking for. His eyebrows rose, causing his forehead to furrow. "Here we go," he said ominously. "Nick has a deficient immune system. That would make you vulnerable to a poisonous spider bite like that. I think we can rule him out as one of the suspicious deaths. He's unpacking a box in the garage, gets bitten, has an immune system that can't handle that kind of thing, and he dies. It's sad, but not unheard of."

Calvo reached over and took the report back. Hilliard watched her as she read it over. After reading the final page, she laid it down on the desk and frowned.

"So, it's just a coincidence that this guy's wife attended a séance with Madame Lorraine and he ends up dead?" she asked. "Hey, wait a minute…"

Calvo opened her leather folder and pulled out the copy of Hilliard's photos from the psychic's sign-in ledger. She found Marsha Jenning's name and the date she was there for a reading. Calvo looked back at the autopsy report's date of Nick Jenning's death. She stared at Hilliard with a look of determination.

"Nick Jennings gets bitten by a deadly spider only days after

Marsha Jennings is at one of Madame Lorraine's seances. That's too much of a coincidence for me," she said heatedly.

"Next up, Waylan Montez." Calvo picked up another autopsy report from her file. "This one is complicated, and once again, Jennings in the lab came through with his advanced tech. Blood, liver, and tissue results using the advanced LC-MS/MS testing show oleandrin in the blood and tissues. It is represented as cardiac glycosides in the body." She looked over at him.

"Translation," Hilliard said. "Did he not die of a heart attack?"

"He died from inhaling the smoke of burning oleander branches! That's where the oleandrin comes from. According to this, there was evidence of smoke inhalation and the oleandrin showed up in the urine, blood, and tissue samples."

"So what are you saying?" Hilliard asked.

"Maybe..." Calvo's face suddenly brightened. "Maybe Madame Lorraine is providing the death weapon *and* the murder plot!" she exclaimed. "In this case, a black widow spider for a garage box, and oleander branches! Unfortunately, there is no autopsy report for Roger Landry because his body was never recovered from Lake Pontchartrain. Strike Two for him is that the food from the boat came back negative for poisoning."

She looked over the list of food items and wrappers obtained from the boat. Caviar, crackers, some jam, and melted brie on two sandwich wrappers, mixed fruit, and a crushed grape branch with a withered grape still attached.

She sighed.

"I'm not sure how that murder was pulled off, but we know his wife attended a séance. I wonder what the asking price is for the Murder in a Box plan?"

****

Brenda Griffin pulled the pot roast from the oven and set it on the stovetop. The kitchen was infused with the mouthwatering aroma of seasonings and gravy. She lifted the lid to the pan of frying parsnips and turned them over to cook for another five minutes. Increasing the heat, she added soy sauce and some seasoning, flipping the sliced tubulars to coat them evenly.

"Ted," she called, "dinner is ready."

Brenda placed the pot roast on a platter and surrounded it with the fried parsnips, adding some parsley as a garnish. The bowl of hot rolls was already on the table, wrapped in a kitchen towel. A bowl of salad greens with her husband's favorite blend of chopped eggs, bean sprouts, and crumbled bacon sat next to a cruet of his favorite vinaigrette.

Ted entered the room, his facial expression sour as if he had been interrupted from something. It seemed to brighten when he saw the feast his wife of eight years had laid out. He took his seat without waiting for her to take hers and picked up the carving knife and fork.

Brenda poured his favorite red Merlot into his wine glass and then poured one for herself. She finally sank into her own chair.

"How is the report coming?" she asked timidly.

Ted grunted and continued to slice the roast.

"Why do you ask me when you know you wouldn't understand it if I did discuss it with you?" he said condescendingly.

She chewed the inside of her cheek and tried again.

"The Porters invited us to go on a Christmas cruise," she began, trying without success to sound casual. "Debbie sent over the dates, and if you want, we could look them over after...."

"No," Ted said sharply, and continued carving. He slid two thick slices onto his plate and scooped up a large helping of parsnips with the serving spoon.

Brenda picked up the abandoned serving fork and helped herself to a slice of meat. She reached for the salad bowl and lifted a helping of the greens onto her plate with the serving spoons. Ted took the bowl from her and shoveled a large helping of the salad onto his plate, making sure he spooned up most of the sliced eggs. He beat her to the bottle of dressing.

They ate in silence, with Ted constantly checking pings coming in on his cell phone that was resting next to his plate. His loud chewing grated on Brenda's nerves as she picked at her lettuce. From the corner of her eye, she watched her husband fork several slices of parsnips and cram them into his mouth, his eyes on his phone. Swallowing them, he followed it with a long drink of wine.

Brenda fidgeted with her hands, absently rolling her wedding ring around her finger. She had lost so much weight from the stress of the marriage that the ring practically twirled around on its own. She watched him as he forced another forkful of parsnips into his mouth. He was chuckling over some text that had popped up on his phone.

Ted's fork suddenly fell from his hand, clattering on his plate. It left a trail of soy sauce from the parsnips down his shirt. His head bent forward, and his facial muscles began to twitch. He quickly reached for his wine glass, but his trembling fingers lost their grip, and it fell to the table, red wine saturating the lace tablecloth. He looked at Brenda with dilated pupils and a look of fear on his face that she had never seen. He reached for her, but she leaned away. His body went into convulsions until he was thrown from his chair. He lay on the dining room floor, twitching and contorting, saliva dripping from his open mouth. After several minutes of agony, he lay still, his body lying on its left side in the fetal position and his fingers clutching his throat.

Brenda sat, her chest heaving as she stared at her husband lying there. Fear hammered at her rib cage, and she felt bile rising in her throat. When he remained still, his eyes open and staring, she got up and went to him. He was dead. Fighting the urge to vomit, she pried his hands away and unbuttoned his shirt. It was cumbersome getting it off, his limp body refusing to cooperate. Finally, she pulled his arm through the last sleeve and stood up. She laid the shirt on the counter and took the roast with the parsnips to the sink.

Carefully, she plucked out the remaining parsnips from the serving platter and crammed them into the garbage disposal. The grating sound filled the kitchen, setting her teeth on edge. From the cupboard, she pulled out a smaller serving plate and put the remaining pot roast on it, sprinkling fresh parsley around it. She took the roast back to the table and set it in the middle.

Brenda studied the table, her mind whirling. She picked up Ted's plate and the dropped fork and took them to the sink. Scraping off the remains of his food into the disposal, she ran it again. Turning the hot water to full blast, she scrubbed the plate and fork, dried them, and put them away. She scrubbed the frying pan and utensils she had used for the parsnip recipe and dried them also, returning them to their proper places. Finally, she took down a fresh plate and walked to the table. Using the serving fork, she placed a small chunk of roast on the plate and moved it around to smear the gravy. She placed a roll on the plate next to it. He hadn't finished the salad on his smaller plate, so she left that alone. The spilled wine worked. She would say he had a sudden collapse and dropped the glass.

Gripping the stained shirt, Brenda carried it to the garage, where she stuffed it down into a large open bag of potting soil until it disappeared from view. She slapped the dirt from her hands and went back inside.

Brenda walked to the back bedroom and returned with a striped button-up shirt. Grimacing, she began redressing the body. When she turned him onto his back to button it, she cried out. His eyes stared sightlessly at her, the pupils mere pinpricks. Drool ran across his face. Her fingers shaking, she finished the last button and turned him back into the position in which he had fallen. She pulled his arms back up to his chest and backed away. The room seemed to spin around her. Finally, looking it all over once again, she picked up her cell phone and dialed 911.

18 A SECRET TO DIE FOR

Lieutenant Adelaide Calvo and Detective Archer Hilliard entered the modest home of Brenda and Theodore Griffin. A patrol officer was just coming out of the house.

"What have we got?" Hilliard asked as Officer Williams paused to speak to him.

"It's hard to say right now," he said. "It's the husband. He's dead. Lying in the dining room. It could be cardiac arrest or some kind of respiratory failure. He seems kinda young, but you never know. What are you doing here?"

Calvo wasn't prepared to share that Davis Miles had called her and alerted her that he had heard the call go out on his police scanner and recognized the name Griffin. She had immediately grabbed Hilliard and headed to the scene.

"We were in the area," Hilliard lied. "Heard it on the scanner. Just thought we'd check it out."

Officer Williams shrugged and walked off just as an ambulance gurney was brought in. The two detectives snapped on latex gloves.

Calvo and Hilliard entered the home and followed the sound of voices to the dining room. A photographer was snapping photographs as an EMT knelt over the body of a man lying on his side, his hands up against his chest. The medic looked up at Hilliard and nodded.

"They're sending detectives out on 10-54's?" he asked.

"A 'Possible Dead Body' is always on my radar," Hilliard said, addressing the code. "What do you think happened?"

"It points to a heart attack at this time, but it's early. He was eating dinner and keeled over, according to his wife. She's in the other room with Olson."

Calvo stooped and looked at Theodore Griffin's face. His eyes were still staring, his face contorted. Drool had crusted across the bottom of his face and cheeks.

"Did she move the body?" Calvo asked.

"Don't know," the medic answered. "Why?"

"He's on his left side. You can see the saliva pooled under his face there. So how did it run across his face in the opposite direction? Gravity doesn't work like that."

The medic looked closely at the body. He nodded.

"Good point. The autopsy will tell us more."

"Make sure you get pictures of his face," Calvo said, straightening.

Hilliard was studying the dining table that still showed the remains of a dinner for two. He was particularly interested in the spilled wine that stained the linen tablecloth in a grotesque, blood-like pool. He lifted the plate in front of the chair where the dead man lay with one finger and peered beneath it.

"What's up?" Calvo whispered to him.

"How come the wine isn't splashed onto the plate?" he asked. "The stain runs all around the plate, and the glass practically landed on it. There's no wine on the plate."

Calvo looked at the remains of a roast and a roll sitting in a smear of gravy on Griffin's plate. Some salad remained on a plate to the right of the plate. She suddenly bent and looked beneath the table. She then turned to the medic and asked, "Did you guys pick up a fork?"

He looked surprised and shook his head, turning to look up at the other medic standing near him. He, too, shook his head.

"Have you looked under him yet?" Calvo asked.

"We're about to load him, so you can see for yourself."

The two medics gently rolled Theodore Griffin onto his back and lifted him onto the gurney, zipping the white body bag closed. There was nothing beneath him. Only a pool of dried fluids marked where his head had been.

"You're not waiting for the coroner to check him?" Calvo asked.

"There are no signs of foul play," he said. "We got the pictures, and they're interviewing the wife. Looks like an allergic reaction to me."

Calvo sighed and waited until they had rolled the body out of the room. She couldn't tell them her suspicions based on a séance reading. The autopsy results would have to do. She walked into the kitchen, which opened onto the dining room. Nothing was in the sink. A roasting pan with concealed gravy set atop the stove. Some remnants of salad preparations littered the island counter. A knife lay among the lettuce clippings. She opened the dishwasher. It was empty. The kitchen garbage can also revealed nothing out of the ordinary. Finally, she turned to Hilliard, who was watching her.

"Where is his fork?" she asked. "It isn't on the table or floor. If he were eating and fell off the chair, then the fork should still be there. He didn't eat with his fingers, and it didn't get up and walk away on little fork legs. You noticed the wine stain doesn't line up with the plate. Do you think she switched plates and forgot to put the fork back?"

Hilliard and Calvo paused inside the living room entry and listened in as Officer Olson questioned the woman hunched over on the couch, sobbing into a tissue. She was young, blonde, and swollen eyed. Calvo studied her, remembering Davis speaking of her as "being too old for him" when he shared a séance table with her. Now, her husband was dead, and the crime scene wasn't lining up.

"Does your husband have any medical issues other than the ones you mentioned?" Olson asked her, making notes.

"No," Brenda said in a choked voice. "He is... was...very image conscious. He worked out, took supplements, and gave strict orders on what food he wanted." She looked up to see Calvo and Hilliard standing a few feet away, watching her. She shifted in her seat and brushed a wave of blonde hair from her face, then immediately put it back, looking about her nervously.

"Could it have been an allergic reaction to the food?" Olson asked.

Brenda now only shook her head and broke into fresh sobs. Looking uncomfortable, he rose.

"Thank you, Mrs. Griffin," he said. "We'll be in touch."

He nodded at Calvo and Hilliard and left the room. Brenda's sobs filled the vacancy. Without a word, the two detectives left her sitting there.

Calvo returned to the dining room, where the photographer was packing up.

"Hold up," she said. "I want photos of that table. Close-ups, the whole thing. The kitchen, too. Lastly, get one of the wine stains under the man's plate."

Sighing, he pulled his camera back out of his bag and walked over to the dining room table.

"We need to get forensics in here," Calvo whispered to Hilliard, "before anything else gets messed with. Something is not kosher."

"A Jewish quote from a native Creole," he said.

"Did you notice her forehead?" Calvo asked him in hushed tones, ignoring his last remark, as they walked out the front door. "She's got a bad bruise. She tried to cover it with makeup, but you can see it. She kept it covered with her hair."

"So he was beating her, and she killed him?"

"Wouldn't be the first time," Calvo said as they walked to their car. "She also had dirt under her fingernails. Seems odd if you had just prepared a meal. Carol and I are headed back to Scripted! tomorrow," Calvo said. "There's a connection there between Dorothy and Malcolm Harris. Carol got a purple notecard in her purse the night she and I attended the séance…just like the purple card that fell out of Dorothy's purse and the one you found in Harris's trash can. I'm going to shake the cage and see what falls out."

"Keep me posted," Hilliard said.

"Call forensics," Calvo said.

****

Beverly Singleton's face lit up when she saw Lieutenant Calvo and her 'niece' enter her shop. She practically leapt from her chair, where she was organizing envelopes at her desk.

"Mrs. Beaufort, Miss Hadley, how lovely to see you again," she cooed, shaking each of their hands. "Are you closer to making a decision?" she asked.

Calvo recognized that the innocuously sounding question had a double meaning. She and Carol had visited the shop the day before their séance, ostensibly for Beverly to meet the 'niece' and begin the selection process for the wedding invitations. As per Calvo's request, Carol, aka Michelle Hadley, had acted nervously, unclear as to whether she should go through with the wedding.

"I'm not used to all that money," Carol said in feigned distress. "His family is from generational wealth, and I, well, my family owns a small restaurant in Shreveport."

Just as Calvo hoped, Beverly took the bait.

"You know, you are not the first young bride-to-be to feel this way," she said. "I have just the person for you. She is marvelous. She can foretell the future and allay your fears!"

Carol's eyes opened wide with interest.

"Really?" she exclaimed. "Why, that would be too wonderful! If I can just feel better about it, I can focus on going forward with all this!"

She waved her hands to encompass the vast array of wedding invitations. Calvo smothered a grin. Carol was better than she thought at all this.

"Here," Beverly said, "this is her card. I will make the arrangements and call you. How does that sound?"

"Madame Lorraine," Carol breathed, reading the card. "She even sounds mysterious! I am so excited! Thank you so much!"

Now, Calvo and Carol had returned after attending the séance.

Calvo was hoping to see what happened next. So far, there was nothing she could actually accuse the medium of doing other than some harmless reading. The note left in Carol's purse, however, was a different matter.

"We are getting closer," Calvo finally answered Beverly's question upon their arrival that afternoon.

"Do come sit down," Beverly offered.

The two took their seats at her desk. Just then, a young man came out of a back room. He looked surprised to see the two women and apologized for the interruption.

"I, uh, just wanted to ask you about the next appointment," he said nervously to Beverly, whose demeanor changed upon his arrival.

"Uh, this is my husband," Beverly offered, flushed. "Sorry about that." She reached into a drawer and pulled out a sheet of paper. Calvo could make out what looked like an address, but she couldn't read it clearly. "There you are," Beverly said, forcing a smile. "See you later."

He took the note, folded it in half, nodded at the two women, and returned through the door behind his wife, shutting it after him.

"He helps with things," she offered. "Where were we?" she said, a bit breathless.

"We went to the séance," Carol said, "and it was amazing! I mean, there was this green smoke and a glowing skull…I was half-scared and half-flabbergasted!"

Beverly laughed.

"Yes, she is quite wonderful. So, are you ready to proceed?"

"I do have a question," Carol said, her southern drawl soft and pleading. "I found this in my purse after I got home. I think it must have been put there at the séance. I'm not sure what it means."

She passed the purple notecard to Beverly. Calvo watched her closely as she read the note:

The Spirits say the conditions are favorable for a union. There are obstacles, but the magic arts can overcome them. With help, you will enjoy a long, happy marriage.

Beverly licked her lips and took a moment. She looked up at Carol and smiled.

"It appears that Madame Lorraine may be able to assist you further with your need to feel confident in your decision," she said. "If you like, I can arrange for her to create something for you that will guarantee your future happiness with this man."

Calvo felt her pulse quicken. This was it! This was how it was done!

"Oh!" Carol said, her eyes wide. "Like a magic amulet or something?"

"Exactly!" Beverly said, beaming. "Like a magic amulet. We are in New Orleans after all!"

The three women laughed. Beverly waited for Carol to take the next step.

"Well, okay, I guess. If it will not harm anyone. I mean, it's just to make it a happy marriage, right?"

"Of course!" Beverly said. "No chicken blood or *gris gris*. No swinging a cat around at midnight!" She laughed.

"Alright," Carol said, clasping her hands. "What do I do?"

****

Rachel found her place on the recorder and pressed Play. She held it up for the parrot to hear the recording again.

"Hi Tiffany. I'm on my way home," the recording said, in a strong male voice.

Socrates tilted his head and listened. He fluffed out his feathers and bobbed his head.

"Come on, Socrates," Rachel coaxed. "Say it. You did it before. Say it like the man's voice this time."

The parrot squawked and walked back and forth along his perch.

Rachel sighed and tried again. She keyed up the recording and hit Play.

"Hi Tiffany…"

"Hi Tiffany," Socrates croaked. "I'm on my way home."

Rachel's face lit up.

"That's good, Socrates! Very good. Please do it again, like his voice. That was better. Try again. 'Hi Tiffany…'"

"Hi Tiffany. I'm on my way home," the parrot said. It was the same inflection, but done with a lower register than the male voice in the recording. It wasn't perfect, but it was close.

Rachel gave the bird its reward for completing the rehearsal. She walked out into the shadowy hallway and listened.

"Lorraine?" she called, just barely catching herself before she yelled out 'Ruby.'

The house settled around her, feeling almost angry that her loud voice had dispelled its quiet. Rachel felt a sudden twinge of nerves. Her sister had gone out without telling her. The only sound was Socrates munching on a toasted treat.

Rachel quickly went to the kitchen door, opened it, and stepped down the stairs to the side yard. She stopped and looked up at the second-story windows in search of her sister's face. There was no one there. She crossed to the bush and looked beneath the azalea bush where she had returned the bag of money the day before. It was gone.

19 ABRACADABRA

Nathan Hennings stopped in the middle of the library, panting. About him were scattered books and decor. Nails protruded from blank squares on the walls where paintings had hung. Other rooms in the large home were in a similar state of disarray. Clothes spilled from bedroom closets, hangers still in place. He had sent the maid home for the day and set about taking the house apart, one room at a time. Somewhere, his wife had hidden a painting worth half a million dollars.

Louise Hennings had lingered on with lung cancer. Her marriage to Nathan had deteriorated long ago. They had filled a home with priceless possessions, but money couldn't buy warmth and love. Neither had a will or life insurance money. There was no pre-nup. What remained were possessions obtained through their twenty years of marriage. In particular, a painting of a European monarch said to be worth over $500,000. It had always hung in the living room above the fireplace.

One morning, Nathan found Louise dead. She had passed during the night. Minutes after they took her body away, he had gone to where the painting hung. It was gone, and a cheap imitation of a Monet waterlily montage hung in its place. It was her one last, spiteful move to underscore her hatred for him. Twenty years his junior, you had begun regretting the marriage in the second year.

While ordering the funeral programs for Louise's service, he had been told about a psychic who could provide answers to any questions he might have. She reportedly helped in the grieving process by holding seances where one could talk to their lost loved ones. In desperation, he went to see her. But the evening had taken a bizarre turn. Louise's face had appeared on a giant mirror in green threading. He had gone to ask where the painting was hidden. Instead, he had a message from the dead accusing him of 'a hurried death, a hurried funeral, and something hidden.'

Now, as he stood in the chaos he had created, his mind went to the séance and the things that had happened since. He walked to the desk and unlocked the top drawer. Three folded notecards in a pale purple stock were lying there. He steeled himself as he read them again, each arriving in his mailbox a week apart.

Eaten like cancer, but not cancer. A death too soon. Hurried cremation. How much did she know? How much do I know?

The second message was more to the point:

Money won't bring her back, but it might buy your freedom. $300,000, cash, Thursday night. Your back porch. Plain brown paper bag. 11:30 PM.

When Thursday night came and went without Nathan complying, the final note, arriving the day before, read:

An autopsy report can be ordered.
Final message. Sunday night. 11:30.

Nathan's hand trembled as he read the final card. The armpits of his shirt were stained with perspiration. A flashback of him switching her blue and yellow pills for ones laced with arsenic shot before his eyes. He felt the heat on his face and the back of his neck as he looked at the barren walls and screamed:

"Dammit! Where is it?"

****

A tap came on the doorframe of the open door to Hilliard and Calvo's office. The two looked up from their reports to see Mike Jennings from the lab standing there, a brown file clutched in one hand.

"I've got your tox report from the Griffin case," he said. "Got a minute?"

Calvo's face couldn't contain its excitement. She waved him to a metal chair next to her. He turned it around backwards and straddled it, his forearms resting on the back.

"What exactly are you guys investigating?" he asked. "These requests you keep sending me are some of the more bizarre cases I've seen. I'm having to use special spectrometry to even find the culprit."

"We're not completely there yet," Calvo said, "but we're closing in. Would you believe it looks like it's revolving around a psychic and messages from the dead?"

Jenning's face showed amusement.

"Well, your spirit board is conjuring up real results," he said, opening the brown file folder. "This Theodore Griffin died of coniine poisoning. His bloodstream showed elevated levels that could have killed him twice over."

"Where did the poison come from?" Hilliard asked, making a note of it.

"Some aloe plants can produce it, but here, we don't have to guess. I can rely on the gastric contents of Mr. Griffin for that answer. The man died of eating poison hemlock."

Calvo gasped.

"Hemlock? How did he get hold of that?"

"His stomach contents showed undigested bits of the tubular root portion of the plant. It can be mistaken for parsnips. As it was mixed in with some soy sauce, and the remains of roast beef and salad, I can only assume someone served hemlock masquerading as parsnips."

Calvo and Hilliard's eyes met across the desk.

"There were no parsnips at the dinner table," Calvo said in a strained voice. "We suspected she cleaned up before the police arrived. She must have gotten rid of it."

"Who's 'she'?" Jennings asked.

"Brenda Griffin," Calvo said. "We finally have something to hang our hat on."

****

Brandon Singleton pulled up to the address his wife had given him. It was the second pick-up that week. Obviously, the séance sisters were raking it in, he thought. As long as he and his wife, Beverly, got their cut, he was happy. Their little print shop did a brisk business, but wedding and funeral announcements did not provide the lifestyle he was after. The side hustle was bringing in real cash.

He pulled up to the curb and peered through the windshield at the imposing three-story home. He reached for his vest lying in the passenger seat and pushed his arms through the sleeve holes. Sliding from the truck seat, he adjusted the vest with yellow neon stripes and the words Meter Reader across the back. He leaned in and retrieved his fake ledger and electronic reading device. Glancing around him, he walked to the front gate and opened it.

Insects swirled as Brandon rounded the corner of the house and strode to the meter box. He paused, pretending to read the data there. He glanced around again for prying eyes and then reached down into the bushes beneath the box. It was there, like the others: a large brown paper bag with the top folded over and sealed with tape. He lifted it out, tucked it under his arm, and left the property.

Nathan Hennings watched him from the parted curtains of a second-floor bedroom, his face working spasmodically. He had caved to the blackmail. He had no other choice.

****

Tiffany Belmont LeBlanc arrived at the Stanton-Mills mansion a few minutes early for her séance reading. She had paid an exorbitant amount of money for a private session. She peered out the passenger window at the large house, sitting back from the road in the darkness. She fought the urge to restart the car and pull away. Her mind raced like a manic hamster racing in a wheel. She glanced at her watch and took a deep breath. *You can do this*, she thought, and opened the car door.

The house loomed above her as she opened the gate to the front walk and paused. She thought she saw a lace curtain fall back into place from a room to the right of the door. Candlelight was coming through the curtain to the left. The upstairs lights were off, giving the house the illusion of sightless eyes.

Rachel answered the doorbell and smiled at the meticulously dressed woman before her. Tiffany LeBlanc's ivory linen suit was put together in understated elegance that screamed wealth. Her simple gold earrings accented her honey blonde hair that was swept back in a fashionable chignon. Her cheeks were highlighted with the faintest touch of plum blush that matched the accent color of her eyeshadow.

"Please come in," Rachel invited and stood aside to allow her to do so. "Madame Lorraine will be with you momentarily. May I invite you to sign our guest list, please?"

Tiffany looked past Rachel's arm to a small hall table where an open book sat. She hesitated.

"I would much prefer to remain anonymous," she said, in a tone that bore the hint of a woman used to getting her way.

"I understand, but it is protocol," Rachel said. "However, I think we can waive that if it makes you uncomfortable. Please leave any devices in the basket, such as cell phones, etc. That I do insist upon!"

Tiffany arched an eyebrow at the directive, but complied, placing her cell phone into the basket. She stood with her arms crossed at the wrists, holding a leather handbag with a Chanel clasp.

"Excellent," Rachel said. "Right this way."

Tiffany followed the woman into the room she had noticed from the front of the house. There was a large candle burning in the center of a round table. Only two chairs were arranged around it, one across from the other. She allowed Rachel to guide her to the chair that had its back to the hallway. Tiffany sat down, placing her purse on the floor next to her.

Without another word, Rachel exited the room. Tiffany sat in the stillness, her heart rate erratic. The room's furniture sat in hulking shadows to her right, and she could make out a fireplace, cold and forbidding, in the center of the back wall. A pervasive musky smell surrounded her. It seemed like an eternity before a woman suddenly appeared from behind her, making her jump.

Madame Lorraine assessed Tiffany from the corner of her eye as she glided around the table to her chair and sat down. The mere tilt of her head carried the look of one studying a specimen before relegating it to a category.

"Welcome," Madame Lorraine said quietly. "I believe your young niece attended one of my gatherings. I do hope I was of help to her."

"Yes," Tiffany said. "She had been having a great deal of trouble with some mean school girls. They can be so cruel at that age. Haley told me you helped her, but she was vague on how."

Madame Lorraine grinned, a thin, feral smile that Tiffany found unpleasant. Without addressing the woman's comment, Madame Lorrain began.

"The spirits will be favorable tonight, I feel it." The thin smile gave off more of a sinister feeling than warmth, and Tiffany shifted in her seat. "Please place your hands on the table, palms down, and remain still throughout," the medium instructed. "We will now begin."

Madame Lorraine closed her eyes, tilted her head back, and began breathing deeply. Tiffany could not take her eyes from the pale face that looked luminous in the candle's single flame. The psychic suddenly took a deep rasping breath, her head lolling.

"Yes!" she cried out. "Yes, Jaziel, we are assembled. We await you!"

Tiffany gasped as a luminescent green fog entered the room from her left. It undulated like a writhing snake, lifting and falling. It swirled behind the medium's head, rising as it did so. Before Tiffany's terrified gaze, it rose into the darkness above the table and was gone. She turned to look behind her, afraid something might be creeping up from the shadows. All she could make out was the silhouette of the open doorway to a pitch black hallway beyond.

"Someone is here," Madame Lorraine said, her voice low and rattling. "It is a man. A young man, in his late thirties. His hands are stained. He is falling."

Tiffany's heart hammered against her ribcage. Her breath was coming in short, staggered bursts.

"Is he dead?" Tiffany breathed.

"I see blackness. A coffin. Many mourners."

"When?" Tiffany asked. "When do you see this happening?"

"Soon," Madame Lorraine said. "But he will not stay at peace. His spirit will be restless…in need of answers."

Just then, a muffled voice came from the hallway. Tiffany turned in her chair to face the inky blackness of the doorway. Seconds passed, and it came again. A voice echoing in the darkness.

"Hi Tiffany. I'm on my way home." The disembodied male voice floated into the parlor from the hallway where the two sat in candlelight.

Tiffany screamed, her hand flying to her throat.

"That's Jackson's voice," she cried.

"The spirit world can show us what is to come," Madame Lorraine said, her green eyes glistening. "Nothing is outside the realm of possibility beyond the veil. His time may be coming sooner than he knows."

"And you can help me," she asked, afraid of the answer.

"Oh, yes," Madame Lorraine said, the same horrifying smile returning to her face. "As I said, all things are possible."

****

Madame Lorraine pushed another treat through the bars of the giant bird cage in the mansion's library. Rachel sat with one leg thrown over the arm of the oversized wing chair, a large hardback book open across her lap. Tiffany LeBlanc had gone, a black satin bag in her purse that Madame Lorraine had secretly handed her at the conclusion of the séance. Inside the bag was a purple notecard with instructions.

"What are you reading?" the medium asked, glancing down at the enormous book in Rachel's lap. "Let me guess…plants in the afterlife."

"The history of New Orleans' historic homes," Rachel said, ignoring her sister's sarcasm. "It's fascinating. Did you know that way back in the mid-1800s, they had voodoo dolls they would hide under floorboards in the home to ward off evil or keep the spirit of someone alive? They would use personal items like hair, a photo, or an article of clothing of the deceased to link the doll to a person, and then "awaken" it by blowing life into it. The dolls were often made of cornhusks or stitched from muslin and stuffed with moss."

Her sister looked at her with mild interest.

"These houses have seen two centuries of history," Rachel continued. "Some even have secret passages and staircases where people could escape from one floor to the next in case of attack or to hide someone. There are hidey holes…"

"How long are you going to prattle on about this?" Madame Lorraine asked.

"How can you not find this fascinating? I could talk about it all day," Rachel said.

"Obviously. I thought you would never shut up telling that tall girl about the flocked wallpaper. There I was, waiting in the kitchen to make my grand entrance, and you went on and on."

Rachel chewed her bottom lip. All her enthusiasm was gone.

"Your lack of curiosity has always amazed me," she said dryly, closing the book. "How can you live in a historic house like this and not want to know its provenance?"

"If you think this is my dream house, you don't know me at all," the medium laughed. "This is a stopping point and a means to an end.

It's perfect for a séance atmosphere, but I have my sights set on something altogether modern and upscale."

Rachel watched her sister's face light up as she pictured some mansion in a gated community.

"Well, that kind of home would cost a lot of money," she said, carefully, studying her sister intently. "We'd have to raise our prices."

Madame Lorraine's shoulders tightened. She shot Rachel a quick look and found only a face looking back at her innocently. For one moment, she worried that her sister had figured out her secret. She turned her back and stepped toward Socrates' giant cage.

"You did well at the seance," Madame Lorraine said, studying the large parrot. Rachel wasn't sure if she was speaking to her or the bird.

"Beverly deserves a lot of the credit," Rachel said. "It must have taken a lot of cunning to get Tiffany's cell phone while she was at the printing store."

The psychic took a chair across from her sister and smiled.

"Just how did she pull that off?" she asked, sinking back into the soft comfort of the worn cushions.

"She said she was showing Tiffany a display at the front of the store after they had been seated at the desk for a few minutes, going over personalized Christmas cards. When Tiffany followed her to the front, Brandon took her phone from her purse, which she had left sitting at the desk, and carried it to the back room. He looked up voicemails from Jackson, recorded several, and hurriedly put the phone back into her purse. I still think it would have been easier just to play the recording than go to all the trouble of teaching Socrates to say it."

"It would have been too obvious it was a recording," Madame Lorraine said, sounding annoyed at repeating her reasoning for the third time. "It needed to sound slightly off, like it was coming from the grave, not a cell phone recording. It was perfect. It even gave *me* chills."

"Awk! Chills!" Socrates repeated, bobbing his head.

"Yes!" Madame Lorraine laughed, leaning her head back to look up at the bird cage. "Chills!"

20 ANOTHER DEATH

Lieutenant Calvo and her 'niece' sat in Carol's car staring at the imposing mansion. Stanton-Mills House, circa 1870, was printed on a bronze plaque stained with green verdigris adorning one of the brick columns that anchored the wrought iron gate.

"Let them take the lead," Calvo reminded Carol. "They think we're here to buy an amulet or potion or something to guarantee your wedded bliss. Keep up the innocent, naïve persona. It's working great. Just remember, your name is Michelle Hadley, and I'm Elena Beaufort!"

"Got it," Carol said, sounding nervous. "How much do you think this will cost?"

"I brought five one-hundred-dollar bills. I doubt it will be that much."

Carol shrugged and opened the car door. She thought she saw a curtain move in a window near the front door. They were already watching, she thought. Time to go into the act.

"I'm so excited, Aunt Elena," she squealed as they walked up the long walkway to the front door.

Calvo grinned. Carol was an accomplished actress. She reached out and rang the doorbell near a small plaque that read By Appointment Only. The grin widened. She was finally unraveling how the whole thing worked.

Rachel opened the door and smiled. For once, her hair was piled high into a neat bun. It made her appear even taller. She was also wearing slacks instead of the long, dated skirts. A hint of eyeliner brightened her weak eyes into something almost exotic.

"Please, come in," she said, stepping back. The same smell of tired furnishings and mildew assailed the couple as they stepped inside.

"You won't need to visit with Madame Lorraine today," she said, sounding confident. Calvo marveled at her transformation. "Please follow me."

The two women followed her into the depths of the hallway. Calvo took advantage of it to peer quickly into the rooms they passed. Most sat in shadows except the room nearest the front door. Here, the curtains had been pulled back, and a large bird cage sat glinting in the morning sun. They finally arrived at a kitchen where the lingering smell of coffee grounds hung in the air. It was tidy and void of unnecessary accessories. Two cups drained in a rack near the sink.

"Please watch your step," Rachel said as she opened a door at the back of the room. The smell of moist earth assaulted the women as they followed her down four wooden steps into a large greenhouse. Calvo was taken aback. You would never guess this was here from viewing the front of the house. Plants with name tags lined low, wooden benches. Trees and vines grew from pots along the east wall. Everywhere was the sensation of things growing. *But for what purpose?* Calvo wondered as she strove to take it all in.

Rachel walked to a small door at the back, leaving Calvo and Carol to wait in the middle of the center aisle. She blocked their view of an old iron lock as she fitted a key into it and unlatched the door. She turned to look at them and smiled, "I'll be right back," she said, and disappeared inside the room, closing the door behind her.

Calvo walked along the middle row, bending to look at the names written in black marker on wooden stakes rising from the earth of each potted plant. Some names were familiar to her: Rosemary, basil, lemon grass. Others were not and smacked of witchcraft, such as Mandrake and Jimsonweed. She straightened and glanced two rows over at the towering young trees and trellises of tangled vines. Her eyes came to rest on a particular vine laden with purple grapes. A branch of grapes, she thought. She had just seen that on a list of items recovered from Roger Landry's fishing boat. Curious, Calvo left Carol and crossed behind two rows of plants until she was standing next to the climbing vine. A tag was attached to one rung of the trellis. The name read: Moonseed. She touched a cluster of grapes, damp from the humidity in the room.

Just then, Rachel exited the back room, clutching a small black velvet bag in her hand. Calvo stepped away from the grapes, casually looking at other plants as though passing the time.

"How in the world do you keep up with all of it?" she asked Rachel. "It's impressive. I suppose you are never wanting for salad makings." She smiled innocently. It seemed to work. Rachel laughed and turned to lock the door. She pocketed the key and walked over to Carol.

"Now, Miss Hadley," she said in a soothing voice. "This is a love potion. You must add a few drops of this to his champagne on your wedding day during the toast. You must do this without being detected. It will bring you a long life of happily ever after."

She handed Carol the small bag, a look of satisfaction on her face.

"Should there be unforeseen tension or road bumps, as will always happen in a marriage, do not despair. You can always return here for any future needs. But this," she said, tapping the bag in Carol's hands, "will get you off to a wonderful start and give you an edge."

Carol clutched the bag, her eyes and smile dancing with happiness.

"How can I thank you?" she gushed. Rachel smiled.

"Four hundred dollars!" Calvo hissed as they slid into the car. "Four hundred frickin dollars? I'm in the wrong business! It's probably just sugar water or olive oil or something."

Carol opened the drawstring on the bag and pulled out an amber brown vial with a small cork. It took a few twists to unscrew it. She brought the open bottle to her nose and flinched.

"Ew!" she said, scrunching up her face. "I don't know what that is! How are you supposed to add that to the champagne, and the groom does not notice it?"

Calvo saw a movement at the window to the room where the bird cage had been sitting. The shadow moved quickly away.

"Let's get out of here," she said. Carol started the engine. Once they had driven a couple of blocks, Carol spoke up.

"Is all this helpful?" she asked. "To be honest, I'm a little lost. I get they are making big bucks off of gullible women. It's actually a pretty smart business model if it's legal."

Calvo was deep in thought as Carol maneuvered past a food truck touting fresh barbecued brisket.

"Earth to Auntie Elena," Carol joked. "Are you listening to me?"

Calvo glanced over at her, a serious expression on her face.

"I am. But if you think this is just a way to milk brides-to-be of a few hundred dollars, you have no idea what's really going on."

Carol's face took on a miffed expression.

"And let me guess, you're still not ready to tell me," she said.

Calvo reached into the pouch on her hoodie and pulled out a purple grape.

"Exhibit A," she said mysteriously.

****

Calvo scraped her metal chair closer to the table and took a long drink of her iced tea. She and Hilliard were seated inside Central City BBQ on Rampart Street. She wiped a smear of sauce from her cheek and shook her head as she eyed the enormous metal tray of food in front of her partner.

"Three meat combo?" she asked incredulously, staring at enough food for four people.

Hilliard pushed a wad of brisket to the inside of one cheek and answered her.

"It's enough for leftovers," he said, picking up two umami pickles with his fingers. "Bachelor, remember?"

"Five bucks says you eat the entire thing right here," Calvo laughed. She finished the last bit of her Sail Sand Pulled Pork sandwich and wiped her fingers. "Down to business," she said. "I snagged a grape from a greenhouse Madame Lorraine has at the back of the property. You should see this place! Anyway, Rachel got a bag of juju oil for Carol to spike her fake groom's champagne on the wedding day. While she was getting that out of a back room, I grabbed a purple grape from this Feed Me Seymour vine at the back of the room."

She laid the grape on the table between them, avoiding getting it into the spilled sauces.

Hilliard wiped his mouth and stared at her.

"Am I to understand this momentous find?" he asked, sarcastically.

Calvo sighed. "The list of things they took out of Roger Landry's boat for testing. All the food items, beer, etc. One of the things listed was a grape branch. All the food stuff came back negative for anything. His buddy said Roger suddenly grabbed his stomach, went into convulsions, and fell overboard. Something set him off. I'm going to hand this little grape to Jennings in the lab and let him do his magic."

"And if it comes back perfect for jam preserves?" Hilliard asked.

"Then you get the first batch."

Hilliard poked at the grape. Calvo snatched it up, rolled it into a napkin, and returned it to her hoodie pouch.

"Does Carol know what you're doing?" Hilliard asked. "We should be careful until we have this nailed down."

"Not about the murders. She thinks I'm just investigating a fraudulent fortune teller. When I dropped her off an hour ago, she was a little miffed, but nothing bad. She's been a big help."

Hilliard nodded and speared an onion. "I have news too," he said. "Marjorie Harris's cell phone data is back. Looks like an affair was going on. That's motive."

"The lawyer? Code name 'Sidebar'? My guess is the handsome young man at her funeral service that Malcolm skewered with a hateful stare," she said. "We have the note from Madame Lorraine, motive, the murder weapon, aka bath bombs. We don't have the evidence that he actually touched them, but close enough. We just need to know how he got them. The purple notecard you found in the trash in his office said October 2. 1:30. Side yard. I say we look at the CCTV footage from his home again."

Just then, a waitress stepped over to their table. Her thick auburn hair was pulled up in a ponytail. She was wearing jeans and a Central City BBQ shirt. Her sprinkling of freckles across her nose belied her age of 50.

"Let me guess, Archer," she said, smiling. "Gonna need a box?"

Hilliard blushed and nodded.

"You know me too well," he said, glancing at Calvo, who was trying unsuccessfully to smother a grin. "Uh, Stacey, this is my partner, Lieutenant Calvo."

Stacey's gaze swept over the young female officer that told Calvo all she needed to know. Was she competition or was she not? Noticing Stacey relax at the introduction, she surmised she had been put into the 'not competition' category.

"Nice to meet you," Calvo said.

"How'd you like pulled pork?" Stacey asked.

"I gotta say, Hilliard wasn't wrong. He's mentioned this place a few times," Calvo said.

"Oh?" Stacey asked, looking pleased. "Isn't that nice?" Her gaze returned to Hilliard. "I'll box that up for ya, Sugar," she said, laying the bill on the table and taking his tray. She touched his shoulder lightly as she walked off.

Calvo dipped her chin, sucked in her lips, and looked at him, her eyes dancing. His cheeks colored as he bent his head over the bill, tallying up the tip. He scribbled out the total, swearing, and started over. Finally, he set the pen down and looked over at her.

"Don't even!" he growled.

"I'm not going to say a word," she said. "Sugar."

She got up from her chair before he could stab her with a table knife. She was still chuckling when they walked out into the sunlight.

Without a word, Hilliard walked one car back to his patrol car and glared at her as he entered and slammed the door. She walked to her Mustang in front of her at the curb and got in.

Neither of them noticed Rachel exit a retail store across the street and stand beneath its canopy, watching them.

****

Jackson LeBlanc picked up a stained work towel and wiped his hands on it. The pecan stain he was using for his latest woodworking project left an indelible brown covering on his hands. It would take several tries with mineral spirits to remove it. He was used to it. He had never liked working with gloves. They hindered him from getting into the small recesses of dovetail joinery for the cabinet he was making. Wiping his hands, he stood back and studied his progress. He nodded contentedly.

The band-aid he had been wearing on the cut of his forefinger on his right hand came off in the towel. He looked at the wound, still open, but not bleeding any longer. Jackson dipped the brush into the stain and applied a thin coat where the drawer pulls would go in. He grabbed the small towel and caught a drip running down the surface. He grimaced as it entered the wound on his finger. Taking a clean paper towel, he tried to wipe it clean.

Jackson lined up the hardware for the drawer pulls on a separate table as he waited for the pecan stain to dry on the cabinet. He measured each, finally happy that even though he had to get batches from two different online stores, they matched. He wiped his forehead as perspiration suddenly formed there. His heart began racing. He sat down on his work stool, blinking as the room seemed to tilt sideways.

"God!" he cried, bending over and clutching his stomach. His hand muscles were twitching, and his mouth was salivating. As his breathing became shallower, he panicked. His legs were trembling with weakness as the dizziness increased. Gripping the table, he stumbled through his workshop, holding onto lathe machines and massive saw tables. He finally made it to the small bathroom at the back of the shop and, gripping the door frame, fell against the counter inside the door. The diarrhea hit him before he could reach the toilet. His body went into seizures as he collapsed to the floor.

Tiffany LeBlanc waited inside her kitchen, heart pounding. She was afraid to check the workshop on the side of the house. It had a private door from the kitchen. She hadn't heard any sounds for several minutes. She finally got up the courage to check on him. Her hands trembled as she opened the door and stepped inside. A rancid smell was coming from the small bathroom at the back. She walked slowly toward it, covering her. She hesitated before she peered in at her husband, curled into the fetal position on the floor. His pants were stained, and his skin was the color of a sheet. She fought back the bile rising from her stomach. She was partly in shock. It had actually killed him. She hadn't been sure, even when she added the liquid nicotine to his paint stain. Getting him to cut himself had been the hardest part.

The house felt alien as Tiffany entered the kitchen and grabbed a glass, filling it with cold water. Downing it, she wiped her face with a wet paper towel and leaned against the sink, taking deep breaths. Her eyes went to the backyard, the sunlight beaming on a world that was suddenly dark and foreboding. She rallied. Pulled a brown paper bag from the pantry, stuffed with $500,000 in hundred-dollar bills, and went outside through the sliding glass doors in the breakfast nook. Rounding the corner to where the electrical box sat anchored to the wall, she forced the bag down into the bushes beneath it. She hurried back inside to get rid of the black velvet bag, the vial of nicotine, and the instructions that Madame Lorraine had given her at the private séance. Only then did she dial 911.

****

"The grapes were poisonous!" Calvo gasped as she hurtled into Hilliard's office the following day. "Positive match to the one found in the boat! Moonseed grapes. Just like the tag on the trellis in Rachel's greenhouse. They're poisonous grapes. They grow wild. No need to add anything to them. They'll kill you all by themselves. I'll be damned. Those two voodoo sisters are supplying people with the means to off loved ones who have become inconvenient. And they're doing it under the guise of 'the spirits made me do it.'"

Hilliard laid down the file he was going over and sat back in his chair. His face mirrored shock.

"They didn't test the one found in the boat?" he asked.

"There wasn't much of it," Calvo said. "It was smashed and shriveled. I don't think they thought it was anything but normal grapes. They were looking for something that might have been put into the food. Diabolical!"

"We have to look into the mechanics behind all those people who went there for a séance," Calvo continued, practically hyperventilating. "The ones who have an obituary tied to someone near and dear to them. We know Harris used bath bombs, Abegail Landry used grapes, Marsha Jennings got hold of a black widow spider, Geraldine Montez used burning oleander branches, and Ted Jennings…"

"Died from water hemlock tubers imitating parsnips," Hilliard interrupted. "I already called the guys in forensics to get a search warrant for the Griffin house. We'll take out the disposal, pipes, utensils, and anything else we can find." He paused and shook his head. "Even though I'm reading these reports, I still can't believe it. How long have these sisters been at this? It's like Lucretia Borgia on steroids."

Calvo was reflective for a minute.

"The funny thing is, the person who started it all, Dorothy Brindle, attended the sisters' séance, but she didn't kill Charlie. It looks like Everett did. But it doesn't look like Everett attended a séance or had anything to do with Madame Lorraine or Rachel," Calvo said in a low voice. "I guess Charlie's exhumation will give us some answers. I'm almost afraid to find out what they are."

21 A DEADLY TRAP

Madame Lorraine looked at the laptop screen at the photo Rachel was indicating. They were seated at the kitchen table.

"It's him," Rachel said. "I saw him coming out of a restaurant and getting into a police car yesterday. According to this, he's a detective."

Madame Lorraine looked at the photograph of a group of police officers standing around a table and raising glasses of beer to toast a man in uniform holding a plaque for some kind of achievement. On the wall behind them was an order counter for a restaurant with a large fake, multi-colored pig head hanging above it.

"That's the same restaurant he came out of," Rachel said. "It's a barbecue place over on Rampart. He got into a squad car, so I looked up the New Orleans Police Department website and clicked on photos on the off chance he might be in one. Sure enough, this photo popped up. The caption under it reads: 'Detective Archer Hilliard thanks the Central City BBQ restaurant for hosting his 25th anniversary with the New Orleans Police Department.' That's him!"

Madame Lorraine recognized the unusually tall man who had accompanied his younger sister for a reading. Her lips curled. She leaned away from the laptop and sat lost in thought. Rachel waited a moment and then added, "The woman who came with her niece about her upcoming wedding…Elena Beaufort… she was with him. She had just been at the house to get a potion for her niece, only an hour before. What if she's a detective, too?"

Ruby's face hardened, and for the first time, Rachel saw fear in her sister's eyes.

"Did you give her a potion?" she asked, her eyes on fire.

"Of course," Rachel said. "That's the whole point of it. I didn't know she was anything but a concerned Aunt wanting to help her niece have a good marriage."

"What did you give her?" Ruby asked, her voice hoarse.

"Just dandelion juice with a little crushed thistle. It's harmless."

Ruby exhaled, but her mind was in overdrive. She sat lost in thought for several minutes.

"Nothing happened during the reading with the detective and his sister that implicates us in anything," Madame Lorraine said, choosing her words slowly as the wheels inside her mind continued to whirl. "It was just a Tarot reading stating the girl had a fortuitous future ahead. She read it to mean she was coming into a lot of money to start some business…I forgot what. She mentioned an Uncle Perry who was elderly and would leave her some money. She asked to come back. Did she book an appointment?"

Rachel nodded. "She called a few days ago. Asking for a séance."

"Did you schedule it?"

"It's for tomorrow night. It's a private session. That means a lot more money. But now… what do we do now?"

"We go on as usual," Madame Lorraine said, her green eyes narrowing.

"He's a policeman!" Rachel said, surprised. "You want him to come back? He's going to be looking for something."

"And we will give it to him," the medium said. "The one with the niece only walked away with a harmless dandelion potion. They can't get us for that. Let me handle the tall guy."

Rachel leaned back into her chair, a sudden visceral reaction filling her stomach. The cruel smile that spread across Ruby's face was one she had seen often, just before tragedy occurred. It had always frightened her.

"Ruby," she said softly, placing a hand on her sister's wrist.

The medium reacted with hatred pouring from her eyes. She jerked her hand away, her chest heaving.

"Get mad," Rachel said, choking back tears. "You are wrong this time. You are playing with fire. You're not infallible. This could take us down! They close down places perpetrating fraud."

"Keep the appointment," Madame Lorraine said, her tone icy as she rose from the chair. Her breathing was still labored, but there was a look of determination on her face. She faced off against her sister, who was still seated, visibly trembling. "I'll only use the Tarot cards," she said. "You can skip the usual theatrics."

Rachel sat in the empty kitchen, staring sightlessly at the marred dinette table. She ran a finger absently along a deep scratch, discolored with age. She felt as if she were having an out-of-body experience. She knew in her gut her sister was doing more than fleecing wealthy clients with phony seances. Where did all that money come from that she had found in the sack? Her sister was capable of horrible things.

Unwanted memories of that night 18 years ago flooded in. The pulse in her neck throbbed. She squeezed her eyes shut, trying without success to block the images hurtling toward her.

"Ruby? What have you done?" She saw herself standing near the prostrate body of Ronald T. Harrington, her sister's husband of fourteen years. He was lying in the driveway near his car, the driver's side door open. It was obvious he was preparing to leave; an overnight bag was on the passenger seat. Ruby held the bloody knife in one gloved hand, looking down at the pool of blood spreading from his neck wound across the cement driveway. The sun was just beginning to crest the nearby hills.

"Shut up and help me get him into the car," Ruby barked. "Move that bag into the back seat, and we'll put him in the passenger seat for now. I'll drive."

Rachel saw herself, rooted in place, staring down at the blood that had found its way to a dividing line in the cement and was flowing off at a right angle. Her stomach roiled, and she fought off the dizziness, reaching for the hood of his car to keep from going down. Why had she answered her sister's frantic phone call?

"Rachel!" Ruby hissed, looking about her. The neighboring houses, flanked by tall hedges, were spared seeing the horror that lay in the driveway of the Harrington home.

Rachel took a deep, steadying breath and looked at her sister, whose face was unrecognizable in the feeble sunlight. Her eyes were manic, bulging in a way Rachel had never seen before. The pale skin was pulled tight in anger, her nostrils flaring like some wild animal.

"I can't," Rachel said, taking a tentative step away from the car. "I can't do this!"

Finding her legs, she turned and bolted to the side of her sister's house, pressing her back to the brick wall, holding onto the cold, rough surface for support. She could hear Ruby groaning beneath the weight of her husband as she tried to load him into the car. With that, Rachel fled into the backyard and through the small garden gate that separated the sisters' houses.

Rachel sat now in the stillness of the Stanton-Mills mansion. A wave of dizziness overtook her, and her head fell to the breakfast table. The terror of that night set her ears ringing. What had she done? Why had she let this go on for so long?

****

Detective Hilliard tucked his pin-striped shirt into his pants and smoothed his hair. Emma looked at him nervously. They were standing at the door of the Stanton-Mills mansion.

"Don't forget," Hilliard whispered, "I'm Bill. Don't mess up!"

The door opened, and Rachel stood there. She was attired in her usual dark, long, sweeping skirt and high-necked blouse. The only color was a green brooch at her neckline. Hilliard noticed the strained look about her and worried that something was amiss. Rachel smiled a taut, forced greeting that only amplified Hilliard's concern.

"Do come in, Emma, and Bill, was it?" Rachel said.

Hilliard's instincts as a detective went into overdrive. Something was wrong, but he couldn't turn back now.

"Correct," he said, trying to sound as nonchalant as possible.

Rachel beckoned them inside and closed the heavy door.

"Please sign in," she said, "and place all electronics in the basket."

This, too, was new, Hilliard thought. *Before, she had only mentioned placing all cell phones in the basket. Did mentioning all electronics mean that she suspected a recording device or something else to monitor the evening's events?*

Hilliard placed his phone in the basket and picked up the pen to sign in. As he gripped it in his right hand, he suddenly recoiled, dropping it onto the table. A cut appeared on his right index finger, and blood was pooling at the wound.

"Oh dear," Rachel said, genuinely surprised. "What did you do?"

A drop of blood landed on the guest sign-in ledger. Rachel grabbed a tissue from a nearby box and handed it to him. Hilliard wrapped it around the cut.

"I think your pen needs to be replaced," he said. "The clip on the top is ragged, and I cut myself on it."

Rachel picked up the writing pen and looked at the clip that ran along the top. It was rough, as though it had been scraped along a hard surface. It was not the ornate quill-shaped pen that was usually there.

"I'm so sorry," she said. "Do you want a bandage?"

"Nah," Hilliard said, removing the blood-stained tissue. "It's already done, I think. He put the injured digit in his mouth. "I'll live," he said, grinning.

Rachel glanced down at the blood drop that was spreading into the weave of the linen finished guest page.

"We can skip you, Emma," she said, sounding shaky. "Let's just go in, shall we?"

The two entered the same parlor and took the same seats they had had the day of Emma's reading. Night had fallen outside the windows, allowing a feeble ray of moonlight to penetrate the sheer curtains. Rather than making the dark room feel more inviting, it only magnified the strange surroundings of vintage paintings, the eyes of long-dead ancestors staring down at them. This time, two small parlor lamps were lit across the room before the window. There was no candle in the center of the table.

Madame Lorraine floated into the world, her long black dress sweeping the worn rug. She passed behind Hilliard, who felt an involuntary chill as she did so. The medium placed a deck of Tarot cards on the table and took her seat.

"Welcome back," she said, without a hint of warmth. Her green eyes settled on Emma. "You are in search of further information for your dream of opening a business," she said, in the form of a statement, not a question. "I assume dear Uncle Perry is still with us."

Emma paused, her mouth dry. She fought the urge to look at her brother for help.

"Yes, uh, that is, I am still interested in opening my business. Uncle Perry is in declining health, but hanging in there," she said.

Madame Lorraine nodded and turned toward Hilliard. Her gaze swept over his glasses, strong jawline, and salt-and-pepper hair. It lingered on something near his chin.

"How did you get that scar?" she asked quietly.

Hilliard's fingers reached for his chin and touched the small indentation.

"A long time ago," he lied. "Playing shortstop and trying to block a kid from sliding into base."

Madame Lorraine nodded, the same indefinable grin crossing her face as he had seen the other time they were here. It was unsettling.

"Some might say a war wound," The thin smile again. Hilliard frowned, his nervousness amplified. "You are not a believer, I think," she said, cocking her head to watch him.

Hilliard looked surprised. He had the uncomfortable feeling he was not in control of the situation.

"Well, not sure," he said, flashing his little boy grin. "Doesn't matter. We're here for Emma, not me."

"The unbelievers fascinate me," Madame Lorraine said, catching movement in the hallway from the corner of her eye. She looked into the darkness beyond the doorway and saw nothing. "The spirits know everything we do not. Why not avail yourself of their knowledge?"

she asked, bringing her gaze back to the man seated next to her.

"I'm sure a lot is going on here," he said, letting the double meaning hang in the air. "But, it's Emma's dime. I'm sure she's eager to begin."

Madame Lorraine smiled, a full, all-teeth-bared smile. She reached for the deck of Tarot cards and pulled the stack from the box. Emma looked confused.

"I thought we were going to do a séance," she said.

Madame Lorraine ignored her. Instead, she shuffled the worn cards carefully and then fanned them out, holding them toward Hilliard with both hands.

"Choose one," she said.

Hilliard looked over at Emma, whose face showed disappointment and confusion. He paused.

"Humor me," Madame Lorraine said. "Let me prove to you that the Tarot knows your heart."

Hilliard's face twisted to one side, but he reached out and chose a card from near the middle of the deck, plucking it out with his thumb and forefinger. He held it in his right hand and waited for instructions.

"You can look at it," Madame Lorraine said, folding the other cards together and setting them aside. "Show it to me."

Hilliard turned the Knight of Spades toward the medium.

"Ah," she said. "The devious Knight. He is known to enter your life and depart just as quickly. He is not to be trusted. Now, the question is, is he warning you of someone, or of yourself?"

Hilliard frowned again. He turned the card back toward him and studied the knight. He was wearing silver armor and carrying a lance with a red cloth fluttering atop it. His white horse was bolting, rising on its two back legs. He smiled and laid the card down on the table.

"I'll keep my eyes open," he said, folding his arms and leaning back into his chair.

Madame Lorraine watched him for a few seconds. The smile returned. Shrugging, she turned to Emma.

"We will begin your séance," she said. "I want you to close your eyes and picture your new business as already accomplished. See yourself as a successful businesswoman. Look around you in your mind. What do you see? What does your office look like? How many employees do you have? Is it a large company or a small boutique brand?"

Hilliard's forehead furrowed. This didn't feel like a séance as much as it did a New Age meditation for manifesting your desires. Something moved in the hallway, and Hilliard turned his head in that direction. Rachel was standing back in the shadows, watching what was going on. She stepped away quickly, disappearing into the gloom.

"Once you have it pictured," Madame Lorraine said, "we can begin. Are you ready?"

Emma opened her eyes and nodded. Madame Lorraine leaned back against her chair and closed her eyes, taking deep, intentional breaths. She lifted her chin toward the ceiling as her head bobbed to and fro.

"Jaziel?" she rasped, "We are assembled. Do you have a spirit present who can show our guest Emma what the future will hold for her?"

Emma looked around the room, expecting some apparition to appear from behind the curtains. Hilliard watched the medium closely, especially her hands that rested on the table. The room was silent, the weight of the 200-year-old house bearing down upon them. He shifted uneasily in his chair.

"Jaziel is here," Madame Lorraine said, her voice low and imposing. "Do you have wisdom for us? Is there someone with you who wishes to speak?"

Emma found herself holding her breath.

"Yes! A woman. She died young, complications of the breast. She shows much love toward you. Toward you both."

Hilliard pushed back from the table, his eyes bulging. Emma's eyes were rimming with tears. Completely forgetting the ruse she and her brother were perpetrating, she leaned in.

"That's our mother," she said, her voice quaking. "She died of breast cancer. She was only fifty years old."

Hilliard swallowed repeatedly, fighting the urge to topple the table.

"She is here with you," Madame Lorraine said kindly. "She shows me that you will be successful in your endeavors. The money will come."

Emma began to ask a question, but Hilliard interrupted her.

"I think we have what we need," he said, resisting the urge to flash his badge and question the medium right there. He had to bide his time a little longer. He stood up and looked at Emma to do the same. She looked back at him, clearly wanting to stay and speak to their mother. She finally rose, holding onto the back of her chair.

"Thank you so much," she said, her voice choked with emotion. "I was young when she passed."

Madame Lorraine nodded sagely. She rose, shot a meaningful glance at Hilliard, and walked around behind Emma, placing a hand on her back. She continued to the open doorway and disappeared. Rachel stepped into the room. Hilliard had the feeling she had been just outside the open doorway the entire time, hiding in the shadows. She looked nervous, he thought.

"I hope your session was successful," Rachel said. "These things can be emotional." She offered Emma a tissue from the same box she had handed Hilliard for his cut. Emma took it, wiped her eyes, and reached into her purse. She withdrew a legal-sized sealed envelope and handed it to Rachel.

"Thank you," Emma said, meekly. She retrieved her phone from the basket and walked to the front door. Hilliard picked up his phone, glanced with sudden suspicion at Rachel, and pocketed it. She walked them to the front door, unlocked it, and swung it open.

"Have a lovely evening," she said, without making eye contact.

The brother and sister walked out into a night laced with the scent of fall flowers and a hint of woodsmoke wafting on a breeze. Emma clutched the sleeve of his shirt and let him lead her to her car. Hilliard offered to drive. He opened the passenger side door for her, and as he did so, he looked back at the mansion. Rachel was still standing in the open doorway, watching them.

22 THE SPIRITS ARE ANGRY

Lieutenant Calvo put her cellphone on speaker and asked Davis Miles to repeat what he had just told her. It had been three days since Hilliard and Emma had attended Madame Lorraine's séance.

"I heard over the police scanner that an ambulance was called to a ritzy part of town in response to a 911 call from a woman named Tiffany LeBlanc. She said her husband was lying on the bathroom floor of his home workshop and appeared to be dead. Was there a LeBlanc on your séance guest list?"

Calvo opened the file and looked again at the photograph Hilliard took of the guest sign-in pages at Madame Lorraine's. No LeBlanc.

"No," Calvo said. "Maybe she was there after he took the photo of the guest book. Then again, not every death in New Orleans Parish can land on Madame Lorraine's doorstep. Do you know how he died?"

"That's your department," Miles said. "Check with your officers. I'm just reporting the latest. How are things going over there? An anybody in handcuffs yet?"

"No, but it's coming very soon," Calvo said. "I promise to tell you once I'm sure it won't get me in trouble." She grinned at Hilliard, who was leaning over, his left hand holding up his head. "Thanks, Davis," she said. "You're the best.'

"Yeah, I know," he said, and hung up.

Calvo looked over at her partner.

"You okay?" she asked. He looked pale and shaky.

Hilliard raised his head and pulled his hand from his bangs. His fingers came away with strands of his hair. He stared at it hypnotically. His head lolling, he wiped the hair off on his pants and reached for a bottle of water he had been guzzling for the past few minutes.

"My legs hurt," he said. "I must have some kind of flu bug. My head feels like it's filled with cotton, and I can't think straight. I've been throwing up too."

"Sounds a little like COVID," Calvo said. "I've heard some people are still dealing with it. It does cause your hair to thin sometimes."

Just then, Jennings popped his head in.

"Early Christmas present," he said, smiling. "We found signs of hemlock in the sink drain and garbage disposal at Brenda Griffin's house. My guess is she did serve it up disguised as parsnips. The report will be ready in a bit, but I was anxious to tell you."

Hilliard suddenly bent over and threw up in the trash can. His face had lost all its color and was covered in a sheen of perspiration.

"Yikes," Jennings said. "You look like shit. Did you eat something that might have given you food poisoning?"

Hilliard put his head on the desk, holding the back of it with his hand.

"You need to go see a doctor," Calvo said.

Hilliard removed his hand and struggled to lift his head. Calvo gasped. A patch of his hair was clutched in his fingers.

Jennings rounded the table to him.

"Are you experiencing confusion?" he asked, his voice filled with alarm. "Neuropathy in your legs, feet, and hands?"

Hilliard merely nodded and grunted. He leaned over the trash can again.

"Get an ambulance," Jennings barked to Calvo. "Now! I think he's been poisoned. Those are the same symptoms of thallium poisoning...the same thing we found in that beer bottle the little old lady brought in. Hair falling out is a huge indicator."

Calvo raced from the room to the front desk and told them to get an ambulance here. She instructed them to have the responders come to Hilliard's office. When she bolted back to the room, she was shocked to see Hilliard lying on the floor, his long legs buckled beneath his desk.

****

Another ambulance had been called to the LeBlanc home. Jackson LeBlanc was pronounced dead at the scene. His wife, Tiffany, was inconsolable as two officers tried desperately to get some information from her. She kept repeating the same details between hysterics.

"He was working on this cabinet," she wailed. "He always does on the weekends. I warned him to open the windows when he was using the stains and thinners. He never did. Is that what happened to him?"

She buckled again and burst into fresh sobs.

"It's too early to tell," Officer Gleason said to her. "Does he have any health issues we should know about? Medications, that kind of thing?"

"No! He doesn't take anything. He is in great health…was in great…" Tiffany leaned over onto the arm of the couch and wailed.

Jackson LeBlanc's body was loaded onto a gurney. His stained hands were bagged. An officer took photos of the workroom and bathroom. Due to the brown discoloration on Jackson's hands, they also capped the can of pecan stain, bagged the stained towel, and took them as evidence. Something didn't seem right about a young man lying dead from obvious gastric distress in his bathroom.

"This town is beginning to look like a plague has hit it," Officer Patterson whispered to Gleason as they finished up and followed the body from the workshop.

****

At 2:30 pm, on a cloudy afternoon, the cemetery superintendent unlocked the family tomb of Charlie Brindle. Dorothy had remained at home. She couldn't bear to watch. Signing the consent form had been hard enough. Curious bystanders, including Davis Miles, who had heard that the exhumation was to take place that day, stood at a discreet distance and watched as several men entered the tomb with the name BRINDLE chiseled into the frieze at the top of the stone building. Among them was Harlow Faregate, the funeral director who would oversee the removal of the casket, two New Orleans police officers, and a court-ordered official with the permits and consent in hand.

Inside the vault, the men removed the ledger stone on the wall, marked with the name Charles M. Brindle. The crowd waited, whispering, as an hour passed. Finally, they were rewarded when a mahogany casket, carried by six men, exited the crypt and was loaded into a waiting hearse. Davis Miles took several photographs for his paper and sauntered away.

****

Calvo entered the ICU room, a vase of flowers from the hospital gift shop in one hand, and a small paper bag in the other. She nodded at a nurse who was checking the monitor, keeping track of Hilliard's vital signs.

"How is he?" Calvo whispered, setting the vase of flowers on a side table. There was another floral arrangement already there; its card read, "Get well, Boss." It was from the other officers with whom Hilliard worked.

"Lucky," the nurse whispered back. She crossed to stand next to the short Lieutenant. "If they hadn't gotten some Prussian Blue into him, he might not still be here. He'll feel out of it for a while, but he's going to pull through. The guy is built like a tank. He may have lingering issues with neuropathy in his hands and legs."

Calvo walked over to the bed and placed a hand on Hilliard's. IV tubes seemed to be coming out of every vein. She noticed some of his hair lying on the pillow next to his head.

"Will he lose all his hair?" she asked the nurse.

"It will keep doing that until the poison is out of his system, but it should grow back. Alopecia is common in thallium poisoning. It's one of the first signs. I'll be back to check on him," she said and left the room.

Calvo pulled a chair next to the bed and took Hilliard's hand again. His eyes were closed, his face ashen. He suddenly looked older, his face gaunt. She realized it was the first time she had seen him without his glasses. Her eyes rimmed with tears. She gripped his hand tighter and whispered, "Don't you dare leave me, you big jerk!"

There was no reaction. The silence was the hardest part. The gray afternoon pressed against the window glass, adding to the room's gloom. She stayed for almost an hour, until she was asked to leave for the detective's sponge bath. She laughed.

"Yeah, I love the guy, but that's one thing I don't want to watch."

She set the small paper bag on the table next to her flowers and walked to the door.

"Don't take any of his crap," Calvo said, one hand on the doorframe. "Believe me, he can be an ornery old cuss." She glanced at him again and struggled not to cry.

Calvo walked down the antiseptic, grey, and blue tiled floor and pushed the down button on the elevator. Several floors below her, an ambulance was unloading Jackson LeBlanc's body into the medical examiner's facility. Right behind him, a hearse was pulling up with the casket of Charles M. Brindle for a post-mortem examination.

****

Calvo collapsed into her usual chair in the office she shared with Hilliard. It was his name on the door, but with the shortage of desk space at the station, they had fallen into an easy relationship, sharing the room. She couldn't bring herself to sit in his chair. She cringed when she noticed a few strands of his hair clinging to his desk calendar. The phone rang, and Calvo answered it.

"Calvo," she said, her voice weak. "I'm sorry, I was at the hospital with Hilliard. When did they bring her in? Did she say anything?" Several minutes went by as Calvo listened. Finally, she said, "Make sure you Mirandize her! I don't want this coming back due to a technicality. Good work, Gleason! You guys did it by the book. I mean it."

Calvo hung up and sat lost in thought. So, Brenda Griffin was in custody. That's one in the bag, she thought. The normal sounds of people packing up for the day could be heard outside her closed office door. Some were shouting orders to meet for drinks, and others were talking about Halloween plans. She had completely forgotten that the holiday that New Orleans waited for was only ten days away. Her mind went back to Davis's phone call. *Who was Tiffany LeBlanc?* she wondered. If he died from natural causes, it would be just a coincidence. If, however, his was another unusual demise, odds were she was one of Madame Lorraine's "guests."

****

Rachel stepped into the parlor and paused. It felt so different in the morning sunlight. Silent. Void of mystery and paranormal paraphernalia. The parlor table sat, still draped in black. Wax puddled on the onyx slab beneath a half-eaten candle. *So many people, she thought,* a shiver going through her. Even the house was still as if listening, gauging her presence. Socrates, for once, wasn't prattling on in his cage. The medium had gone into town ostensibly to buy a black wreath for the door in honor of Halloween. Rachel suspected there was another reason for her absence.

She walked past the round table to the corner at the left and pressed a concealed button in the dark wood paneling. A tall, narrow door slid silently open in the wall, revealing an elevator. A breath of air emanated from it, carrying with it the smell of a contained space. Sitting at the far back was a fog machine. Next to it was a container of phosphorus liquid. She checked to make sure there was enough liquid in the bottle for at least two more seances. After doing so, she pressed a button with an up arrow to the left of the open door. It slid shut, and the small compartment began to silently rise.

The door opened into a dark, curtained room. Rachel stepped out and pressed the button to send the elevator back down to the parlor. It made no sound as it descended. She walked into the room and lit a hurricane lamp on a small table. The lamp, which had been transformed into an electric device, gave off a soft glow into a room void of warmth. A four-poster bed stood against the back wall, its heavy velvet comforter dusty and emitting a faint, musty odor. The fireplace across the room sat, its gaping maw dark and unused for years. It was the master bedroom of the house. The former owner had died in this room. Rachel and her sister had chosen other, smaller bedrooms on the same floor for just that reason.

Rachel crossed to the fireplace and got down on her knees. She reached for an andiron in the shape of a dark bronze cupid. Wrapping her fingers around it, she twisted it hard to the left. A grating sound came from within the brick fireplace as a small compartment door swung open. She withdrew a black bag and undid the tied drawstring. Inside, there were several bundles of one-hundred-dollar bills.

****

Calvo navigated the herd of departing staff, leaving only the night shift on duty, as she made her way to the front doors.

"Wait up," came a male voice from behind her. It was Jennings from the lab.

"How's he doing?" he asked, holding the door open for her.

"He's going to be okay, thanks to you," she said. "I thought he got hit with round two of the pandemic."

They walked to her Mustang, streetlights already diffusing the early October gloom. Her stomach rumbled as the intoxicating aromas of the Big Easy mixed into one decadent combination of smells.

"How bout I treat you to dinner?" Jennings said, hearing the noise coming from her stomach area. "I have some news that will make your day."

Calvo's eyes lit up. She wasn't sure if it was because of his invitation or his tempting hint at something important.

"Do I have to wait for the entrée to find out?" she smiled, looking up into the blue eyes twinkling at her.

"I'm not that mean," he said, opening her car door. "The LeBlanc guy? The one they found in his woodworking shop? Don't even need to wait for the full report. Guess what was on his hands?"

"I thought I heard it was wood stain," she said.

"There was that. But mixed in with it was liquid nicotine."

Calvo stopped and held onto the door frame, one foot inside the car.

"You're not serious?"

"I never joke about poison," he said. He walked around to the passenger side and got in. Once she was settled behind the wheel, he continued. "Pretty ingenious," he said. "There was a fresh cut on his finger. If nicotine, in its pure form, enters the bloodstream through a cut like that, you're dead in a matter of minutes. Poor guy would have gone through some horrific pain before his heart stopped."

Calvo turned and looked out the windshield as the autumn wind sent an empty beer can clanking across the street in front of her. All she could think of was how many more would there be before this all ended?

"The spirits must be really angry," she muttered, and started the car.

Jennings chose the restaurant he thought would be less crowded. They entered the small Mom-and-Pop bistro filled with the smell of boiled crawfish and frying oysters. Calvo realized at that moment that she had missed lunch and had only drunk a smoothie for breakfast. They were escorted to a small wooden table at the back, where a metal bucket, napkins, and a menu were waiting. Jennings ordered a local brew, and Calvo raised two fingers, signaling she'd have the same.

"Get whatever you want," Jennings said, grinning. "It's payday."

Calvo smiled at him and found herself looking into the bar mirror across from their table. In its reflection was a middle-aged woman, seated at the bar, drinking a martini. Calvo frowned, trying to remember where she had seen her before. It wasn't until the woman

204

signed her bill at the counter and rose from her stool that Calvo got a good look at her. Her eyes flew open as she watched her walk out the door.

"That woman," she whispered to Jennings, leaning over the table and gripping his wrist. "She was at my séance! She asked a question about where something was. Madame Lorraine was doing this automatic writing thing, and finally scribbled something and gave her the paper. All I could see was a capital 'P.' I need to talk to her! Be right back. Please order me the Cajun Combo."

Before Jennings could protest, she was on her feet and hurrying for the door. She stepped outside to a burst of human traffic. Dodging inebriated locals and wide-eyed tourists, she looked in vain for the woman. She finally admitted defeat and returned inside. She walked to the bar and addressed the bartender.

"I need that lady's credit card receipt," she said. "That one that just left. She was sitting right here and had a martini."

The man behind the counter, wearing a Voodoo skull t-shirt, looked at her with a sardonic grin.

"Yeah? And I want a paid vacation to Belize." He picked up a rag and began to wipe up the moisture from the bar top. Calvo reached into her back pocket and slapped down her badge. The man seated on the stool next to where she was standing raised an eyebrow.

"You get me that receipt, and I'll get a bottle of suntan lotion for your vacation," she said, leaning in.

His jaw clenched as he turned to a girl behind him at the cash register and whispered something to her. She reached for a stack of credit card slips, looked at the top two, and handed him the second one.

"Here," he said. "Wanda Milieau. Is that who you're looking for? Three lemon drop martinis and an oyster tray."

Calvo looked it over and nodded.

"That works," she said, smiling. "Enjoy the tropics."

23 PAY NO ATTENTION TO WHAT'S BEHIND THE CURTAIN

The ICU nurse entered Hilliard's room and smiled.

"You look much better this morning," she said. "You even managed to stomach the oatmeal."

"Oh, was that oatmeal?" Hilliard asked, his voice weak. He was propped up on two pillows, the bed bent at an angle beneath him.

She grinned and came around to his monitoring machine.

"Your blood pressure is looking better," she said. "We will be moving you to a private room today. Won't that be nice to get out of here?"

"After three days of drips and poking and prodding? Hell yes! Does it come with a wet bar and mini fridge?" His eyes followed her as she moved about the room, tidying and adjusting things.

"They just retired the wet bar," she said, without missing a beat. "I'm hearing it's been replaced with a Jello dispenser and saltines. Yummy!"

She turned to leave the room and paused, looking back at him over her shoulder.

"Oh, and uh….the drips and prodding will continue."

She laughed and walked out, letting the hydraulic door hiss to a close behind her.

Hilliard pushed himself higher onto his pillow, his head protesting the movement. Sighing with boredom, he looked about the room. His eyes came to rest on the floral bouquets on the table next to him, some of the blooms drooping. For the first time, he noticed a small paper sack sitting next to them. Grimacing, he reached for it with his right arm, the IV tube straining to accommodate him. He pulled it onto the food tray across his bed and slowly opened it. Reaching inside, he pulled out a bag of hard caramel candies and smiled. Something else was in the sack, and he pulled it out. A nurse outside his door jumped as his grating laughter exploded from his bed. He was holding a coffee mug with six garishly colored dancing kittens encircling it.

****

Lieutenant Adelaide Calvo sighed as she pored over the paperwork accumulating during Hilliard's three-day absence. Pink telephone message notes mixed with reports and coffee stains. Officer Peterson appeared in the open doorway.

"Why don't you sit in the big guy's chair instead of that uncomfortable one?" he asked.

"Habit," Calvo said, feeling her partner's absence keenly. "Whatcha got?"

Peterson laid a batch of glossy 8" x 10" photographs on the desk in front of her, moving a stack of papers as he did so. He took the steel chair next to her and pulled it a little closer to her than she would have liked. She was immediately overwhelmed by the overpowering scent of cologne.

"Ok," he said, pointing to the top photo. "These are the stills Hilliard ordered from the CCTV footage at Malcom Harris' house. As you can see by the timestamp, these reflect the day of the murder of Marjorie Harris, October 2nd."

Calvo leaned over the photograph and studied it. It was the front of the house early morning. She had watched the video several times. She didn't expect to see anything new. The quality of the photographs was less grainy than the video, however. Peterson seemed to read her mind.

"The guys in the lab enhanced the film and cleaned it up a bit, brought down some background interference, etc."

Calvo went through the photos. She could see Marjorie leave and enter the house at various times during the day. Camille also left and returned with sacks of what looked like food and a few hangers of dry cleaning. Malcolm left the house in the late afternoon, dressed in a three-piece suit, ostensibly for his lecture at the hotel. He was carrying the same overnight bag he had brought in the door with him the morning Calvo and Hilliard were there with other police officers. She sighed. Nothing looked noteworthy. The times at the bottom of each photo aligned with what they already knew of the threesome's actions that day. She cringed at the final photo of Marjorie Harris arriving home in a sequined gown, her long hair pinned up in fancy clips.

"Thank you, Peterson," she said, leaning back in her chair and placing a hand against the dull ache in her neck. Suddenly, she straightened and picked up the stack of photos, shifting furiously through them. "Wait a minute!" she cried. "Wait just a damn minute!"

She got to three photos and set them on the desk, side by side, in order of their time stamp.

"Look!" she said, excitedly. "Hilliard found a note in Harris's trash can in his home office… It was something about a product and instruction being delivered to the side yard at 1:30 on October 2nd. Look at this!" She pointed to the second photo in the layout of three. "Look at the time. 1:32 pm. And look who's in the picture! The meter reader. I didn't think anything of him at the time. It's not unusual to see these guys in everyone's backyard at one time or another. But he's there at 1:32!"

Officer Peterson leaned closer to the photo. His heavy cologne was giving Calvo a headache.

"Is that something under his clipboard?" he asked. "It's hard to see, but maybe…"

Calvo leaned in, her eyes straining.

"It's too blurry to tell," she said. "But if you look at the next picture, it looks like he's bending over the bush beneath the electric box. No one would have even noticed this if we didn't know what we were looking for." She pulled the last photo of him exiting the yard, his hard hat obscuring his face.

"Is this all there is?" she asked. "I need a clean look at his face."

"That's it," Peterson said. "I'll double-check if you want."

"Here's what I'm thinking," she said, scooting her chair over a few inches. "If the meter reader is involved in this, then the odds are good he might show up in CCTV footage from the houses where the other mysterious deaths happened. I mean, everybody has cameras nowadays. And if the homes where we think a murder took place don't, I bet their neighbors do. Many of these deaths happened to well-to-do individuals. Security cameras would be a must. Can you and Gleason get on that? I'll give you the addresses, but you'll need search warrants, unless these people hand the camera cards over to you willingly. Try that first. You can be charming, right?"

"Sure thing," he said, inching his chair closer. He turned toward her, and she suddenly felt claustrophobic.

"That would be great, and I appreciate you bringing these to me." She stacked the pile of photos from Harris' security footage and opened her ledger, extracting a file. She handed him a page of names and addresses associated with the names deaths of people revolving around the guests of Madame Lorraine's seances.

"I really need the footage from Tiffany LeBlanc, Brenda Griffin, Marsha Jennings, and Abigail Landry," Calvo said. "We checked for cameras at the cabin where Waylan Montez died from oleander poisoning. There weren't any. Thanks so much. Let me know as soon as you get the footage, please."

She smiled at him and picked up a pen and a report to continue her work. If she was hoping he would take the hint, it failed.

"Lunch today?" he asked, flashing an uncomfortable smile.

Calvo blanched. She had hoped to head off this very conversation. For the first time, she was grateful Hilliard wasn't here.

His teasing would be merciless.

"That's very nice of you," she said. "I have to take Hilliard some lunch at the hospital and check into some other things."

"Another time, then," he said, a note of disappointment in his voice. He rose from his chair. "I'll ask about those photos, and Gleason and I will look into the security camera footage from these homes."

He exited the office, but his cologne remained, cloaking the air. There was no window to open. Calvo sighed. Finally, gathering up her ledger and a pen, she walked out of the room and headed for her car and some fresh air.

****

Calvo walked along the polished corridor of the ICU hallway, nodding at nurses who recognized her as the lady who had been there every time they turned around.

"They moved him," one of the nurses called out to her from behind the nurse's station desk.

"He got to you, too, huh?" Calvo said, smiling. "Is he in the morgue or a holding cell somewhere?"

Several nurses laughed, obviously grateful to have him out of their charge.

"He's in a private room on the third floor," the nurse said. "Room 312. Do you need directions?"

"No, thank you. I'll just follow the sound of screaming nurses."

She walked away to the sound of laughter behind her. The aroma from the take-out container of gumbo she was carrying in a sack was causing her stomach to growl. She took the elevator to the third floor and found his room. The door was closed.

"Well, look who's back among the living?" she said, smiling, as she opened the door and walked in. The first thing she noticed was the mug of dancing kittens sitting on his food tray. His eyes followed hers, and he grimaced.

"I use it in case I need to spit," he said, wanly.

Calvo crossed to the tray and peered into the cup.

"Interesting how Diet Coke can look like spit." She set the bag of food on the tray and stood looking at him.

"Seriously, how are you? What are they saying about your recovery?"

Hilliard adjusted the pillows behind his head.

"I'll live. Sorry to disappoint you. I'm told my legs will give me some trouble for a while. It might interfere with my Olympic basketball dreams."

She smiled at him fondly as she pulled two Styrofoam bowls and plastic spoons from the bag. Lifting the large container of gumbo, she said, "I know how popular fifty-year-old Olympic athletes are. Sorry you missed out on that."

He grinned and drew in a deep breath.

"Oh, please tell me that's Maggie Olie's gumbo!"

"But of course," Calvo said, smiling. "If you're a good boy, I'll share."

Once the two were happily spooning down hot gumbo, Calvo gave her partner an update on what was happening while he was away.

"First, I saw Wanda Mileau. She was at my séance, and Madame Lorraine had handed her a paper with writing. It was supposed to be an answer to where something was that she was looking for. All I know is that the answer started with a 'P.' Turns out, it was a nothing burger. She was asking her dead grandmother where a diamond bracelet was that had been in the family for years. The 'P' word on the paper belonged to the phrase, "Potted plant." According to Wanda, they dug up every potted plant inside and outside the house. They never found it. She thinks Madame Lorraine made it up to bilk her out of $800 for an automatic writing. There haven't been any deaths with the last name Mileau, so I tend to believe her.'

"What a scam," Hilliard said, gumbo dribbling onto his chin. "At least that one was just the usual flim flam. Any updates on the others?"

"Yes. Peterson brought in the stills from Harris' CCTV footage. The meter reader shows up at the exact time the delivery is listed on the card you found in Malcom's trash can. We couldn't see if he was carrying anything, but he did bend down by the bushes there. It could have been the bath bombs. I couldn't see his face clearly, and we needed more, so I sent Peterson and Gleason to check out four of the other murder suspects' homes to get a look at their security camera footage."

"You should have gotten Bullard and Gleason to go. Peterson's only been on the force for a year. Besides, it's hard to be sneaky when your cologne advertises your whereabouts a mile away."

Calvo sucked in her cheek and looked down.

"Moving on," she said, using Davis Miles' favorite phrase. "Brenda Griffin is in jail. As you know, they found hemlock in the drains and garbage."

"The parsnips?"

"Yep," Calvo said, nodding. "I asked a couple of the guys to get a search warrant for her house. I noticed she had dirty fingernails, which didn't jive with a woman like her, or that she had just prepared a dinner. Hopefully, they find something, like the fork."

"Andddd," she said, sighing. "Jackson LeBlanc died of nicotine poisoning, added to the paint stain he was using. They're bringing in Tiffany LeBlanc for questioning. Andddd, they are finishing the report on the autopsy performed on Charlie Brindle two days ago. There's some other stuff, but those are the headlines. Now, can we please address the elephant in the room?"

"Don't talk about Nurse Beecher like that," Hilliard said, stone-faced. "She eats the treats left behind when patients are released."

Calvo squeezed her eyes shut and took a deep breath. Finally, she said, "You were poisoned with thallium."

"This I know."

"Where did you come into contact with thallium?"

"Where do you think I came into contact with thallium?" he barked, rising up off the pillows. "At the Voodoo Queen's house."

Calvo glanced toward the closed door and hushed him.

"Settle down," she said, her hands in front of her. "I waited until you could think straight to bring it up. Now think. Emma isn't sick, so it must have been something you did at Madame Lorraine's séance that Emma didn't. What did you do? What did you touch? I assume you didn't eat or drink anything."

Hilliard sighed loudly and leaned back against the pillows, his head throbbing.

"I don't know," he said, feebly.

"Hilliard, I need you to think."

He opened his eyes and reached for the kitten mug without thinking about it. Taking a long drink of soda, he set the mug back onto the tray and suddenly noticed the band-aid around his right forefinger.

"I cut my finger," he said, holding up the injured digit to study it. "I was signing that book of theirs, and I cut it with the writing pen."

Calvo leaned forward eagerly, placing her empty bowl on the food tray.

"Did Emma use the same pen?"

Hilliard's forehead furrowed as he tried to remember the evening four days prior.

"Uh...no. No. The tall lady, Renee..."

"Rachel," Calvo corrected.

"Rachel. When she saw the blood from my cut dripping onto the ledger, she told Emma, 'Never mind signing in.' She offered me a tissue for the cut." Hilliard's eyes flew open wide. "I wrapped the cut with the tissue! Is that it? Was the thallium on the tissue? The pen was set up to cut me, and the poison was on the tissue!"

24 LONG SHADOWS

Rachel finished drying the breakfast dishes and was reaching for her teacup when she saw a shadow fall across the lawn through the kitchen window. She leaned across the sink and looked out, craning her neck and turning her head to the right. She was just able to catch sight of the same man she had seen before, walking hurriedly away toward the front of the house. She felt the same rush of panic she had been feeling for over a week now—ever since the detective had been there for a séance with his sister. It was that drop of blood, spreading across all those names in the guest book. All those names…

A soft thud sounded overhead from the direction of her sister's bedroom. The medium had finished her breakfast and gone upstairs to change out of her robe and get ready for the day. Rachel's heart was racing. She'd have to hurry.

Rachel opened the kitchen door to the backyard and took the wooden steps down onto the walkway. She went immediately to the azalea bush and pushed her hand down behind the branches. Her fingers closed on the sack.

She thought she heard a sound from the bedroom window overhead and froze. She glanced up, her heart pounding. No one was there. The sack felt heavy as she pulled open the neck of the bag and pulled out a stack of $100 bills, a rubber band holding them together. Dozens more remained in the bag. She closed it back the way she had found it, put it back behind the bush, and hurried up the stairs.

Upstairs, the hand holding the sheer lace curtain of the window above the kitchen let it fall back into place.

****

Lieutenant Calvo sat with Detective Gleason in Interview Room 2. A small utilitarian table was pressed to the back wall, strategically placed for the camera lens nestled in the corner above the door. At the right-hand side of the table, Tiffany LeBlanc sat, her face strained. Calvo noticed that despite the lady's obvious tension, not one hair was out of place. The tailored blouse and slacks were probably hanging in a dry cleaner's bag only minutes before.

Gleason inched his chair over closer to the recently widowed Mrs. LeBlanc, a strategy used in most police interviews. It closed the distance between the interviewer and the suspect, invading their personal bubble and increasing their stress level.

"Mrs. LeBlanc," Detective Gleason began. "First of all, our sympathy on your husband's tragic passing."

Calvo watched Tiffany's face closely, looking for tells or fluctuating expressions. Gleason's offering of condolences did nothing to soften her face. She watched him with the wariness of a cat sizing up its prey.

"That being said," Gleason continued, "some things have come to light that we need to look into. Let's start with a couple of questions. Was it routine for your husband, Jackson, to be in his woodshop? Was this a frequent pastime of his?"

The wariness in her eyes intensified. Calvo could sense the tumblers falling in her mind as she chose the correct responses to his questions.

"Very much so," she said, her voice tight. "He spent thousands on all that machinery and tools. He said it relaxed him."

Gleason smiled and ran his hand over his shortly cropped hair.

"Relaxed him? He wasn't even 40 yet. Did he have a lot of stress in his life?"

Tiffany stiffened. She crossed her legs and then immediately uncrossed them.

"No, that's not what I meant. It was a hobby."

"Did your husband smoke?" Gleason asked.

Her reaction was immediate. She drew in her cheeks and Calvo could see her blouse trembling with her increased heart rate.

"No."

Gleason tilted his head. "No?"

"No."

"Perhaps, then, you could tell us how a lethal dose of nicotine was found in his system?" He inched his chair closer until their knees were almost touching. Tiffany leaned away from him.

"Nicotine?" she asked, feigning surprise. "I don't understand. My poor Jackson must have had a heart attack or something." She pressed a tissue to her dry eyes.

Calvo coughed and leaned forward.

"As much as I'm enjoying this dog and pony show of yours, let me help you out," Calvo said. Gleason leaned back and let her take over. "You got the nicotine from Madame Lorraine or her sister after attending a séance at their house. We have the list of names of all those who attended her little events," she said, omitting the fact that Tiffany's name wasn't on the list Hilliard took a photo of.

"You heard she was helping unhappy wives become rich and joyful widows," she pressed. "You added the liquid nicotine to his paint stain, and that was it. Very clever. Liquid nicotine turns brown when it comes into contact with air. Brown nicotine, brown pecan stain. No one would notice it. One little mistake. There was a drop of nicotine found on the cuff of one of your blouses at the house. We also reviewed the CCTV footage that we obtained under the same search warrant. Do you usually leave large paper bags inside your bushes by the electric meter?"

Tiffany's cheek muscles broke into spasms. She looked wildly at

Gleason as if pleading for him to save her.

"I...I...," she began and stopped. Her shoulders sagged, and she burst into tears.

"Madame Lorraine gave you the nicotine, didn't she?" Calvo asked, a vein protruding from her forehead.

Tiffany nodded.

"Did she ask you questions about his habits or his health?" Calvo continued. "Did you tell her he does woodworking and was staining something, so nicotine was recommended?"

Tiffany nodded again, her face a roadmap of pain.

"How did you get him to cut his finger?" Calvo asked in a calmer voice. They got their confession.

Tiffany looked up with the expression of a trapped animal, but one that was resigned to its fate.

"I...I dropped a wine glass. It broke. He bent to pick up the pieces. I did the same and made sure one of the larger pieces cut his right hand. It bled a lot." She burst into fresh tears. "He told me not to touch the glass because he didn't want me to get hurt!" She buried her head in her hands and sobbed.

Calvo fought her disgust.

"Why?" the Lieutenant asked. "Was it money--insurance money? Was he cheating?"

Tiffany slowly raised her head. It lolled to one side as she gathered herself. Her perfect posture had collapsed.

"No. I just didn't want to be married anymore," she said in a monotone voice. "It was all so boring."

Gleason caught up with Calvo outside the interview room. She was walking quickly down the hallway toward her office, her face red.

"Slow down!" he called.

"I don't want to talk about it," she said hotly. "I can't stomach this job sometimes. I really can't. She had a husband who cared about her, and she was bored? BORED?"

"I know. I threw up too. Just one question," he said, catching up to her. She stopped, panting. "We didn't find any blouse with nicotine on

217

it. Did you make that up?"

"Leave me alone," she said and walked off.

Gleason stopped following her and let her go. He'd lied about evidence to catch a suspect himself. Cops did it all the time. He grinned as he turned and headed back to Interview Room 2. It was going to be a pleasure to watch Tiffany LeBlanc pose for a mug shot.

Calvo made it into her office and slammed the door. She stood in the middle of the small room, huffing and trying not to throw something.

"That damn woman is making money off of providing the means to kill poor unsuspecting people and using a phony séance to do it!" she said aloud to the empty room. "Buckle up, bitch! I'm coming for you!"

A timid knock came on her door.

"What?" she yelled.

The handle turned, and Officer Peterson timidly peered around the door.

"I don't have a white flag to wave," he said nervously. "Can I enter?"

Calvo managed a grin.

"Yeah, come on in. I'm just venting."

"So, I heard," he said. He came into the office and laid a brown file down on the desk. "I can leave these for you. They're all tagged. It's the stills from the CCTV footage of the four houses you sent us to. Your meter reader shows up in all of them but the Landry house. Nice going, Lieutenant."

He smiled and turned to leave the room.

"Peterson?" Calvo said. "Thank you. You don't know how much I needed that evidence."

He smiled at her, but something was different. The flirtation was gone. His professional demeanor was reassuring. Just before he walked out into the hallway, Calvo stopped him.

"What happened to the cologne?" she asked, smiling.

"Oh," he said, blushing. "A girl I took out for drinks told me it was too much. Can you believe that?"

He walked off, leaving Calvo chuckling and shaking her head.

Calvo sank into her chair and quickly opened the file. She thumbed through several glossy 8 x 10s and then stopped. The picture had a sticky file tab attached to it. It was from the LeBlanc residence with the date and time stamp. There, in one of the back yard photos, was a man in a striped utility vest walking up an incline, his hard hat tipped back just enough to see his face. Calvo yelped and did an air pump with her fist.

"Yes!" she yelled.

Just then, the desk phone rang. Calvo walked around to Hilliard's side and punched the glowing button that was numbered 2.

"Calvo," she said. "Of course, put her through."

Seconds later, a voice filled the receiver with wailing. It took a minute for Calvo to discern who it was.

"Camille?" Calvo asked. "Calm down. What's wrong?"

The wailing continued with unintelligible words mingled in.

"Camille! I can't understand you. What's happened?"

"Maxwell found kitty!" she wailed.

It took Calvo a moment to process what she was hearing. She paused and asked, "Who is Maxwell? Found kitty where?"

"Maxwell is neighbor's dog. He digging in our garden and he find kitty! Kitty is dead!"

****

The afternoon sun disappeared behind a bank of angry clouds. The wind was whistling around the corners of the old house, testing the shutters' grip against the clapboard, and moaning down the chimneys. Rachel peered out of her bedroom window at the tree limbs thrashing against the peeling paint. A neighbor's Halloween witch decoration escaped its mooring and flew off above the trees. She watched it in fascination as the figure on the broomstick whipped through the bruised clouds. She shivered. It felt like October.

Rachel walked out of her room into the dark upper hallway. The threadbare carpet runner was curled on its edges, a tripping hazard if ever there was one. She paused and listened for her sister. It always made her nervous when she didn't know where she was. Her nerves had been on edge lately, wondering if Ruby had discovered she knew about the bags of money and that she was helping herself to some. She needed the money to escape. To find somewhere to live.

The muffled sound of the refrigerator door closing in the kitchen below reached her. Ruby must have been tired of waiting for her to make lunch. She stood there in the gloom and glanced off to her left. Her sister's bedroom door was standing open. She bit her lip. It would be risky. Ruby's bedroom was right above the kitchen. If she heard her in her room, there would be hell to pay. But she had to know. Ever since the séance with the man whom they now knew was a detective, Rachel had worried over something she saw.

Rachel tiptoed in bare feet to the open door and looked in. The bed was made, and a shawl was thrown over the bedspread, part of it hanging to the floor. The curtains were open, but with the storm outside, it didn't help much in the way of light. She stood there in the doorway, listening. The blender in the kitchen suddenly roared to life. This was her chance.

She quickly crossed the room to the tall wardrobe in the far corner. One of the doors was ajar. She opened it and pushed the array of long, dark dresses to one side. The small shelf at the back held various things her sister used in her seances. The crystal skull watched her with hollow eyes. A small black ball sat atop a Ouija board. She reached for the deck of Tarot cards sitting off to the right. She picked them up and glanced at their back. It was her sister's deck that she used for every reading. Rachel replaced them and continued to search the closet. Fearing her sister would come looking for her, she gave up.

Rachel pulled the dresses quietly back into place. As she tugged on the long black dress her sister used regularly in her seances, it fell from the hanger and landed with a *thunk* on the cupboard floor. Confused as to the sound, Rachel picked it up. There was something weighty in one of the pockets. Reaching in, she pulled out something wrapped in an old handkerchief. She opened the folds and peered inside. Nestled in the lace was another deck of Tarot cards, worn and used like the other deck. On the back of the cards was a raven standing on a branch of thorns. Her heart pulsed in her neck. She hurriedly folded the delicate fabric back over the cards.

The grating sound of the blender below stopped, and she froze. She held her breath as the silence closed in. Moments passed. Rachel listened for a footfall on the staircase. Instead, the sound of water running in the kitchen sink echoed from the kitchen. She exhaled sharply and pushed the wrapped card deck into her pants pocket. Quickly, she hung the dress back up and partially closed the cupboard door as she had found it. She began tiptoeing toward the open doorway. Her left foot caught in the shawl hanging from the end of the bed, and she stumbled.

Rachel froze in place, hunched over and listening. Her erratic breathing was interfering with her ability to hear the sounds from below. After several minutes, she heard her sister walking toward the staircase. Silence again. And then…

"Rachel?" Ruby called out. "Do you want any lunch?"

****

Calvo was leaving the office for the day. It was six o'clock, and her head hurt. Skipping meals was catching up with her. She would stop by the hospital and see Hilliard, and then head home to her cat. She desperately wanted a cat cuddle and a beer. As she reached for her baseball jacket, the desk phone rang. Sighing, she picked it up.

"Calvo?" she said, her voice thick.

"Whoa, somebody's had a long day," Peterson said. "Just wanted you to know, one of the guys helping me at the Griffin house found what you were looking for. After digging up half of the landscape outside, they went into the garage and found a big bag of potting soil. Guess what?"

Calvo hated the 'guess what?' questions, but she played along.

"What?"

"A man's dress shirt. Rephrase, a really stinky and messy man's dress shirt. There are brown stains on it and, well, other stains. He's bringing it in. Nice catch, Lieutenant. You're on a roll!"

She laughed, a tired, happy laugh.

"Good work, Peterson," she said. "Tell the guys thank you as well."

She had no sooner replaced the receiver than the phone rang again.

"Calvo? Yes, Jason. Say that again," she asked the front desk officer.

"Someone just called in," Jason said. "They asked if Detective Hilliard was still in the hospital. I said, 'As far as I know. Who is calling, please?' They didn't answer that. Instead, they said, and I quote, 'Tell him to look to the Tarot cards.'

25 BURIED TRUTHS

The week leading up to Halloween seemed to fly by. Calvo felt like a juggler with far too many balls in the air. She went home each night exhausted, falling asleep on her worn couch with her cat resting on her stomach. Take-out containers littered the small apartment.

Calvo pulled her Mustang up to the hospital doors and entered into the massive lobby. Hilliard was waiting in a wheelchair at the discharge desk.

"I can walk, dammit!" he was yelling at a nurse who looked like she could take over a linebacker's position if needed. The large woman merely looked at him with the expression of one who had dealt with a hundred Hilliards and always came away victorious.

Calvo was smiling as she reached to pair.

"I believe I can relieve you of this man," she said to the nurse. The linebacker gave her the same look she had just given the detective.

"Hospital policy. I wheel him out. Then you are more than welcome to take over," she said, her tone making it clear the deal was done.

Calvo picked up a paper bag of Hilliard's belongings and two empty floral vases. She followed the nurse to her car and opened the passenger side door. Hilliard rose unsteadily and folded himself into the car seat, his knees practically reaching his nose. The nurse turned on her heel and departed with the wheelchair without another word.

"How's it feel to be out among the living?" Calvo asked as she slid into the driver's side. She reached behind her and set the vases and paper bag on the back seat.

"I'll let you know when I've eaten real food," he said, grumpily. "Whoever designed this car has never had a person over six feet ride in it."

"You're welcome," Calvo said sarcastically. "Heck, I didn't have anything else to do but come here and give you a ride home."

"I'm not going home," Hilliard said. "We've got a lot of work to do. To the office, James."

Calvo looked over at him and frowned.

"I've already filled you in on everything. It's under control. We've got both Tiffany LeBlanc and Brenda Griffin in the lock-up. Theodore Griffin's shirt stain was soy sauce with indicators for hemlock. Tiffany confessed. Both Tiffany and Brenda will be denied the right to attend their husbands' funerals today. Abigail Landry is a tougher nut to crack. We know there were Moonseed grapes in the boat, but she denies knowing anything about them. She says he could have bought them or picked them himself. They grow wild near the water. Her surveillance cameras don't cover all of the areas around her house."

"And the Montez case?"

"It's hard to prosecute that one for one reason: the oleander branches were burned up. We know the toxin was in his body. We also know that in Geraldine's 911 call, she said, 'He *would have* been 70 in two months.' Most people who have called for an ambulance and are in shock from seeing their spouse lying on the ground in an emergency situation, are still hoping for a miracle. They are not already thinking of them in the past tense. Can we get a conviction on either of those two things? Probably not. We'll have to keep digging. There were no cameras at the cabin. All we know is that Geraldine Montez was a gust of Madame Lorraine's, and, her husband ends up dead from inhaling oleander smoke."

"Well, it there were no oleander trees growing on the property, doesn't that nail it down?" Hilliard growled.

"We need more," Calvo said.

"Have they located Harris yet?" Hilliard asked, shifting in his seat.

"No. When the cat was found in the garden bed, he took off. We'll find him."

Hilliard sighed and watched the houses go by littered with carved pumpkins adorning doorsteps, waiting for their time to shine. Vampires, ghosts, an inflatable Beetlejuice, and a scarecrow wearing a mask of the governor of Louisiana flew by as Calvo navigated the heavy traffic.

"You aren't going to throw in my face that you were right about the cat?" Hilliard finally asked.

"Nope. This is your pity pass. I'll bring it up down the road when you're in better shape." He grinned.

"I want to be there when you talk to Dorothy Brindle," Hilliard said. "Is that today or tomorrow?"

Calvo sighed. "If you overdo it, you'll be back in there with your favorite nurses." The look he gave her ended the conversation. Sighing again, she said, "It's today. 11:30. Tell you what. Let's grab some BBQ to go from your favorite place, and we'll eat it at the office while we're waiting for her."

Calvo tried without success to smother her grin. She could feel the steam coming out of her partner's nose. She glanced at him with her most innocent look.

"Am I incorrect? Is Central City not our favorite BBQ place? I saw how many empty containers of theirs were in your hospital trash can. I'm sure Stacey will hand you the takeout bag with her own little hands." She lifted her shoulder as if to ward off a blow. Hilliard turned his red face to the window.

"Just drive," he said hotly, but Calvo noticed a small grin on his face.

✶✶✶✶✶✶✶✶✶✶✶✶✶✶✶✶✶✶✶✶✶✶✶✶✶✶✶✶✶✶✶

Madame Lorraine set the skull into place on the parlor table. She went over the other items set out on the tea cart behind her chair. Noticing how low the pillar candle was getting, she made a mental note to buy a new one, and then stopped, smiling. After tonight, she wouldn't need another candle. Or another séance. Or Rachel. It was time to pack up the tent, she thought to herself. News of the arrests of Tiffany LeBlanc and Brenda Griffin had made the papers. She scanned them daily, nervously looking for anything that would implicate her in their husbands' deaths. So far, nothing. Geraldine Montez and Abigail Landry seemed to have slipped the noose. Their names had not appeared in print.

The medium looked around one last time and exited the room. She crossed to the dark oak staircase and started up, one hand on the worn railing. Rachel was out getting Halloween candy for the following night. They usually received more raw eggs and toilet paper in the trees than they did trick-or-treaters, she thought ruefully. Being the premier haunted house in the area had its downfalls.

Reaching the landing, she turned to her left and stopped. The heavily draped curtains at the only window let in a sparse amount of light. The gaping hole in front of her bedroom door showed like a dark gash in the floorboards. Her breath caught in her throat as she walked to the hole and stooped over to get a better look at it. It was empty, except for some mouse droppings and a few cobwebs. The board belonging to it lay on its side nearby, the rusty nails protruding from it like a hag's ragged teeth.

Madame Lorraine stood in the shadowed hallway, staring down at the rectangular opening. What did it mean? Stepping over it, she opened her bedroom door and hurried inside, closing it behind her. She turned around to face the room and screamed.

There, its red color incongruous with muted shades of her walls and furnishings, was a baseball cap, sitting atop her bedspread. Her hand was pressed to her chest, where she could feel her heart hammering against it. Eyes bulging with fear, she took several tentative steps toward it. Her fingers trembled as she pulled the small chain to her night table lamp.

She stumbled back, reaching for a wall to steady herself. She tried to swallow, but the saliva wouldn't come.

"No," she hissed. "No. It's impossible. It's not real."

She fell against the bedroom door frame, gasping, her eyes glued to the red baseball cap and the black oil stain smearing its right side.

****

Dorothy Brindle sat in Calvo's chair, her small, gloved hands clutching the handle of the leather purse she carried with her everywhere. She sat with her shoulders back and waited. Hilliard was seated in his chair across the desk from her, and Calvo was in the metal chair next to her. Calvo could see she was shaking—the small white eyelet sweater trembled. The purple paisley skirt was moving as well, as the elderly woman's knees shook.

Hilliard's face was pale, and perspiration pebbled his forehead and upper lip. Calvo glanced at him repeatedly, worried he would fall over. The tremors in his hands were still there and would be for some time from the effects of the poison. She decided to take the lead.

"Dorothy," she began quietly, squaring off to face the woman who refused to make eye contact. "We have Charlie's autopsy results. You know that, don't you?"

Dorothy's lips trembled. She swallowed a few times and finally nodded.

"You were right," Calvo said. "There was poison found in his body."

Dorothy turned quickly to face her, her eyes open wide, magnified by her glasses. A look of shock was on her face. It took her a moment to recover. Calvo was having a difficult time reading her reaction. It was one of shock, yes, but mixed with something else. Happiness?

"I knew it," Dorothy finally breathed, her voice weak. "I knew he killed my Charlie."

Calvo looked over at Hilliard as to how to proceed. It was like walking a tightrope.

"Dorothy," Calvo said again, placing a hand on Dorothy's. "We found poison, but there's a problem. It wasn't thallium."

Dorothy's eyes glazed over. Her shoulders rose and fell with her breathing. She was chewing on her lips from inside her mouth, her face ashen.

Calvo gave it a minute to sink in.

"Dorothy. It was thallium in the beer bottle you brought in. But it wasn't thallium found in Charlie's body. It was arsenic. How do you explain that?"

****

Rachel entered the kitchen from the side door, huffing under the weight of two sacks of groceries. She fell against the counter, releasing them with a sigh. She turned to put her purse on the table and jumped. Ruby was standing in the hallway doorway, watching her.

"You scared me!" Rachel said, laughing nervously. When her sister didn't respond, she hurried on, her voice jittery. "You should have seen all the people buying candy," she said, turning her back to her sister to unpack the grocery bags. She set several bags of mixed miniature candy bars on the counter, a bag of rice, and a produce sack of apples. "I got your apples," she said, talking a little too fast. "You go through them faster than I can buy them."

The silence filled the small room. She finally turned to see her sister studying her with a look Rachel couldn't decipher. She waited, pushing a loose strand of hair from her forehead.

"Did you know apple seeds are poisonous?" Ruby finally said. "If you chew them, that is."

Rachel flinched. Her sister's tone was flat yet menacing.

"I did know that," she said. "So, don't eat the seeds."

She smiled, hoping to diffuse the tension, but Ruby's face remained inscrutable.

"There's a floorboard pried up in the upstairs hallway," Ruby said, taking a step into the kitchen. "Don't you find that odd?"

Rachel could feel perspiration under her armpits. She felt trapped.

"That is odd," she said, her voice sounding feeble.

"Yes," Ruby said, taking another step closer. "Weren't you telling me about Louisiana Creole dolls they hid under floorboards? Wasn't that something you read in that book of yours? Voodoo or something if I'm not mistaken."

Something in Rachel stirred. Years of fear. Years of dread. She lifted her head and met her sister's glare. Her voice took on a determined tone.

"Are you saying you think something was under the floorboard by your door? Something that wanted to get out?"

Ruby's eyes flashed as she crossed the final few feet to her sister.

"Don't mess with me, Rachel," she hissed into her face. "You have no idea what I'm capable of."

Rachel closed the rest of the space between them, her eyes steely as they bore into those of her older sister.

"Oh, but Ruby," she whispered. "I know exactly what you're capable of." Years of pent-up anger flared up like a pyre. "Shall we count the ways? Let's start with a hysterical phone call one early morning before the sun was up. 'Help me, Rachel,' she mimicked. You had it all planned! I would come running, see Ronald lying in his own blood on the driveway. Then, oh, and this is the really insidious part, you ask me to help get him into the car…and move his bag to the back seat. So that my fingerprints would be all over it. You were wearing gloves if I'm not mistaken. How clever you are, Ruby! How sickeningly clever. For 18 years, you've held his murder over my head. Every time you felt me pulling away, you threatened me with going to the police."

Ruby's anger matched her sister's as Rachel continued, and the two sisters squared off against each other in the kitchen.

"And here's where it gets really good," Rachel said, her eyes brimming. "When I told you I had nothing to do with it, and that I hadn't touched his body or his suitcase, you played your trump card. You reminded me I had touched the hood of his car. The car they never found. The car that, if they did find it, would have Ronald's blood all over it. And my husband…Mark," she broke into tears, unable to finish.

The weight of the words hung in the air. Ruby took a step back, her face one of surprise. Racheal had rarely stood up to her. Something about her had changed. She paused, watching as Rachel collapsed into a kitchen chair. She decided not to mention the baseball cap. Not yet. She would play her own game and win.

She turned angrily and marched out of the room. Rachel heard her climbing the stairs to her bedroom. Moments later, she could hear her walk into her bedroom and slam the door.

The medium walked to her wardrobe and opened the double doors. She took down the long black gown that she hadn't worn since the séance with the detective and his sister. Lying it across the bed, she reached into the side pocket to remove the deck of cards she had wrapped in a handkerchief and placed there.

They were gone.

****

Dorothy held the autopsy report in trembling hands, her lips mouthing the words she was reading. Finally, she glanced up to see Hilliard staring at her.

"Dorothy," he said, his voice weak. "Explain to us how arsenic is found in the report but not thallium. You need to be honest here. You could go to prison for killing your husband."

Her eyes flew open wide. She turned her head to face Calvo, her mouth hanging open in surprise.

"I didn't poison Charlie!" she cried. "I would never hurt him. I miss him so much," she sobbed.

"You have to tell us all you know," Calvo said. "This is serious."

Dorothy's shoulders fell forward, and she cried, tears dripping onto her purse. In shuddering sobs, she told them what happened.

"I knew he did it," she sputtered. "I knew Everett killed him. He waited until I was out of town, and he went there to kill him. To get the inheritance. There was no doubt in my mind." She paused and pulled a handkerchief from her purse.

"I didn't know what to do. But I had to focus on Charlie's funeral. I was at this little print store that the funeral director recommended for the service program. The young lady there was very kind. I think it was her kindness that made me say it. I told her I wanted so much to ask Charlie something that I needed to know. Whether or not to go forward with it. I didn't say what.. She said there was this woman who helped people talk to their loved ones who had passed on. That this woman could help me.

"I thought if I could talk to Charlie, I could ask him if I was right, that he was murdered. So, she made the arrangements for me to attend a séance, and I went. Charlie came through and gave me a note. A note in a black bag. It said he was okay and to 'proceed.' I took that to mean I was on the right track, believing Everett killed him. I found a note in my purse after the séance. It instructed me to return on another date if I needed further assistance, and a solution would be provided to me. When I went back, I was asked some questions. I told her about my suspicions regarding Charlie's grandson. She asked some more questions about Everett's visit to Charlie the day I called him, and Everett was there. After I told her about Everett's routine when he came to call, she told me to go to his house and get a beer bottle. She gave me this little bottle of liquid and told me to put the liquid into the bottle, and then take it to the police."

Calvo and Hilliard looked at each other with a look of shock on their faces. The sound of the wall clock ticking filled the room. Hilliard took a deep breath, which made him dizzy. He took a long drink of cold water and faced the little woman who was trembling with terror.

"So, you set him up by putting the poison in the bottle...and that poison came back to be thallium. We told you as much as you sat in that same chair that day. So, how in the world did arsenic end up in Charlie's body?"

Dorothy blew her nose and folded the handkerchief. She sniffed and said, "Everett must have used arsenic to kill Charlie. I knew he had killed him. I didn't know with what. I thought if you found something in the beer bottle, that would be that. You would arrest Everett, and it would be over. But you didn't. I kept waiting. You had his fingerprints, you had the poison. I was afraid he was going to get away with it, so I did the only thing I could think to do. Have his body examined." She broke into fresh tears.

Calvo's head reeled back in surprise.

"You went through the pain and expense of having his remains removed from the vault and examined, not knowing if they would find anything?"

Dorothy faced her with swollen eyes.

"He's my Charlie. My world. I knew that evil boy killed him. I knew it. It was the only way to prove it. Besides, Charlie told me himself to 'proceed.' It was all I needed to know to go forward with it."

Hilliard looked incredulous.

"Charlie told you to go ahead?" he asked, not wanting to believe she could be that gullible.

"Yes. He came through the veil. And I brought him justice," she said.

"And just how much did that 'justice' cost you?" he asked, the nausea he was feeling coming from something other than his illness. "How much did you pay Madame Lorraine for the poison?"

She paused and looked down at her purse. When she answered, it was in a soft voice.

"$150,000," she said.

Hilliard bent over the trash can.

26 HAUNTED HALLWAYS

The morning dawned dull and foreboding. Dorothy Brindle looked out the window of her small bedroom and shivered. It would be a hard few hours ahead, but she was ready. She adjusted her small hat with the white netting, kissed Charlie's photograph by her bedside, and left for the cemetery.

Detective Hilliard, Lieutenant Calvo, Faregate from the funeral home, and the cemetery superintendent were already at the vault when Dorothy stepped from her Cadillac. Unfortunately, so were a few reporters, including Davis Miles. She tugged on her eyelet sweater nervously and walked over to the group, who were waiting for her. The sound of cameras snapping filled the sodden air, rain threatening to break loose at any moment.

Dorothy's eyes shifted to the funeral hearse. Her breath caught, and long, bent-up emotions rose to the top. Hilliard reached out an arm to steady her as she stumbled on the first step to the vault.

"I've got you," he said kindly. "It's over. You may have gone about it in a convoluted way, but you brought a murderer to justice and did what you knew in your heart was right."

Dorothy looked up at him with appreciation. Hilliard felt her frailty as she clung to his arm.

"So, no handcuffs for tampering with evidence?" she said, a small smile pushing her wrinkles into her cheeks.

"Nah! I'd be blocked from family gatherings if they knew I threw an elderly woman in with New Orleans' bottom-dwellers. Next time, trust us."

She nodded gently and let him guide her up the final two steps and into the vault where Charles Brindle was laid to his final rest.

****

Rain exploded in a true Louisiana downpour as Calvo and Hilliard drove to Scripted! The car windshield wipers could barely keep up with the deluge.

"Lord!" Calvo said, trying to see the traffic lights that were mere red and green blurs. "The trick-or-treaters will not be happy."

They finally made their way to the small print shop and pulled up to the curb. The bakery next door highlighted Halloween-themed cakes and cupcakes in its window. Small pumpkins set among the delicacies looked out through the rain-soaked window with electric smiles.

The shop bell rang, and Beverly Singleton looked up in surprise to see the two people standing there, shaking droplets from their hair and clothes. Her face tightened as she rose slowly from her desk chair and came toward them. Calvo was struck by her demeanor. Gone was the vivacious saleswoman who had worked with her and Carol on wedding invitations.

"Good morning," she said. "What brings you out on this beastly day?" The tension in her body was palpable.

"I think you might know why we are here," Hilliard said. "How about we don't waste each other's time? You and your husband are involved in a scheme to not only defraud people of their money through phony seances, but also to give them the means to commit murder."

Beverly stumbled back, catching the center display table behind her. She was gasping for breath.

"No…" she managed. "No…I …I."

"You can save the theatrics," Hilliard said. "All I need to know now is if Brandon is here. You are both under arrest."

Beverly's eyes looked at him with sheer terror. The color drained from her face, and her knees gave out. Calvo caught her and placed her in a chair.

"Beverly," Calvo said, her voice gentler than she would have wanted in the moment. "You helped Madame Lorraine by supplying her with names of people with money who were unhappy in their marriages. They came here for various reasons in the beginning— party invitations, itineraries, funeral programs, weddings. You used your gift of ingratiating yourself with people to learn about them. The funeral programs were the easiest. You encouraged them to go to Madame Lorraine to talk to their loved ones. You ensnared them at their most vulnerable moments."

Beverly bent over and sobbed.

"It didn't start that way," she whimpered. "She came in one day. She wanted some business cards and purple note cards. A few customers came in while she was here, and she watched me handle them. She mentioned how good business seemed to be going for me, and I said something like, 'It could be better. We're just a small shop', kind of thing. She asked if I would like to make a little money on the side. If I supplied her with names of people who had just lost someone, or for any reason, as long as they looked like they had money, she would pay me a percentage of what she charged for her seances."

Calvo sighed. Beverly looked up at her, her face ashen.

"You can't judge me," she said, "I didn't know. I mean, a lot of people find comfort in hearing from people who have passed. I didn't see the harm. I would give her information that I had on each person. I'd make the appointments for the seances. Brandon was to pick up our share of the money."

Hilliard had already hurried to the back of the store, where the desk and office were. He disappeared through the office door.

"So, how did the Meter Reader gig start?" Calvo asked, not buying the watered-down version of events.

Beverly paused, the panicked look returning. It was clear she wasn't aware they knew that part of the scheme.

Several minutes passed as she worried her wedding ring with trembling fingers.

"Brandon got greedy," she said, her voice barely discernible. Madame Lorraine needed a way to collect money from the people who went beyond just wanting a séance. She also needed a delivery boy for some of the…uh…"

"Murder devices?" Hilliard offered sharply as he reentered the front of the shop.

Beverly looked over at him, terrified. She pulled in her lips and remained quiet. Calvo was afraid they had lost her.

"Where is your husband?" Hilliard said. "He isn't here, so where is he?"

****

By the time Beverly had completed her formal recorded police interview at the station, the rain had stopped. Low-lying clouds, their bellies pregnant with rain, warned this was just a momentary reprieve. The gutters gushed with rainwater, spilling out across streets in waves. Calvo and Hilliard sloshed their way to Calvo's Mustang and headed out toward the Garden District.

"Will there come a time when I'm deemed worthy to drive again?" Hilliard asked grumpily. "It feels like when my Mom took me to school."

"Let's give it two more days," she said, smiling. "You're finally getting some color back. Being mistaken for a vampire, even on this day, is not good optics."

Hilliard sighed and looked out the window as a plastic pumpkin floated down the gutter. Low rumbling sounds grumbled from the clouds periodically, adding to the tension the pair was already feeling.

"Do you really think Camille knows where he is?" Calvo asked, addressing the unspoken question hanging in the air.

"Maybe, maybe not," Hilliard said, trying to refold his legs into a more comfortable position. His right knee was beginning to throb. "She's afraid of him, that's for sure. All we can do is try."

Calvo pulled the car into the long driveway of the Harris home. Nothing had changed, except a few waterlogged newspapers sitting out front. Knowing Camille's steadfast routine of bringing in the mail and newspapers, Calvo felt a sudden apprehension. Had something happened to the maid?

Hilliard pressed the doorbell for the third time. Calvo was just about to go around back when the front door opened a few inches. A pair of frightened eyes looked out.

"Camille?" Calvo asked, tilting her head to peer at the partial face. "It's us. Are you okay?"

The door opened wider, and Calvo rushed in, grabbing the maid.

"What's wrong?" she asked, as Camille fell into her arms.

"Oh, Missus Lapolis," she cried, "help me! There is a ghost in the house!"

****

Thunder crashed above the rooftops of New Orleans. Old house frames shuddered under the assault. Rachel lit a few lamps on the main floor of the mansion, but they did little to dispel the darkness that pressed through the windows and settled into tired fabric. She could hear her sister moving about upstairs as ticking clocks measured the early evening hours. Minutes later, the tapping of raindrops sounded against the balconies outside and the vintage window glass. Within moments, the wind whipped it into a deluge of water. Rachel darted into the library and whispered something to Socrates.

Madame Lorraine paused outside the bathroom door in the upstairs hallway. She turned her head toward the top of the staircase and listened. There had been a voice. She was sure of it. The house groaned beneath the wind as rain continued to pound on the roof like bowling balls. Nervously, she glanced at the floor in front of the open doorway to her bedroom. The floorboard was still in place from where she had repaired it from the day before.

"Come and find me!"

The voice filtered up the stairs, as invasive as an intruder.

"Rachel!" she called out. "What are you up to?" She could hear the nerves in her voice.

Rachel appeared at the bottom of the stairs, the dim light turning her form into a silhouette.

"Are you calling me?" she asked, her head tilted up to where her sister was standing.

"What was that voice?" Ruby asked.

"What voice?" Rachel asked.

"I heard someone saying, 'Come and find me,'" Ruby said, clutching the newel post at the top of the stairs. "It sounded like a child."

Rachel paused, cocking her head to one side. Thunder filled the silence.

"It must have been the wind," she said mildly. "I was going to fix a light supper. Are you hungry?"

Ruby stared at her, anger pulsing in her veins. She waited before answering, "I'm not hungry."

"Suit yourself," Rachel said and turned into the dark hallway, vanishing from view.

Ruby went into her room and closed the door. She could hear the sounds of Rachel preparing food in the kitchen beneath her. A pot rattled. The sink faucet came on. Sounds that used to be comforting were now filled with menace. She crossed to her wardrobe to pull out her evening robe. There would be no one out on a night like this, not even an intrepid trick-or-treater.

BOOM!

Thunder ricocheted off the side of the house. Glassware tinkled as picture frames rattled against the walls. The lights suddenly went out.

Ruby stood in the dark room, her heart pounding. The storm surged in all its fury, threatening to tear the vintage roofing from its frame. She stumbled to her bedside table and opened the drawer.

Feeling around in the darkness, her fingers finally closed on a taper candle and a small box of matches. She struck the match against the striking strip, and the little flame leapt to life. Lighting the candle, she blew out the match and walked slowly to her bedroom door. She could hear Rachel in the kitchen, stumbling about, obviously looking for the matches herself.

Ruby opened the door and held the candle before her, looking out into the long hallway, encased in shadows. She looked down before stepping out onto the worn carpet runner and gasped.

The floorboard had been pried open again, its interior a dark maw.

Ruby fell back into her room, her eyes glued to the hole in the floor.

"Rachel!" she screamed.

There was no answer. The sounds had stopped in the kitchen.

"Rachel!" Silence.

Holding the candle before her, Ruby stepped over the floor opening and hurried to the top of the stairs. A drop of hot candle wax fell onto her thumb, and she cried out.

"Rachel! Damn you…answer me!"

BOOM!

Something hit the roof with the force of a wrecking ball. The two-hundred-year-old boards wailed as the house felt as if it were tilting beneath the attack.

In the sudden silence that followed, a small voice came from the front of the house on the main floor and floated toward her.

"Come and find me!"

Her heart exploded in her chest. She knew those words, knew the childlike register. Fear turned to burning hate as Ruby grabbed the banister and started down the sweeping staircase, each antique rung creaking beneath her weight. When she reached the first floor, she stopped. Listened. The sounds of rain and wind whistled around her.

She could see the outline of the front door and the opening into the library, both dimly outlined in stark relief. No sound came from the parrot. No lights were shining from any of the rooms. The glow from her candle sent out a feeble halo, exposing only a few feet around her. She turned toward the kitchen. It was dark.

"Rachel?" she called out again.

"Come and find me!"

Ruby's head swiveled back to the staircase, and her eyes lifted to the dark landing above. The voice was upstairs now. The candlelight illuminated the fear in her eyes. Her breathing lifted the silk fabric of her robe, her exhalations sounding like an accordion's wheezing rhythm. She put one foot on the first rung of the stairs and held the candle up in front of her, trying without success to see the upper hallway.

"Come and find me!" It was the voice of a young boy. A voice that should have sounded playful, but the tone now felt ghostly and horrifying.

"Stop it, Rachel!" she called out into the dark house. She sounded near tears.

Rachel suddenly appeared behind her in the hallway outside the kitchen.

"Ruby, for Pete's sake. Whatever is wrong?"

Ruby whirled on her heel to face her, her eyes bulging.

"What are you doing?" she screamed. "Where is Socrates?"

Upon hearing his name, the parrot squawked from the library a few doors away. Ruby took a step toward the library, stopped, looked up at the second-floor landing, and then at Rachel, her face terrified. She stood there heaving. Suddenly, her face changed from terror to anger.

"You're using the elevator," she shrieked. "You're going between the two floors with that parrot to say things and try and scare me!"

Ruby ran down the hallway to the parlor, the candle dripping wax on the carpet runner like paraffin bread crumbs. Rachel followed her, keeping her distance. The shutters rattled against the side of the house.

Tap, tap, tap.

The sound of something knocking against the front door echoed down the hallway. sounding like skeletons dancing against the siding. She stepped into the parlor in time to see Ruby pushing on the hidden button to the elevator in the dark paneling on the far left-hand side wall. She pressed harder and harder, finally pounding on the hard wall.

"Ruby," Rachel said softly.

Ruby whirled to face her. Her eyes were those of a wild animal, and her pale skin glowed eerily in the single candle flame.

"The power is out, Ruby," Rachel explained in a voice meant for a young child. "The elevator can't work without electricity."

"Awk!" Socrates cried out in the room across the hall as another thunderbolt split the night air.

"I'm going to find the old hurricane lamps," Rachel said. "Can I borrow your candle?"

"No! No!" Ruby yelled. "You cannot. I'll come with you. I'm not letting you out of my sight!"

"Suit yourself," Rachel said and walked out into the hallway. She waited for Ruby to catch up to her. They stood for a moment, staring at each other as the house groaned around them, their faces highlighted in the candlelight.

"Just tell me," Ruby finally said, controlling her anger. "If it's a Halloween joke, you did a good job. You had me there for a minute. How did you do it? You taught Socrates to say something, didn't you?"

Just then, echoing throughout the second-floor hallway, came the adolescent voice, cajoling, tempting—

"Come and find me!"

Ruby ran for the staircase, the candle flame sputtering in the draft. She reached the top landing, panting. Her eyes went directly to the floorboard opening that was still gaping. Her breath was coming in spasms, her body trembling. She tried to swallow, but her throat was too dry. With legs threatening to give way, she walked slowly to her bedroom door, careful not to step into the long rectangular hole in the floor, and held the candle out a few feet in front of her, casting her room in a ghostly pale.

She screamed. The red baseball cap with the oil stain sat in the center of her bed. Next to it, creased and worn, was an old Missing Persons flyer with a photo of Timothy Bridgersn in its center.

"Rachel!" she wailed. The wind answered her, screaming around the corner of the house like a banshee.

Rachel stood in the dark kitchen below and listened. Somewhere in the distance, she could hear a siren screeching through the night. Something banged against the side of the house, and she jumped. Debris was flying everywhere. She heard her sister call her name again with more panic than she had ever heard. She stepped out into the hallway to end the scare.

A male voice suddenly sounded from the second floor. It wafted down the hallway near Ruby's bedroom. It filtered through the thunder and clung to the walls.

"I am on my way home!"

Ruby screamed. A terror-filled cry that shook the house every bit as much as the storm outside. Rachel recoiled. She was at the bottom of the stairs, heart pounding. It was Jackson LeBlanc's voice. The same voice and words she had taught Socrates to say for the séance. But the voice was coming from upstairs. She could hear the bird prattling from its cage in the library only a few feet away.

Ruby appeared at the top of the stairs, her eyes blazing. Rachel could see the candle wax dripping onto her sister's hand, but she was oblivious to the pain.

"You're doing this!" Ruby screamed, her body trembling. "Because of Mark. It won't work! I'll kill you. You know I will. I'll kill you!"

"I didn't do that!" Rachel cried, her own terror pounding in her ears.

Ruby grabbed the banister and had one foot on the first rung. Rachel was backing up, her mind whirling as to which door to flee out of.

The voice came booming from behind the medium, so loud the hallway picture frames vibrated.

"I'M ON MY WAY HOME!"

Ruby whirled around to look behind her. Her foot became tangled in her long robe. Eyes bulging, she clawed at the air as she tumbled backwards. With a terrified shriek, she plummeted down the stairs. The candle went out on the third rung.

27 THE SPIRITS ARE WITH US!

Detective Hilliard huddled in the shadows of Harris's kitchen. It smelled damp from the storm. The rain had finally stopped, the sound of thunder rumbling becoming farther and farther away. A shard of moonlight fell into the room through the kitchen window, reaching across the floor like an accusing finger. He looked at the luminous dial on his watch. It was nearly midnight. Midnight in New Orleans on a Halloween night, he thought. Here he was, staked out in a house where a murder had been committed, and it was the witching hour. The power was out. He listened for werewolves to pass the time.

A footfall sounded on the backyard walkway to the kitchen door. Hilliard pressed his bulky frame back into the far corner of the kitchen and crouched down. Knowing the electricity was out gave him a sense of comfort. No one would enter and turn on a light.

That safety net vanished as he saw the beam of a flashlight pierce the sheer curtain of the window nearest the door. Swearing beneath his breath, he moved a few feet to the kitchen table and bent down behind it.

A key sounded in the lock. He held his breath and watched the door between the spindles of a dinette chair. Slowly, the handle turned, and a bright beam of light shot into the room. He pulled his head down as far as he could go. Someone walked slowly into the room, closing the door softly behind them. The beam of light paused. Silence. The footsteps began again, and Hilliard peered out through the chair back. As soon as the figure had crossed the room and was heading for the hallway, Hilliard sprang. He tackled the man with such force that they both crashed into the doorframe and went down. The flashlight rolled a few feet away and came to rest with its beam playing fully upon the man Hilliard had in a choke hold.

Brandon Singleton's purple face stared up at him.

****

Hilliard drew his chair in closer to the young man who was sitting across from him in the police interview room. Calvo was seated next to Hilliard, a small tape recorder whirring on the table.

"Why don't you tell us how you're involved in this whole mess?" Hilliard asked him.

Brandon Singleton glared at the detective and then turned his gaze to Calvo. She could tell he recognized her from the print shop. He took a drink of the coffee, glancing up at the camera filming everything.

"Why don't you tell me how much you know?" he said, finally, a look of annoyance on his face.

Hilliard leaned in, his jaw muscles working. Brandon leaned away from him, the arrogant look on his face vanishing.

"Listen to me," Hilliard croaked. "There's a trail of dead bodies out there, an elderly woman who had to dig up her husband, and I nearly died from poison. It's 1:30 in the morning. I'm tired. I smell. And I'm about two seconds away from risking my badge and beating the shit out of you!"

Calvo's highbrows met her hairline. Singleton's face registered sheer terror. He looked to Calvo for help.

"Don't look at me," she said. "I'll hand him the club."

Brandon's face collapsed along with his shoulders. He looked off

244

to his right, eyes downcast.

"It started with just some extra cash," he said. "Beverly would suggest Madame Lorraine to clients who came in for various reasons. We were told to look for the ones with money. People who just had someone die, or seemed unhappy in a relationship, that kind of thing. Bev is really good at drawing people out. We would get a cut of the séance money. It wasn't a lot, but it helped. Madame Lorraine would leave the money for me to pick up at her house behind a bush."

He paused with the look of one who hoped that might be all he had to cough up. Hilliard's face told him otherwise.

"When was the first time you helped with a murder?" Hilliard asked bluntly. Brandon paled, his face registering shock.

"In all fairness," he said, becoming emotional, "I didn't really know that it would lead to someone dying. I thought it was just some potion stuff…voodoo kind of thing. I just picked up the bags of stuff and delivered them. Then I went back to the same people and picked up bags of cash. Our cut suddenly got a lot bigger. It wasn't until I recognized the names of people in the newspaper who were dying that I tied them to the addresses I had been delivering to. I started to figure out what was going on…sort of. The money was so good. I convinced myself that I didn't have anything to do with the actual…"

"Murders!" Hilliard said. "Whose idea was the meter reader get-up?"

"Mine," he said sheepishly. "I told Madame Lorraine that people in these swanky neighborhoods would be suspicious of some guy going into back yards and probably call the police. It worked. Bev printed out a magnetic sign for my van to make it look official."

"So, last night," Hilliard said. "You had a key to get into Harris' house…"

"Yeah, he gave it to me to deliver a bag from Madame Lorraine. He didn't want it left outside. The key was under a potted plant near a little shed by the kitchen door."

"The CCTV footage shows you stopping by the meter out back of his house," Hilliard said.

"That was to pick up the money he left me," Brandon said. "I had left the delivery the day before inside his office at the house the way he told me to. He said the maid doesn't go in there and mess with his stuff."

"What were you doing there last night?" Hilliard asked.

Brandon paused. His right knee was bouncing up and down. Calvo wanted to reach over and press down on his thigh.

"I've been hiding out there," he said. "When the newspaper said they were exhuming that guy's body to test for poison, I panicked. Things were unraveling. Harris was on the run, and I was afraid the death of his wife might fall on me. I didn't have anywhere to go, and I didn't want Beverly to get pulled in."

"It's a little late for that," Calvo said. "She's already told us her side of the story. "So, you're the ghost Camille has been hearing."

"I just came in for some food after I thought she was asleep," he said, visibly upset that his wife would share his fate. "I was sleeping in the shed."

"Well, now we know why Harris flinched the morning after the murder when I asked him if anyone else had a key to the house," Hilliard said. "Do you know where Harris is?"

"Me? No! If I did, I would tell you. I didn't do anything but play the errand boy. If his wife was murdered, I had nothing to do with it."

Hilliard's face reddened.

"You had everything to do with those deaths," he said. "You're an accomplice, young man. You can sugarcoat it all you want, but you're looking at prison time."

Brandon finally broke. He leaned against the table and looked the detective straight in the eye.

"They killed my friend!" he said, shaking. "Jackson LeBlanc was in college with me at LSU. We did everything together. I was just asked to record his voice off of Tiffany's phone while she was at the shop with Beverly. They said it was just for a séance, to get money from Tiffany. I never liked her. I told Jackson not to marry her. She's a bitch. She was only after his money. I was happy to set her up. I didn't know it would lead to him dying. What was in the bag that I delivered?" Brandon asked, tears running down his face.

"Pure nicotine," Hilliard said, his voice flat and tired. He sighed. A sigh that came from the depths of his soul. "At least now, we can arrest that evil fake," he said.

Brandon looked at him. His eyes were hollow.

"No," he said, "no, you can't. She's dead."

****

"This feels like Déjà vu," Hilliard said, "and not in a good way."

He and Calvo were exiting the Mustang in the driveway of the Stanton-Mills mansion. Broken tree limbs dangled about the yard like broken baseball bats. Puddles filled the walkway to the front porch. Most devastating of all, half of the giant magnolia tree that stood near the street was now leaning against the roof. Broken tiles littered the lawn.

"This part of town was hit hard," Hilliard said, noting the other houses with similar damage. The gutters were still overflowing, their runoffs blocked by debris.

The pair stepped up to the front door and pressed the bell. Calvo stared at the plaque reading 'By Appointment Only' with fresh eyes. It sent a shiver down her spine. After several minutes, the door opened slowly. Rachel stood there in a simple pair of slacks and a pullover. Her eyes were vacant, giving her an otherworldly feeling that Calvo found unsettling. Without saying a word, she stepped aside to let them in.

Calvo hesitated once inside the foyer. Lit candles seemed to be everywhere. Candelabras holding six or more candles each stood on every available side table. Despite the abundance of flickering flames, the house felt dark and cold.

"Have they said when the power will be back on?" Calvo asked, easing into the uncomfortable discussion that would follow.

Rachel looked at her with the same vague expression before shaking her head no. She turned and led them into the parlor. Hilliard felt an involuntary shudder as they passed the séance table and settled into the worn armchairs in front of the window. Rachel chose to sit on a large hassock facing them.

Hilliard nodded to his partner, a silent prodding to take over the interview.

"Rachel," Calvo said, leaning toward the woman to get her attention. She appeared drugged. Rachel lifted her eyes to meet the Lieutenant's. "Tell us what happened to your sister last night, please."

Rachel's brow furrowed as if thinking was a weight too much for her to take on. She looked past Calvo at the window and then said, "She fell."

"Yes," Calvo said, "I know. But what happened? How did she fall?"

"The voices," Rachel said. "The spirits came and took their revenge."

Calvo looked at Hilliard with raised eyebrows. She contemplated her next question.

"Rachel, why would spirit voices make your sister fall down the stairs?"

"They frightened her and she fell."

"Do you really believe the voices made her fall?" Calvo asked gently. This time, there was a reaction.

"Of course I do," Rachel said, her eyes pulling focus and fixing Calvo with an uncomfortable stare. "Timothy came back. After all these years, he came back."

Calvo's face echoed the confusion she was feeling.

"Timothy? Who is Timothy?" she asked.

"Timothy Bridgers. Little Timothy Bridgers. He disappeared the morning Ruby's husband died."

Hilliard shifted in his chair. The lady was clearly off in La La Land somewhere.

Calvo frowned.

"Who is Ruby?" she asked, her voice filled with skepticism.

Rachel looked at her with a smirk that was totally incongruous to the flatline emotion she had been showing.

"Ruby is my sister," she said, as if that should be evident. "That's her real name. Ruby. Ruby Harrington. She murdered her husband,

Ronald, eighteen years ago. October 31st. Halloween. She stabbed him in the driveway as he was getting into his car to leave her. No one leaves Ruby."

Hilliard sat forward in his chair.

"I don't remember this case," he said. "Was it in this parish?"

Rachel shook her head slowly, watching him with the same vacant stare. A shiver went through him.

"We were living in Florida. Ruby inherited our mother's old house. She was the oldest. I bought the little house behind it. Our back yards were connected by a gate." She paused, her gaze returning to the window. "I heard them fighting in the driveway from my back bedroom window. I heard them fight often, but never like that. She called me in a panic. She wanted me to come over right away. I went through the backyard and came around the corner of her house. So much blood. He was lying in the driveway by his car. The car door was open. I fell against the car. And then, and then, Timothy was there."

She trailed off. Calvo took a moment to process the information. There was too much detail for this to be something she fabricated.

"I don't understand," she said, finally. "Who is Timothy?"

"He was the paperboy. It was still dark out. Ruby wanted me to help with the body. She was trying to pull him into the back seat of his car when we saw him. Little Timothy Bridgers. He was just sitting there, at the end of the driveway on a bike with a basket filled with newspapers. It was a Sunday, and he always came early on a Sunday. Ruby saw him and let go of Ronald's legs. The rest of his body was inside the car. Timothy just stood there looking at us, one foot on the ground to hold up his bike. Then his eyes went to the blood that was flowing down toward him.

"I remember thinking, 'Why doesn't he run away?' He just watched the blood until it touched his shoe, and then he freaked out. He began screaming. Ruby began running down the driveway toward him. He tried to get his bike upright to take off, but he was too scared. He fell off of it. I couldn't watch. I turned and ran through the dark just as the sun began to come up. I cut myself on the gate hinge.'

Rachel lifted her forearm and looked absently at a long scar there. She touched it with her forefinger.

"They found his bike. They never found Timothy. I remember the flyers with his face everywhere. His parents were always on the TV, begging people with information to come forward. The hardest part was when they posted film of Timothy at some of his birthday parties. In one of them, he is peeking over the table where a cake and presents are waiting, and is grinning. He looks into the camera and says, "Come and find me!"

Her eyes misted over, and her head lolled.

"He came back last night. It was the anniversary of his disappearance, you see. I think it may have been a voodoo doll under the floorboard by Ruby's bedroom. They can bring things back from the dead. Ruby told me she found Timothy's red baseball cap in her room. Timothy came back, and now Ruby is dead."

Calvo had gotten so caught up in the story that it took her a moment to come out of her trance. She blinked several times and slipped back into a detective's thinking.

"Do you have the cap?" she asked, feeling somewhat stupid for asking. Rachel's look of incredulity didn't help.

"Of course not. It's not from this world. It's gone home with Timothy."

Hilliard groaned softly, and Calvo shot him a look.

"Rachel, you said 'voices.' Were they all Timothy's?"

Rachel's face suddenly flooded with fear.

"No! Jackson LeBlanc was here! The voice said he was on his way home. It's the same thing he said at the séance."

Hilliard couldn't hold it in anymore.

"Cut the BS," he said, hotly. "We already know Brandon Singleton supplied you with a recording of Jackson's voice saying 'I'm on my way home' from Tiffany LeBlanv's cell phone messages. He already confessed to your little organization."

Rachel's reaction was one of calm, not surprise.

"Yes. Brandon helped us create the right atmosphere for the seances. It was just to bring comfort to people and maybe sell some harmless potions. Ruby did the seances, and I made the fake potions. I grow plants. They were harmless. We rigged the candle to light itself, the glass skull to turn green or red depending on Ruby's clues to me. I was in the hallway with a remote control. The green ghost was a fan and a phosphorous liquid hidden inside a secret elevator. It was no worse than what they are doing on Bourbon Street."

Hilliard's nostrils flared.

"I don't think they're facilitating murders over on Bourbon Street," he barked.

Rachel looked at him. It was as if she had regressed to a child. Even her voice when she spoke was in a higher register and pleading.

"I didn't know until much later," she said, tears slipping down her cheeks. "Ruby was doing it behind my back…taking the poisonous plants and using my little room in the back of the greenhouse. I found out for sure the day you and your sister came back," she said, looking at Hilliard.

His face hardened, and his hands gripped the threadbare armrests.

"The pen was not the one that was always by the sign-in sheet," she said, her voice trembling. "She must have done something to it so it would cut you. That was my first fear that something was wrong. I watched from the hallway as she prodded you into a Tarot reading. The cards were not the same. I called your police station and told them to warn you to look at the Tarot cards."

"That was you?" Calvo said, surprised. "What do the cards have to do with it?"

Rachel stood unsteadily and walked over to a bookcase. She pulled out two books and took out a white handkerchief wrapped around something rectangular that was hidden there. She told the two detectives to come over to the table. Hilliard hesitated, but Calvo was already on her feet.

"Don't touch them," Rachel warned, as she carefully let the handkerchief folds fall away, revealing a pack of Tarot cards. Hilliard walked up to stand next to Calvo.

Rachel carefully picked up the top card and held it up to the candelabra in the center of the table. The candlelight reflected off the tip of the card.

"She laced the tops of the cards with thallium," she said. She turned the card back and forth to show them the shiny top of the card. "I could tell from the hallway that it was the wrong deck. She always uses the one with the vines and planets. This is an old deck with a back showing ravens that she quit using a long time ago."

Hilliard almost reached out to grab it. He looked at her in confusion.

"But I watched her shuffle them," he said. "She wasn't wearing gloves. How could she shuffle them and hold them out to me if they had poison on them? Even if she didn't have a cut, you can absorb that poison through your skin, just not as quickly."

Rachel gently lifted the pack from the handkerchief despite Calvo's protestations. She rounded the table until she was standing across from the two detectives. She carefully took the deck, halved it, and shuffled it. Then she picked it up and spread out the cards in her hand in a fan shape and pushed them toward Hilliard. He stepped back.

"I don't understand," he said.

"If you watched me, you saw that my hands never touched the top of the cards. I shuffled them, holding only their bottom half, and I spread them out from the bottom, just as you'd normally do so that the subject can pick a card by pulling it from the top edge. And if you pick a card," she said, her voice pregnant with meaning," you typically pull it out with your dominant hand, using your forefinger and thumb. You sign in with those same two fingers gripping a pen."

Hilliard stood frozen. The sheer diabolical planning of it staggered his mind. Madame Lorraine wanted him dead.

"We found out you were a detective," she said, reading his mind. "I saw you come out of a restaurant and get into your squad car. You were with him," she said, glancing at Calvo. "We looked you up on the internet for the police department and found out your name: Archer Hilliard. A little more searching found your mother's obituary, listing you and your sister Emma as surviving children. That's how Ruby knew what to say in your sister's reading concerning your mother."

Rachel looked down again at the cards in her hands.

"Put them away," Calvo said meekly. She, too, was in shock. "If you knew all this, why didn't you stop it? Why, once you knew people were dying, didn't you turn her in?"

Ruby laid the cards down onto the handkerchief. Her body seemed to shrink before their eyes. It was like watching a balloon slowly deflate.

"My husband Mark fell down the stairs at our home one night after a big fight. The irony is that the fight was about Ruby. He hated her. He told me she was bad news. He wanted us to move away. The fact that her house sat just on the other side of a garden gate made him nervous. I told him she was my sister, and she was all I had for a very long time. He was so angry. He threw a suitcase on the bed and told me to pack. I sat down on the bed and sobbed. He went out into the hallway, and the next thing I knew, I heard a scream and a series of loud thuds. When I came running, he was lying at the bottom of the stairs. I could tell from the angle of his head that his neck was broken."

The two detectives looked at her incredulously.

"Ruby threatened me!" Rachel cried, reading their faces. "You have no idea how afraid I was of her. When we were little, I saw her drown a burlap bag of kittens in a pond once, just for the thrill of it. She told me that if I ever told what happened to her husband, Ronald, or the little Bridgers' boy, that she would tell the police I pushed Mark down the stairs after a violent quarrel. She also threatened to set me up for the murder of her husband. My handprint was on the hood of his car, and I found out later that the knife she killed him with was from *my* kitchen. She set up her own sister for two murders I didn't commit! She's held it over my head for the last eighteen years. We moved here, changed our names, and Ruby thought of holding seances to make money. She said New Orleans was perfect for it."

She hung her head, her shoulders quivering.

"The spirits pushed Ruby down the stairs last night," she said. "Just like she pushed Mark that night. Karma does come back around."

"So, you haunted her last night, with fake voices, causing her to fall in the darkness when the power was out..."

"I was downstairs when Timothy's voice was calling her from

253

upstairs. The elevator wasn't working. She thought she heard him downstairs, too. I can't be everywhere at once. And I did NOT have anything to do with Jackson LeBlanc coming back through the veil to haunt her."

"No," Hilliard said, "but I think I know who did."

28 SUMMONING GHOSTS

Lieutenant Adelaide Calvo sat in the opulent living room of the Harris home on St. Charles Street. It had been a long day already as the late afternoon November sun began to slide down beneath the tree line. Camille sat across from her on the same couch she had occupied the first day Calvo met her. Everything else about her had changed. The maid's uniform was gone. She wore a simple dress of muted colors, her hair pulled back away from her face. She looked younger.

Calvo explained to her that it was Brandon Singleton, not a ghost, that had been inside the house the times she heard things moving around. Judging by the fear on the maid's face, Calvo felt she would have been happier hearing it was something supernatural than that a strange man had been so close to her bedroom door.

"Where will you go now?" Calvo asked her gently, finishing her tea.

"I go to my sisters in Shreveport," she said. "I can get work there and maybe help her with the children. Any money I bring in will be welcome to her."

Calvo smiled.

"Well, that's one of the reasons I've come today," she said. "We looked in Marjorie's will. It's routine to see who would benefit from her death. Turns out, all of her money is going to *her* sister in New Zealand, some cat shelters, and....you."

Camille stared at her, not quite comprehending.

"She loved you, Camille," Calvo said warmly. "She calls you her 'White Light' in the will. You may have been the only real thing she had in the midst of fake friends and a husband who wanted only to possess her. She left you $250,000, some jewelry, and a coat. I don't know which coat, I'm afraid."

The tears that were always so close to the surface spilled over and ran down Camille's face.

"I know this coat," she cried. "She loaned it to me once when I first come to work here. I did not have one. It was a cold day for my marketing, and she handed it to me. She wanted me to keep it, but Mister told her not to do that. That it was not good to give servants things. It give them courage to steal things."

"Encourages them," Calvo said, smiling. "But that is not true." She placed a hand on the woman's knee. "Camille, did you hear what I said?" Calvo asked, leaning closer. "She left you $250,000!"

"Is that good?" she asked innocently.

Calvo laughed. "Yes, Camille. That is very, very good. You and your sister won't have to worry about money for a long time."

Calvo rose.

"Oh, I wanted to return this to you," she said. She handed Camille the photograph of Richy that the maid had loaned her when she came back to speak to her two days after Marjorie Harris' murder.

Camille sniffed and hugged it to her chest, nodding.

"Are you sure I can't give you a ride somewhere?"

"No, Lapolis," she said. "My sister is coming for me."

Calvo paused and looked intently at the woman.

"Camille, please, one last thing. Can you think of anything the Mister did or said that could tell us where he is? Did he make any reservations for a plane or a hotel, or anything at all that would help us?"

Camille shook her head slowly.

"I would tell you. I never see him again after kitty is found. I know now he kill the Missus," she said, wiping her face. "I cannot stay here anymore. I hope you find the Mister. I think he is sick. I didn't know he was sick."

"Why do you think he is sick?" Calvo asked, surprised. "You mean mentally? That he would kill his wife?"

"No. Sick. He say he is going to where there is oxygen," Camille said, shrugging.

"Oxygen?" Calvo said, shocked. "What does that mean?"

"I don't know, Lapolis. He say it the day before they find kitty. I ask him if he need anything when I am going out for the marketing. He say, "No, I am going out myself. I am going to oxygen.""

****

Hilliard leaned back in his desk chair and sighed. He was still dealing with some nerve damage in his hands and a relentless headache, but he could see light at the end of the tunnel. He smiled wearily across the desk at Calvo, who was shaking her head.

"How many murders do you think there were?" she asked, tiredly. "How long had this been going on? It scares me to think what we may have missed."

"If Beverly and Brandon are to be believed, they were brought in around September of this year. That doesn't mean the séance scheme wasn't going on long before, probably under the radar. We know the sisters bought the Stanton-Mills mansion twelve years ago…"

"From my aunt," Calvo said, smiling ruefully.

"From your aunt, the realtor to the stars," Hilliard said, nodding. "At what point this plan was hatched, I don't know. The guest book that all the clients signed into shows only about two months of names. That's a good sign. Were there other books? Who knows. We can keep looking. Your pal at the paper can help there."

Calvo blushed.

"He's good at his job," she said, trying to deflect Hilliard's
257

twitching grin. "He left me a file of photos he took from Charlie Brindle's exhumation at the cemetery. Poor Dorothy. I hope her heart heals. She started us down this road."

Hilliard nodded and took in a deep breath. He rolled his head, cracking his neck.

"I just want to get that bastard in handcuffs," he said.

"Everett? We got Everett. Is your memory still whacked?"

He lowered his eyes at her.

"Not that punk! Harris! Where the hell is he? He's got enough money to go anywhere in the world and disappear for a long time."

"Somewhere where there's oxygen," Calvo smiled.

"What?" Hilliard looked at her in surprise.

"Camille said Harris told her that he was going where there was oxygen. I assume he meant he needed to breathe because the walls were closing in."

"When did he say that?" Hilliard asked.

"The day before they found Richy buried in the back yard."

Hilliard stared at her. Suddenly, his face lit up.

"Oh my God," he said, jerking forward. "I know where he is!"

Calvo waited impatiently as his mind kept whirling.

"He's in Greece!"

"And just how do you arrive at that deduction, Sherlock?" she asked.

"First and forever, he's a military man," Hilliard said. "His office is practically a museum to the wars. What day did they find that cat?"

Calvo thought back.

"Friday, the 24th.

Hilliard's grin went from ear to ear.

"Oxi Day is on October 28th! It's a major public holiday with huge military parades celebrating Greece's resistance to surrendering during World War II. The biggest commemoration is in Thessaloniki, Greece!"

"So we, what, go check out every parade route in Greece?"

"No. We find the most expensive hotel in Thessaloniki, Greece, overlooking the parade route."

"Speaking of checking things out," Calvo said, I forgot to tell you, there is no evidence that Malcolm stopped for breakfast between leaving the hotel and arriving home the morning we were at the house."

"I wonder what he was doing for over an hour," Hilliard said.

"We may never know," Calvo answered. "All because Marjorie was having an affair with their lawyer. He could have afforded a divorce."

"I wonder if 'Sidebar' would have represented Marjorie."

Beaming, he pushed off from his chair and stood, stretching his arms over his head until his fingertips practically touched the acoustic ceiling tiles.

"Are you buying Singleton's story that he didn't cause Madame Lorraine to fall down the stairs?" he asked, gathering up some files.

"He told me when I talked to him an hour ago in jail that he did play the recording of Jackson's voice to scare her, but he adamantly denies having anything to do with the little boy's voice or anything else. He said Lorraine tripped on her robe and fell in the darkness. Do I think his playing Jackson's voice caused her to trip? Probably. He's going to prison, either way."

"He tried until the end to implicate Rachel," Calvo said. "I believe her. I don't think she knew what Lorraine was doing, not until the very end. She did call and try to save your life by warning you about the Tarot cards."

"Yeah, a little too late," Hilliard said, stiffly. "The court decided to let her off the hook, not mine. I can't believe she's going to stay in that creepy old mansion. Brandon Singleton said he thinks it's haunted. And I'm sure you buy that," Hilliard said sarcastically. "The only magic I saw going on at that house was my $1500 I gave Emma to pay for her séance disappeared! I think you'd believe anything that has to do with the supernatural."

"Speaking of that," Calvo said, grinning. She opened the folder of photographs Davis Miles had taken of the cemetery. In the pictures were Dorothy Brindle, the funeral director, other police officials, and a man she assumed was the cemetery superintendent. They were carrying Charlie Brindle's casket back into the vault. She selected an 8" x 10" glossy photo and handed it to Hilliard. "Notice anything unusual?" she asked.

He took the photo and studied it. He leaned closer to the photo and then looked up at her, her face red.

"No," he said. "No, you don't. Not again! I'm not buying it! Nice try. Tell your reporter friend, "Ha ha!" He angrily threw the picture that floated onto the floor.

He walked around the desk and reached for his old college basketball jacket that was hanging on a coat tree.

"Where are you going?' Calvo asked. "I was going to treat you to dinner to celebrate. And you owe me. I was right about the cat."

"I have plans," he said, his cheeks coloring.

"Oh! You have *plans*?" Calvo said, smiling. "Might those plans include barbecue sauce?"

"That's none of your business," he said. "And, I'm happy to announce I'll be driving myself! Get Gleason to start checking the guest registers at the swanky hotels in Thessaloniki, Greece, for starters."

He walked out, shoving one long arm into the jacket sleeve. Patterson was walking up the hallway with a box of Halloween decorations from the front desk area.

"Did you have a fun Halloween, Boss?" he asked.

"Bite me!" Hilliard said and kept walking.

"Oh, a little vampire humor?" Patterson called after him, grinning. He paused at the open door to Hilliard's office. Calvo was putting on her Saint's jacket.

"Dinner?" he asked, the hopeful look on his face tugging at her conscience.

"I'm sorry," she said, "I have…"

"Plans," Davis Miles said. He was standing in the hallway behind Patterson.

The officer nodded, a restrained look on his face. He stepped back to let Calvo exit into the hallway.

"Have a nice evening," Calvo said gently, touching his sleeve.

The pair walked off.

"Do we have plans?" she asked, smiling.

"Thought you might need rescuing from the guy with the cologne issue," he said, grinning. "O'Brien's?"

"Does anyone ever tell you No?" she asked, smirking.

"No."

"A hurricane would be perfect!" she said, referring to the restaurant's signature drink.

Officer Patterson looked into the empty office. A large glossy photo lay on the floor near the desk. Shifting the small box of decorations to one arm, he bent and picked it up. He was about to lay it on the desk when he stopped. He pulled it closer to his face and blinked. It was a picture of a casket being taken up the steps to an open vault on a dreary, cloudy afternoon. A small, elderly lady was standing off to the side, a handkerchief pressed to her face. Next to her, a diaphanous shape of an elderly man was standing, his transparent arm wrapped around her shoulders.

Patterson recoiled as if he had picked up a writing snake. He tossed the photo onto the desk and hurriedly left the room.

****

One month later, Rachel sat at the head of the round table in the parlor of the Stanton-Mills mansion. Her long hair was pinned up atop her head. Her slender frame was draped in a long, dark black dress that had been her sister's favorite. The room was ensconced in shadows as four strangers sat around the table, their palms flat on the black tablecloth, fingers splayed and pinkies touching. The flame from the large pillar candle sputtered in the silence. Rachel began to groan, her head swaying from side to side. Her chin suddenly jerked up toward the ceiling, and she cried out.

"Yes! Madame Lorraine, we are here! We await your spirit to guide these poor souls to the resolution they seek!"

Upstairs, in the dark master bedroom believed to be haunted, the dust stirred. The fireplace opening loomed black and cold. On the right of it was the hidden elevator, now active again. To the left, secreted behind a floor-to-ceiling tapestry, was a secret door. Behind the door was a series of stairs leading down into the darkness to the first floor.

A shelf sat near the turn in the stairs, anchored to the ancient brick. Sitting atop it were three things: a boy's red baseball cap with an oil stain, a tape recorder with Timothy Bridgers' voice from his parents' TV interviews, and a Missing Persons flyer.

ABOUT THE AUTHOR

Rebecca F. Pittman is a bestselling author in several genres. Her non-fiction History and Haunting series highlights the most haunted venues, events, and people in the world. The Countdown to Murder series covers the incredible murder cases of famous cases, such as those of Pam Hupp and Alex Murdaugh. She is also a bestselling author for her books on how to create businesses in the creative arts arena.

Ms. Pittman's foray into psychological thrillers comes as no surprise. They are a natural segue from her paranormal and true crime interests. Her love of Agatha Christie and Shirley Jackson is a huge inspiration to her. The Hilliard and Calvo thriller mysteries are primarily set in New Orleans and are infused with the delicious influences of that city and its culture, be it a nod to voodoo, its mansions, or its sumptuous food fare. Book One in the series is When Shadows Walk! Book Two is The Widow's Séance Society. Coming in April 2026 is The Lady in the Pool, followed by The Wrong Address and The Diamond Peacock Club.

Ms. Pittman is featured on myriad TV, radio, and podcast forums to discuss her books and her research. She lives in the beautiful Colorado Rockies. You can join her free newsletter on upcoming books, giveaways, and an upcoming interactive murder mystery game. Simply go to her website, rebeccafpittmanbooks.com, and sign up. It's free and packed with fun surprises.

If you enjoyed this book, it would be kindly appreciated if you would leave a review on Amazon or Goodreads. Authors are not only dealing with the talent of other writers, but now, with the advent of AI, we are in the trenches. Thank you so much for your support and purchase of this book.

Other Books by Rebecca F. Pittman

The History and Haunting Series:

The History and Haunting of the Stanley Hotel. 3 editions
The History and Haunting of the Myrtles Plantation. 2 editions
The History and Haunting of Lemp Mansion
The History and Haunting of Lizzie Borden
The History and Haunting of Salem: The Witch Trials & Beyond
The History and Haunting of the Palace of Versailles
The History and Haunting of the 1771 Enfield House
The History and Haunting of the Bell Witch
The History and Haunting of the Smurl Horror

Coming Fall 2026: The History and Haunting of Haunted Dolls

The Countdown to Murder Series:

Countdown to Murder: Pam Hupp
Countdown to Murder: Alex Murdaugh

Business Books for the Arts:

How to Start a Faux Painting or Mural Business
Scrapbooking for Profit

Relationship Advice:

Troubleshooting Men: What in the World Do They Want?

Novels:

Hilliard and Calvo Series

When Shadows Walk!
The Widow's Séance Society
Coming April 2026: The Lady in the Pool

T.J. Finnel and the Well of Ghosts (Juvenile Fiction, Pegasus Publishing)

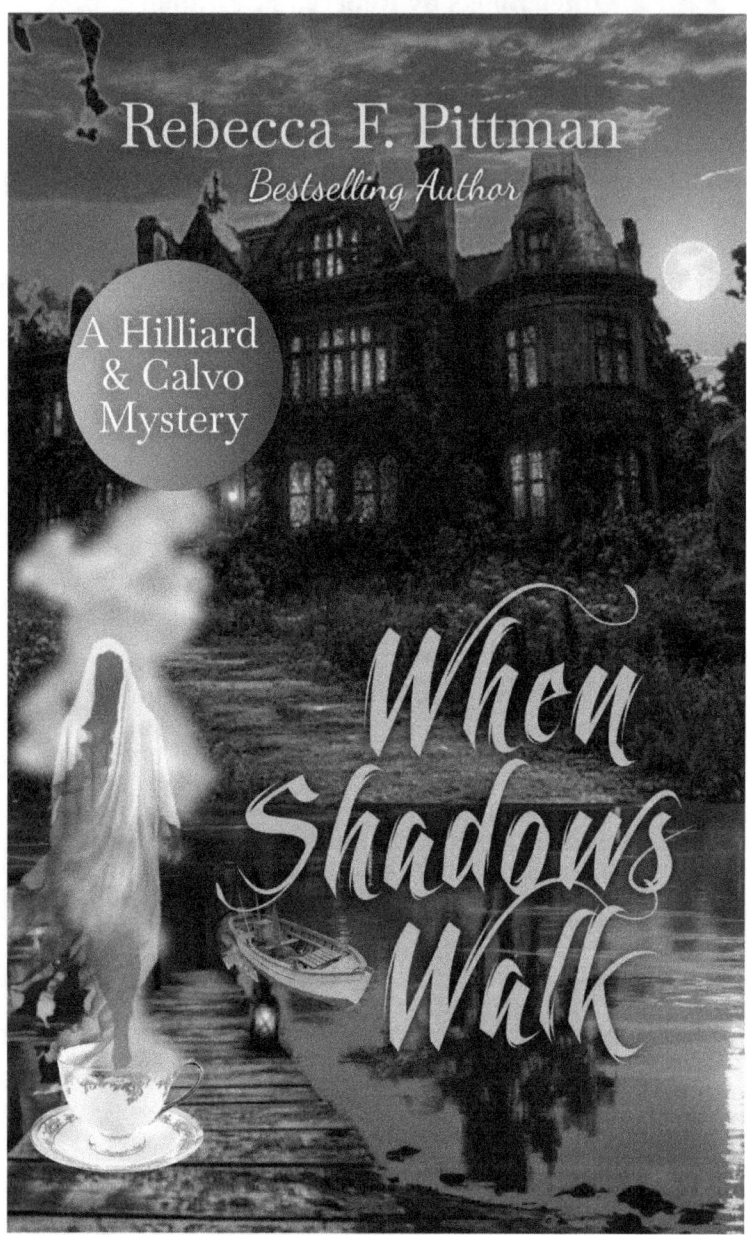

Book One of the Hilliard & Calvo Mystery Series

All 5-star reviews!

Now for sale on Amazon

www.ingramcontent.com/pod-product-compliance
Lightning Source LLC
Chambersburg PA
CBHW052023020726
47501CB00004B/1201